**Praise for the *New York Times* Bestselling
Magical Cats Mysteries**

Cat Trick

"An entertaining series." —Fresh Fiction

"The mystery is well plotted, though the suspects aren't all that obvious. Small-town charm and a charming cat duo make this every cat fancier's dream."

—The Mystery Reader

Copycat Killing

"I've been a huge fan of this series from the very start, and I am delighted that this new book meets my expectations and then some. . . . Cats with magic powers, a library, good friends who look out for each other, and small-town coziness come together in perfect unison. If you are a fan of Miranda James's Cat in the Stacks Mysteries, you will want to read [this series]." —MyShelf.com

"This is a really fun series and I've read them all. Each book improves on the last one. Being a cat lover myself, I'm looking at my cat in a whole new light." —Once Upon a Romance

"A fun whodunit. . . . Fans will appreciate this entertaining amateur sleuth."

—Genre Go Round Reviews

continued . . .

"This charming series continues on a steady course as the intrepid Kathleen has two mysteries to snoop into. . . . Readers who are fans of cats and cozies will want to add this series to their must-read lists."

—*Romantic Times*

Sleight of Paw

"Kelly's appealing cozy features likable, relatable characters set in an amiable location. The author continues to build on the promise of her debut novel, carefully developing her characters and their relationships."

—*Romantic Times*

Curiosity Thrilled the Cat

"A great cozy that will quickly have you anxiously waiting for the next release so you can spend more time with the people of Mayville Heights."

—Mysteries and My Musings Blog

"If you love mystery and magic, this is the book for you!"

—Debbie's Book Blog

"This start of a new series offers an engaging cast of human characters and two appealing, magically inclined felines. Kathleen is a likable, believable heroine and the magical cats are amusing."

—*Romantic Times*

Also Available from Sofie Kelly

Curiosity Thrilled the Cat
Sleight of Paw
Copycat Killing
Cat Trick

FINAL CATCALL

A MAGICAL CATS MYSTERY

SOFIE KELLY

AN OBSIDIAN MYSTERY

OBSIDIAN
Published by the Penguin Group
Penguin Group (USA) LLC, 375 Hudson Street,
New York, New York 10014

USA | Canada | UK | Ireland | Australia | New Zealand | India | South Africa | China
penguin.com
A Penguin Random House Company

First published by Obsidian, an imprint of New American Library,
a division of Penguin Group (USA) LLC

First Printing, October 2013

ISBN 978-0-451-41470-0

Printed in the United States of America
10 9 8 7 6 5 4 3 2 1

ACKNOWLEDGMENTS

I owe a debt of gratitude to many people for the success of the Magical Cats Mysteries. Thank you to all the readers who have embraced Owen, Hercules, Kathleen and everyone else in Mayville Heights. Thank you as well to my agent, Kim Lionetti, whose guidance and enthusiasm keep me on track. My editor, Jessica Wade, makes every book better and does so with unfailing good humor—and a little help from her assistant, Jesse Feldman. Thanks to both of you. Fellow writer Laura Alden can always be counted on for a pep talk and a laugh when I need one. Chief Tim Sletten, the now-retired police chief of the Red Wing, Minnesota, police department, once again answered a barrage of questions and was very gracious when I played with the facts. Any errors are mine, not his.

And as always, thank you to Patrick and Lauren, the two best things that ever happened to me.

PROLOGUE

The cats were waiting in the kitchen. I kicked off my shoes and knelt beside them. Owen immediately began sniffing the sling on my left arm. Hercules climbed up on my lap and licked my chin. I took a shaky breath against the prickle of tears I could feel about to fall. I wasn't going to sit around on the floor crying. I was going to fix things with Marcus. I was going to keep apologizing until he listened. The problem was that when Detective Marcus Gordon was hurt, it wasn't easy to get him to listen.

I sat on the footstool in the living room and tried his number. His cell phone went to voice mail. (He didn't text.) There was no answer at his house, either. I heard something clatter to the floor in the kitchen. I went back out to find Owen and Hercules with the keys to my truck lying between them. "You're not exactly subtle," I said, bending to pick up the key ring. "Then again, if I see him in person, maybe I can get him to listen."

Owen meowed loudly. I looked at Hercules, and

after a moment's hesitation, he gave a soft meow as well. I knew it was a bad idea to be driving one-handed, but I was past caring.

The cats followed me out to the truck, and there didn't seem to be any reason not to let them come along. Owen looked out the passenger window while Herc sat beside me and stared out the windshield.

Marcus wasn't down by the tents set up alongside the water beside the Riverwalk for tomorrow's food tasting. A couple of hours earlier Maggie and I—and Hercules—had been there while the police took away a killer we'd helped catch.

"Are you all right?" Maggie had asked as we stood on the grass next to the boardwalk. She touched my shoulder, which had been twisted almost out of its socket, and I winced. "Okay, obviously you're not." She pulled out her cell phone.

"What are you doing?" I said. I had my good arm wrapped around Hercules. The air had gotten colder when the sun went down, but holding the little black-and-white cat was like having a portable heater.

"Calling Roma." She shrugged. "I know you won't go to the emergency room, and since you're stub-born as a mule, it seems appropriate to get her to take a look at that shoulder."

Roma was a vet, and one of my closest friends, but she also had first-aid training, so it wasn't really that outlandish of an idea to call her. I talked quietly to Hercules until Maggie put her phone away.

"Roma is going to meet us at your house in a little while." She gestured at Hercules. "How did he end up here?"

"The cats like to ride in the truck. I guess I didn't see him jump out when I got out." I figured that was more believable than the truth: He walked through the closed truck door because that happens to be his superpower. Maggie didn't know that both my cats had some unbelievable and unexplainable abilities. No one did.

A few minutes later Marcus came out of the tent. Maggie had spotted Liam Stone, one of the organizers of the food festival, and had gone to speak to him. Marcus stared at me for a long moment and then walked across the grass to me.

"Is your shoulder all right?" he asked.

"I think so."

"Someone should take a look at it." His voice was cold and emotionless.

"Maggie's already taken care of that." This wasn't the first time I'd gotten mixed up in one of his cases, but it was the first time I'd seen him this angry. "I tried to call you," I said. I stopped and looked away for a moment. "What did you want me to do?"

I expected him to say, "Nothing," but instead he just looked at me. "Trust me," he said, pulling a hand through his dark, wavy hair.

"I do trust you."

He looked past me, over my shoulder. Then his

blue eyes came back to my face. "No, you don't, Kathleen. I almost think you trust those cats more than you trust me."

"I'm sorry." I was barely able to get the words out, and my heart felt like it was pounding in the hollow at the base of my throat.

His lips pulled into a tight line. "Just once, Kathleen—just once—it would be nice if you had a little faith in me."

Maggie had started back across the grass toward us.

"You can go," Marcus said. He didn't look at me, and his voice was as cold as winter ice in the lake. He turned and walked away, and I felt tears start to slide down my face. I'd been trying to talk to him ever since.

He wasn't at the police station. I drove all over the downtown, but there was no sign of Marcus or his car. I ground my teeth against the gnawing pain in my shoulder and drove out to his little house. It was in darkness and there was no navy blue SUV in the driveway.

I tried his cell again and his home phone. Voice mail both times.

"He doesn't want to talk to me." Hercules leaned against my side and Owen walked across the front seat to rub his furry gray cheek against my good hand. "Let's go home," I said.

I pulled into the driveway, turned off the truck and yanked the key out of the ignition. "I ruined everything with Marcus," I said, sucking in a shaky breath. "It's over, and maybe it never really got started."

I walked around the side of the house with the cats trailing me. I didn't see the chair until I almost fell over it. It was sitting on the path in front of the back stairs.

My rocking chair. The one Marcus had been fixing for me.

It wasn't in pieces anymore. It was all there, every joint strong and tight, with a new leather back and seat. It was back together, every single piece.

The chair looked wonderful. Absolutely wonderful.

But not nearly as wonderful as the long-legged detective who was sitting in the shadows on my back step.

I felt my knees go rubbery with relief. "I'm so glad you're here," I said.

"I wasn't sure you'd say that." The denim-clad legs stretched and stood up. At the same moment Hercules began to hiss because he could see what I now saw.

It wasn't Marcus waiting by my back door.

1

It was Andrew.

Andrew, who was part of the reason I'd ended up in Mayville Heights, Minnesota. Andrew, who I'd once thought I was going to spend the rest of my life with in Boston, until we had a fight and he went off on a fishing trip with his friends and came home married to a waitress from a fifties-themed diner.

"What—what are you doing here?" I stammered.

"I came to see you," he said. He gave me that smile my friend Lise back in Boston always said would melt the elastic in your underpants.

"I don't understand." I'd been living in Mayville Heights for a year and a half. Why was he here now? "What do you want?" My hair was coming out of its ponytail. I pulled off the elastic and shook it loose.

He shrugged. "I want you."

"I'm serious, Andrew." It was late and I was exhausted. I didn't want to play word games.

"So am I." He gestured at my arm. "What happened?"

Hercules had stopped hissing, but both cats had moved in front of me so Andrew couldn't get any closer without tripping over them.

"It's not a big deal. I wrenched my shoulder. The sling is just to keep me from using it for a day or two."

Andrew was studying me, his green eyes serious. I wondered what he was thinking. My hair was longer, and I was a little thinner because I walked so much. I probably looked rumpled and sweaty and tired. That was certainly how I felt. He looked good. His sandy hair was a bit shorter than the last time I'd seen him, but he still had the same broad shoulders, strong arms and, of course, that smile.

"So you're all right?"

I nodded. "I'm fine. Andrew, what are you doing here?"

I'd spoken to him exactly one time since I came to Mayville Heights, and then only because I'd needed his help when it looked as though Maggie might be a suspect in a murder investigation—another one of Marcus's cases.

I suddenly remembered the rocking chair. It was still sitting in front of the back steps. "Was that here when you got here?" I asked before Andrew could answer my first question.

He nodded. "It's a nice piece. Where did you get it?"

Marcus had done a beautiful job. The seat and the back of the rocker had been reupholstered with what looked to be black leather, and I was guessing the finish on the wood was walnut. "A friend of mine was clearing out an old house," I said.

Hercules seemed to decide then that he was tired of all the talking. He stalked around Andrew, climbed the steps and meowed loudly at the porch door. The end of his tail was twitching, a sure sign that he was annoyed. At least he hadn't done what he usually did—walk directly through the heavy wooden door.

"Are the cats yours?"

I nodded and pointed from one to the other. "The gray tabby is Owen and that's Hercules at the door."

Owen made a low murp at the sound of his name. He was still watching Andrew, and his whiskers were twitching, which meant he was still deciding whether this was someone to like or someone who should get the kitty cold shoulder.

"Andrew, it's late—" I began.

"Come home," he blurted.

I looked around. "I am home."

"I mean come home to Boston. With me. Give us another chance. You wanted to know why I'm here? That's why."

Why now, of all nights, did he have to show up at my door? Why couldn't it have been any of the other five-hundred-plus nights since I'd left Boston?

"There is no 'us,'" I said, exhaling softly. "And I have a life here. I have friends. I have a job."

"There's a life waiting for you back in Boston. And friends. And your family." He swiped a hand over his chin.

I knew that at this time of night it would be covered with red-gold stubble that would scrape my cheek if I laid my face against his. Why on earth had I remembered that?

I rubbed my left arm with my free hand. At my feet Owen meowed softly.

"You're tired, Kathleen," Andrew said, his expression softening. He reached a hand toward me and then pulled it back. "I'm going back to my hotel. I'll pick you up for breakfast in the morning. We can talk then."

"You're wasting your time," I said. Out of the corner of my eye I could see Owen still eyeing Andrew suspiciously.

Andrew shook his head. "No, I'm not. Anyway, would having breakfast with me really be so bad? It has to be better than trying to cook for yourself with only one hand."

I had to admit that having one of Eric's breakfast sandwiches did sound better than trying to make oatmeal and cut up fruit one-handed. "Okay," I said. "Seven thirty?"

He nodded, then gestured at the rocking chair. "Unlock your door and I'll put that inside for you."

I hesitated. I couldn't get the rocker into the porch one-handed, but I didn't want to leave it outside all night.

"I'm not going to use it as an excuse to stay, Kath." He made an X on his chest with his index finger. "I promise."

As long as I'd known Andrew he'd made that gesture to show he was serious about something. After I left Boston I would feel my chest tighten if I saw someone else do it. He wasn't a bad guy.

"All right. Thank you," I said.

Hercules narrowed his eyes at me as I unlocked the door. I snapped on the porch light and he jumped up on the bench by the back door. Owen darted in around my legs, and Andrew brought up the rear with the rocking chair.

He set it down in the middle of the floor and pulled out a set of keys. The little red car I'd noticed parked on the street must be his. "I'll see you in the morning," he said. He leaned down as he passed me and kissed the top of my head, then was gone.

I sank onto the bench next to Hercules. He touched the sling with one paw and cocked his head to one side. "I'm okay," I said in answer to the question I knew he was asking.

Owen launched himself onto my lap. He walked his paws up my chest, stuck his face close to mine and meowed.

"That was Andrew," I said. "But you know that."

Herc scraped his claws on my sling. When I looked at him again, he scrunched up his furry black-and-white face.

"Yes, *that* Andrew." The cats exchanged a look. On occasion I got the feeling that they had some kind of telepathic communication going.

Owen and Hercules had heard more about my relationship with Andrew than either Maggie or Roma, who were my closest friends. I'd gotten into the habit of talking to the cats after I'd found them abandoned as kittens out at Wisteria Hill, the old Henderson estate that was now Roma's new home. Talking to them helped me work things out in my own mind—at least that was what I told anyone who asked. I didn't say that sometimes it seemed as though they were taking part in the conversation.

It wasn't as far-fetched as it might seem. Herc and Owen weren't exactly run-of-the-mill cats. Hercules had that walk-through-walls-and-doors ability, and Owen could disappear at will—and did—generally at the most inconvenient times possible.

I nudged Owen off my lap and got to my feet with a groan. "How about some sardine crackers and hot chocolate?" I asked.

Both cats murped their agreement. I ran my fingers over one arm of the rocking chair as I went past it. Owen darted past me into the kitchen, while Hercules jumped down from the bench and waited at the door. "I'm not giving up," I said to him. "Remember what Yogi said."

He immediately looked over at the picnic cooler on the floor next to the window bench.

"No, not the bear," I said. "The baseball player." I leaned over and scooped him up with my good arm. "Yogi said, 'It's not over till it's over.'"

Hercules didn't get it, but the words made me feel a little better.

*   *   *

It was about twenty after seven the next morning when I heard a knock at the back door. I was already on my second cup of coffee. "He's early," I said to the cats. Neither of them bothered to look up from his bowl or even so much as twitch an ear.

I went out to the porch and discovered it wasn't Andrew at all. It was Abigail, who worked for me at the library.

"Kathleen, hi. I'm sorry to stop by so early but—" She stopped when she caught sight of the sling on my left arm. "What on earth happened to you? Are you okay?"

"I'm fine," I said. "I twisted my shoulder. The sling is just to keep me from moving my arm for a couple of days. What's going on?"

"Have you heard of the New Horizons Theatre Festival?"

I nodded. "It's coming up in a couple of weeks over in Red Wing, isn't it?"

"Not anymore." She made a face. "There was a fire last evening at the theater there. Nobody was hurt and it looks as though the building can be repaired, but there's an awful lot of smoke and water damage."

"What are they going to do?"

"Move the whole thing here."

I felt a cat wind around my ankles and glanced down to see Owen at my feet. "And you're . . . ?"

"Part of the organizing committee that was pretty much thrown together late last night." She smiled down at Owen, who leaned against my leg and seemed to smile back at her. "That's why I'm here. How would you feel about using the new gazebo at the library as a temporary stage during the festival? There are half a dozen short plays on the schedule that we're hoping can be presented somewhere other than the Stratton."

The Stratton was the theater where Marcus and I had met when I discovered the body of conductor Gregor Easton. I gave my head a little shake. Thinking about Marcus wasn't going to do me any good right now.

"I think that's a wonderful idea," I said. "But I should check with Everett and the board, to be certain. I'll give Lita a call just as soon as I get to the library."

Everett Henderson was the head of the library board. He'd funded the recent library renovations as a gift to the town and hired me as head librarian to supervise everything. Lita was his assistant. Not only was she the fastest way of getting in touch with Everett, but she would know whether the board would have any objections to Abigail's plan. In fact, she'd know if *anyone* was likely to object. Lita seemed to be related, one way or another, to pretty much everyone in Mayville Heights.

"Thanks, Kathleen," Abigail said. She gestured toward my arm. "You know, if you need me to come in today, I can."

"Thanks," I said. "I think I'll be okay." I raised my left arm in its sling. "But I'll call you if I need a hand."

Abigail shook her head and grinned.

"I'll be in touch as soon as I talk to Everett," I promised.

"Sounds good." She started down the porch steps and almost ran into Andrew, who was peering at his cell phone as he came around the corner of the house. "Oh, I'm sorry," she said, teetering on the bottom step.

He reached out a hand to steady her. "No, it's my fault for not watching where I was going." He smiled. "Hi, I'm Andrew."

For a moment Abigail just stared at him. Then she remembered herself. "It's, uh, nice to meet you. I'm Abigail."

He could still make grown women get all flustered and discombobulated with just a smile. The fact that he was over six feet tall and all lean muscle in his plum-colored sweater and jeans didn't hurt, either. And though he'd always claimed the smile was the result of four years of braces and had nothing to do with him, I knew he liked flashing that killer grin.

Abigail looked back over her shoulder at me, clearly curious, but all she said was, "I'll talk to you later." She flashed her own smile at Andrew. "Enjoy Mayville Heights," she said, and then she went back down the path and around the side of the house.

Andrew took the porch stairs in two strides. "Good morning. How's your arm?"

"Better," I said. The pain had settled down to a slight ache in my shoulder.

He pointed to the little gray tabby, still sitting by my feet, clearly checking him out. "That's Owen, right?"

"Merow," Owen said, before I had a chance to answer.

"Hey, Owen." Andrew leaned forward as though he was going to stroke the cat's fur.

"Don't do that," I said, putting out my right hand to stop him.

His eyes narrowed in confusion. "Why?"

Owen continued to sit in the same spot, the picture of kitty sweetness with his head tipped to one side, no hint of the whirling dervish he would turn into if Andrew tried to pet him.

"He's feral—at least he was. Hercules, too. I found them both when they were kittens, at an old estate just outside of town. They'll let me touch them, but pretty much no one else."

"You're kidding, right?"

Andrew's skepticism didn't surprise me. Owen looked harmless, but the last person who had disregarded instructions not to touch him had ended up needing a paramedic. And Marcus had had to vouch for the cat.

Why did everything make me think of Marcus? I

shook my head again. "He has claws and he's not afraid to use them."

Right on cue Owen held up a paw, almost as though he knew what I'd just said and was trying to plead his innocence.

I narrowed my eyes at him. "Don't get cute," I muttered.

He flicked his tail at me and went back to the kitchen.

Andrew laughed and straightened up. "So, are you ready for breakfast?"

"As long as you understand it's just breakfast."

"I figured you'd say that." He braced a hand against the doorframe, took a deep breath and exhaled slowly. His expression grew serious. "Look, Kath, I messed up big-time. Yeah, I was drunk and I was pissed at you, but neither one is any kind of an excuse for marrying someone I didn't even know." His mouth moved, as though he were testing the feel of what he wanted to say next. "After I talked to you back in the spring, all I could think about was how badly I'd f— screwed things up. I'm not that person anymore. Have breakfast with me and you'll see that."

"Okay," I said.

His eyes narrowed. "Okay? That's it? You're not going to argue with me? I have another speech I haven't even used."

I shrugged. "Sorry. I'm hungry. But if it will make

you feel better you can give me your speech on the way down the hill."

"You've ruined the effect." He folded his arms across his chest in mock indignation and his lips twitched as he tried—and failed—not to smile.

"I have to get my sweater and my briefcase," I said. "I'll just be a minute."

The cats were sitting by the coat hooks in the kitchen. I got them fresh water and draped my blue sweater over my shoulders while they watched, turning their heads in perfect synchronization to follow me.

"I'll tell you all about it tonight." I reached over to scratch Hercules under his chin. "Have a good day," I said.

Owen leaned sideways and seemed to be looking at the piece of paper stuck to the front of the refrigerator that listed the days Marcus and I fed the feral cat colony out at Wisteria Hill. Was he asking about Marcus or thinking about the sardines that were in the fridge?

I leaned down and stroked the top of his head. "Yes, I'm going to talk to Marcus—or at least try to— and no, you can't have any sardines."

He turned his back on me and started washing his tail. Whatever he'd been asking, he hadn't liked my answer.

Andrew was a contractor who specialized in old houses, and he kept the conversation to his latest restoration project as we drove to the restaurant. "Where are we going?" he asked, as we came to the intersection at the bottom of the hill.

"Turn right," I said. We were going to Eric's Place, my favorite spot for breakfast.

Andrew found a parking space on the street and managed to wedge the little red car he was driving into it. We got out and headed for the restaurant. "What's the food like?" he asked.

"Excellent," I said, as we stepped inside.

"Oh, good." His tone told me that he didn't exactly believe me. He looked around, taking in the space that looked more like a small-town coffee shop than a five-star restaurant.

Claire smiled from behind the counter. She grabbed a menu and came toward us. "Hey, Kathleen. What happened to your arm?" she asked.

"I twisted my shoulder. It's nothing serious," I said.

The smile got wider. "I'm glad. Table for two?"

I nodded.

She gave Andrew a quick appraising glance. "Window or wall?"

"Window," I said before Andrew could suggest we get a slightly more private table along the end wall of the small café.

Claire showed us to the table with the best view of the sidewalk. "Welcome to Eric's," she said to Andrew as she handed him a menu.

He gave her the full power of that smile. "Thank you."

"Claire, this is my friend Andrew from Boston," I said.

"Nice to meet you," she said. Her eyes flicked from me to Andrew, but that was the only giveaway that she was curious about who he was and what he was doing in town. She turned to me. "Would you like a couple of minutes for your friend to look through the menu before you order?"

"Actually, no," I said. I looked across the table at Andrew, who was still checking the place out but trying not to be obvious about it. "How about letting me order for you?"

"Uh . . . okay," he said slowly.

I knew if Andrew ordered his own breakfast he would go for ham and eggs, and while Eric did a good job with that breakfast basic, I wanted to show off just a little.

"Two breakfast sandwiches," I told Claire. "The new one."

She nodded approvingly. "Good choice." Then she picked up the menu, tucked it under her arm and turned to Andrew. "Coffee?" she asked. She didn't have to ask me that question.

"Please," he said.

"I'll be right back."

Eric came out of the kitchen then and raised his hand in hello when he caught sight of me. I lifted my good hand in return. I saw him give Andrew a second look and then say something to Claire before she returned with the coffeepot and a little pitcher of cream.

"I heard what happened last night," she said quietly as she poured my cup.

For a moment I wondered how on earth she could know what had happened between Marcus and me. Then I realized she meant what happened before that, at the tent set up for the food tasting that was scheduled for this afternoon.

The tasting—and an art show—had been planned as part of the town's presentation to a corporate tour company—before one of the partners in the firm had been killed down near the Riverwalk.

"Did Liam cancel everything?" I asked.

Claire shook her head. "Nope. The tasting is starting an hour later, but otherwise everything is a go. Mary was in about an hour ago. They're already starting to get the booths ready." She gave Andrew a curious glance. "You're still coming, right?"

"Absolutely."

She smiled. "I'll save you a bowl of pudding cake."

Andrew added sugar to his coffee and took a sip. "Hey, this is good," he said.

I folded my free arm across my chest and studied him across the table without speaking.

"What?" he said, holding out both hands. "I said it was good."

I continued to stare silently at him.

His face flushed. "Okay, so I thought I was going to end up with a cup of something closer to paint thinner. How did you know that?"

I gave him my Mr. Spock eyebrow and reached for my own cup. "I know you."

"Yes, you do," he said, his expression serious.

I took a sip of my coffee so I wouldn't have to say anything.

"What's so great about this breakfast sandwich?" Andrew asked after the silence had gone on just a little bit too long.

"You'll have to wait and see," I said. "But if you don't like it, I'll buy you anything else on the menu."

He grinned. "You're on." Then he shifted sideways in his chair and reached for his cup. "Tell me about this tasting thing you were talking about to our waitress."

"It's this afternoon, by the boardwalk along the water. A Taste of Mayville Heights." I folded my hand around my mug. "Where are you staying?"

"The St. James Hotel."

"Did you see the tents across the street?"

He nodded.

"That's where it is."

"Sounds like fun," he said. "How about showing me around?"

"I have to work." I shifted to one side so the back of the chair wasn't digging into my shoulder.

"I heard you say you were going."

"On my lunch hour."

"I'll meet you at the library, then. What time?"

I shook my head. "You don't give up, do you?"

"Nope." He tented his fingers over the top of his cup. "I told you—I came here to get you back. I'm not giving up. I'm just getting started."

I didn't have a chance to answer because Eric was on his way to the table with our order. "Hey, Kathleen," he said with a smile as he put a heavy oval plate in front of me.

The aroma of pan-toasted sourdough bread and bacon tickled my nose. "Hi, Eric," I said. "It smells wonderful."

"Thanks." He eyed my left arm. "You okay?"

"It looks worse than it really is." It struck me that maybe I should make a little sign that read I'M ALL RIGHT and stick it on the front of the nylon sling so I didn't have to keep explaining myself all day. On the other hand, it was nice to have so many people who cared about me.

Eric slid Andrew's plate in front of him, assessed him with a quick look and then held out his hand. "Welcome. I'm Eric."

"Andrew," he said.

They shook hands.

"Andrew's a friend from Boston," I added.

"Good to meet you," Eric said. "Enjoy your breakfast." He looked at me and his eyebrows went up just slightly, but all he said was, "Claire will be over in a minute with more coffee."

Andrew reached for half of his sandwich and took

a large bite. That was followed, after a moment, by a grunt of pleasure. "This is good." He gestured at the plate. "What's in it?"

I moved my own plate a little closer. "Bacon, to-matoes, a little fresh mozzarella, a little thyme, and sourdough bread."

"Don't tell me everything on the menu is this good." He took another huge bite.

"Just make sure you try the chocolate pudding cake if you go to the food tasting." As I looked over his shoulder, the front door opened and Maggie and Roma came in.

Perfect timing.

2

Maggie and Roma looked around, smiling when they caught sight of me.

I waved hello and they made their way over to us.

"Hi," Maggie said. She looked from me to Andrew, curiosity obvious in her blue eyes.

"Hi, Mags," I said. I smiled up at Roma. "Hi."

"How's your shoulder?" she asked.

"Better," I said.

"Honestly?"

"Yes."

"Can you move it?"

I nodded.

She reached out a hand and then stopped herself. "May I?"

"Go ahead." I shifted forward in my seat so she could lean down and feel my shoulder. Her fingers were gentle as they probed around the joint.

"I think most of the swelling has gone down," she said, straightening up after a moment.

"Are you Kathleen's doctor?" Andrew asked.

Maggie laughed. "In a manner of speaking, she is."

I leaned back in the chair again. "Actually, Roma is Hercules and Owen's doctor."

"You're a—?"

"Veterinarian," Roma finished.

"And a first-aid responder," I added. "She knows how to take care of four-legged and two-legged patients."

"Good to know you have friends who have your back," Andrew said. He stood up. "I'm Andrew. I'm a friend of Kathleen's from Boston. Would you two like to join us?"

Roma smiled and offered her hand. "It's good to meet you. I'm Roma Davidson."

"And I'm Maggie Adams," Maggie said. "Welcome to Mayville Heights, and yes, we'd love to join you."

Andrew moved aside and Maggie slipped into the chair next to him. Roma came around the table and took the seat next to me. Out of the corner of my eye I saw Claire, already on her way over with coffee, along with a teapot and hot water for Maggie, who didn't drink coffee.

"Hi, guys," she said, giving Maggie her tea and pouring coffee for Roma without setting down the tray she'd carried everything over on. "What can I get for you?"

"I'll have what they're having," Maggie said, tipping her head toward the last half of the sandwich on my plate.

"It smells wonderful," Roma said. "Me too."

"It'll just be a couple of minutes," Claire said. She topped up my cup and Andrew's. I saw her hold up two fingers to Eric as she went back to the kitchen.

"So what are you doing in Mayville Heights?" Maggie asked, dropping a tea bag into the little stoneware pot and pouring in the hot water. "Are you here for business or is this a vacation?" Subtlety was not one of Maggie's strengths.

"I came to win Kathleen back," Andrew said. Then he tipped his head to one side and gave me a sweet—and very phony—smile across the table.

Beside me Roma cleared her throat and picked up her coffee. Since Maggie wasn't the type of person to beat around the bush, Andrew's directness didn't faze her. "So what took you so long?" she asked.

I blew out a breath. "Mags," I said softly. I should have guessed she'd ask a question like that.

Andrew was already shaking his head. "It's okay, Kathleen," he said. "I don't mind answering your friend's questions." He propped his elbow on the back of the chair so he was turned partly toward Maggie. "You know about the fishing trip."

She nodded, reaching for her cup to pour the tea.

"At first I was still married. It took a while to have the whole thing annulled."

"And after that?"

He played with his fork. "After that I was mad."

"At Kathleen," Maggie said. She took a sip of her tea and watched him over the top of the cup.

"Yes."

"She's not the one who married a waitress from a fifties diner," Maggie said, her blue eyes locked on his face.

He blushed, but he didn't look away. "No, she wasn't," he said. "Look, I know I'm the one who messed up. I'm not saying I had a right to be mad because Kathleen left Boston. I'm just saying that I was."

"Okay, I can understand that," Maggie said.

Claire returned then with Roma's and Maggie's breakfast orders and more hot coffee. Once she'd taken a couple of bites of her sandwich, Maggie turned her attention back to Andrew.

"So, when did you stop being angry? I'm assuming that you're not anymore."

He smiled at me across the table, a genuine smile this time. I remembered when that look used to make my heart race and, truth be told, it was thumping just a beat or two faster now.

"No, I'm not angry anymore," he said, letting his gaze slide off my face and back to Maggie.

Was I imagining that he did it with just a bit of reluctance?

"I stopped being mad the first time I saw her again."

"The first time you saw me again was less than twelve hours ago," I said. I'd thought he was going to say it was when we'd talked on the phone several months ago.

Andrew's face flushed.

"You saw Kathleen when she was back in Boston this summer," Roma said.

He exhaled slowly before he answered. "Yes."

"When?" I asked.

He ducked his head. "You were playing football in the park with Ethan and Sara. Your mother and father were there, too."

And my best friend in Boston, Lise.

I remembered that day. Lise had taken a photo of the five of us and surprised me with it, in a small frame, the day I'd flown back to Mayville Heights. I kept it on my desk at the library. It was one of my favorite photographs of my crazy family.

"Why didn't you come say hello?" I asked, adding more sugar to my coffee.

He made a face. "Oh yeah, that would have been a good idea. Walk over and say, how the heck have you been, after a year and a half, with your whole family standing there."

I nodded and smiled, picturing in my mind what might have happened if he'd just walked up to us in the park that day. "He's right about that."

Heaven knows what the twins would have done, not to mention my mother. She'd always thought Andrew was good for me, but when it came to taking sides she was one hundred percent on mine.

He leaned back in the chair so he was facing all three of us. "Short version of a long story—when I saw Kathleen in the park it showed me just how much I'd screwed up, and just how much I'd lost. So I moved my schedule around and decided I'd come here in person and try to win her back."

"What if she doesn't want you back?" Maggie asked. She looked around for Claire and when she caught the waitress's eye pointed at the little stainless-steel water pot.

"I have two weeks before I have to deal with that," Andrew said. "I plan to spend those two weeks trying to show Kathleen that I've changed."

Maggie looked at me.

"I already told Andrew to go back to Boston."

He folded his arms across his chest and shook his head. "I'm not going anywhere. Not yet."

Claire appeared at the table with a carafe of hot water for Maggie's tea. As she stirred the tea, Maggie began asking Andrew about his life in Boston. Roma took the opportunity to lean over to me. "He's determined," she said softly.

"That he is," I whispered. "I'm not sure what to do."

She gave a small shrug. "Why do you have to do anything?"

I thought about it for a moment. Maybe I didn't. I hadn't led Andrew on or given him any reason to think he could win me back like I was a big plush dog at the county fair. I couldn't stop him from trying, though. Marcus had told me once that I liked to control things. Maybe this time I needed to take my hands off the steering wheel and see what happened.

Thinking about Marcus, I automatically looked

out the window, hoping I'd see him headed up the sidewalk for a cup of take-out coffee and one of Eric's famous cinnamon rolls. All I saw was Burtis Chapman driving by in his truck.

Seeing Burtis made me think about Lita. I'd seen Everett's secretary and Burtis in the library parking lot a few days ago, and I now had a suspicion that the two of them might be a couple. I wasn't sure if they'd seen me because I'd done a swan dive onto the front seat of my truck when I caught sight of them standing close together in what looked like a very private moment. I felt a little embarrassed about that. Burtis and Lita were adults, and there was no reason for them not to see each other. If they were a couple, though, how had they managed to keep it from the entire town? Again, none of my business. I had library business with Lita. That was all.

Roma was studying my face. "Have you talked to Marcus yet?" she asked. There was concern in her dark brown eyes.

"Maggie told you what happened." I shifted again in my chair and rubbed my shoulder.

"Last night." She paused as though she was weighing her words before she committed to them. "Kathleen, Marcus is an intense man and being a police officer isn't just what he does; it's part of who he is. But he does care about you. I'm certain about that. You'll work it out."

I thought about the rocking chair that Marcus had to have spent hours fixing for me. I thought about the one and only time we'd kissed. "I hope so," I said.

I reached for my mug, drank the last of my coffee and glanced at my watch. It was time to head to the library.

Roma had seen me check the time. "I have to get going as well," she said. Across the table Maggie and Andrew were still deep in conversation.

"Thank you for coming," I said, turning sideways in my chair so I was facing her. The meeting wasn't just by chance. I'd called Roma and Maggie and asked them to meet us at the café.

"You're welcome. You'd do the same for me." She smiled and put her napkin on the table. "Andrew isn't what I expected."

"What did you expect?"

"I don't know, exactly. Someone a little . . . cockier, maybe." She folded her napkin and set it next to her plate. "He seems genuinely sorry."

I turned to look at Andrew for a moment. As if he could somehow feel my eyes on him, his gaze flicked in my direction and he smiled at me before giving Maggie all his attention again.

"Yes, he does," I said. I pushed back from the table and got to my feet.

Andrew stood up as well and gave Roma and Maggie his killer smile. "It was good to meet you both," he said. "Breakfast is on me."

That got him three "no's" in response.

He looked at me. "Yes. I invited you."

Roma nodded. "You invited Kathleen. Not Maggie and me."

"Kathleen invited you," he said with a slight shrug. He looked at me. "I'll be right back and I'll walk you to the library." He was on his way to the cash register before I had a chance to object to that, too.

Maggie came around the table and hugged me, careful not to squeeze my left arm. "How are you?" she asked, concern making tiny lines around her eyes.

"I'm okay."

"I don't just mean your arm."

"I know," I said.

She pointed at Andrew, who was at the counter talking to Eric. "He's nice. I tried to dislike him, but I couldn't."

"It's all right. He is nice." I reached for my sweater. "And he's wasting his time. Things were over between us a long time ago." I slid my right arm into the sleeve and Roma draped the other side over my sling.

"Don't overdo it, Kathleen," she warned.

"I won't," I promised. "If I need extra help Abigail already offered to come in for a few hours."

She still looked skeptical.

I held up three fingers. "Librarian's honor."

Roma laughed then. "Oh well, *that* puts my mind at ease." She turned to Maggie. "Would you like a ride over to River Arts?"

Maggie shook her head, making her blond curls jiggle. "Thanks, but I'll walk. I need to stop at the co-op store. You're coming to the tasting this afternoon?"

Roma nodded. "Absolutely. I have to go out to the Kings' after lunch to check on Taylor's horse and the rest of my afternoon is clear, assuming there are no emergencies."

They both looked at me. Roma had had to use her medical skills on me more than once. "I'm not going to do anything risky," I said solemnly. Then I held up the three fingers again.

"I better get going," Roma said. She squeezed my good arm. "I'll talk to you later."

Maggie wrapped her in a hug. "Call me if anything changes," she said.

Roma nodded and threaded her way through the tables to go say good-bye to Andrew.

"Have you spoken to Marcus?" Maggie asked.

I shook my head.

"It'll work out."

"I don't know, Mags," I said. "Marcus and I have some pretty big differences. Maybe there isn't any way to work them out."

She was wearing three twisted silver bracelets and she pushed them up her arm. "It'll work out," she repeated. "What's meant to be always finds a way to be."

I waved at Roma as she headed out the door. "So you think Marcus and I are meant to be?"

Maggie laughed. "Where have you been for the last year and a half?"

Andrew joined us again.

"I'll see you this afternoon," I said to Maggie.

"I'll be back and forth between the tents and the community center," she said. She leaned around me to speak to Andrew. "Are you coming to the food tasting and art show this afternoon?"

"Yes, I am," he said. He shot me a sideways look. "If someone takes pity on me and agrees to show me around."

At that moment, outside the diner, Burtis Chapman was coming up the sidewalk, likely on his way back to his truck. Burtis was a big block of a man. He looked as though he could wrench the top off a bottle with one hand. Or someone's head off his neck.

"I think I could find someone to do that," Maggie said sweetly. She pointed out the window. "There's Burtis. I'm sure he'd be happy to show you around."

Andrew just laughed. "It was good to meet you, Maggie," he said.

She smiled. "You too."

We walked out together. Maggie went down the street and Andrew and I turned left toward the library. "So did I pass inspection?" he asked after we'd walked a few feet.

"They liked you," I said.

He wiggled his eyebrows. "I'm very likable."

I ignored the comment. "How did you know I asked them to meet us?"

"I know you," he said. "You haven't changed that much." He reached over and brushed a stray piece of hair off my face. Andrew had made that same gesture dozens of times when we were going out, but it felt too personal this time. Without really thinking about it, I took a step sideways, putting a little more space between us.

His face flushed. "Sorry," he said softly.

We walked in uncomfortable silence to the corner. I was trying to think of some new way to tell Andrew to go home and I wasn't paying any attention to people coming down the hill. So I didn't see Marcus until I literally walked into him.

He caught me by my shoulders to steady me. "I'm sorry, Kathleen," he said. "I wasn't looking where I was going. Are you all right?"

I nodded. "It's not your fault. I wasn't paying attention, either." I stared up into his blue eyes, feeling ridiculously happy just to be standing there.

He seemed to realize then that he was still holding on to me. He dropped his hands and I caught the scent of his citrusy aftershave before he stepped back.

"You did hurt your arm." He gestured at the sling.

"It's not serious," I said, rubbing the shoulder where his hand had rested just a moment before. Was I imagining that I could still feel the warmth from his fingers?

"It looks serious."

"It's not—I promise. Roma and Maggie took me

to the emergency room. The sling is just to keep me from using my arm for a few days."

"That's good." He jammed both hands in the pockets of his jacket, his gaze never leaving my face. "I'm glad you're all right." I waited for him to say he'd gotten my messages, that he was sorry, angry, anything. But he didn't.

Beside me Andrew shifted from one foot to the other.

I cleared my throat. "Marcus, this is my friend Andrew Reid. He's here from Boston." I turned to Andrew. "Andrew, this is Detective Marcus Gordon."

It seemed to me that Marcus stood just a little straighter as he held out his hand. Andrew definitely did, squaring his shoulders and taking a step forward to shake hands.

"Welcome to Mayville Heights," Marcus said. "Are you here for the food tasting?"

"No, I'm not," Andrew said with a cool smile that was nothing like the charming grin he'd used on Maggie at the café. He shot me a quick sideways glance.

I'd never told Marcus about my relationship with Andrew, but it was clear from the way his face shifted into his unreadable police officer expression that he'd figured out there had been something between us. Both men were sizing each other up and not being very subtle about it. I felt a little like they were a couple of German shepherds and I was a fire hydrant.

"I need to get to the station," Marcus said abruptly. "Take care of your arm, Kathleen." He gave Andrew an almost imperceptible nod and continued down the sidewalk.

Andrew and I crossed the street and continued on to the library. "I suppose in a small place like this you get to know pretty much everyone," he said after a couple of minutes of silence.

I knew a fishing expedition when I heard one. "That's one of the things I like about Mayville Heights."

"You know a lot of people in Boston."

We were almost at the library. "I know that," I said, stopping again so I could look at him full-on. "I know my family is there. And Lise, and a lot of other people I care about. But you're still wasting your time. I'm not going to fall into your arms and ride off into the sunset with you." I started walking again and he scrambled to keep up with me.

"Sunrise," he said after a moment.

I frowned at him. "Excuse me?"

"Sunrise." He made a gesture in the general direction of the river. "We'd be going east, so we'd be riding off into the sunrise."

I took a deep breath and turned toward the library steps. I thought it was a better idea than pushing him into the nearest flower bed, which was what I'd suddenly had an intense urge to do.

Mary was just coming from the parking lot. "Good morning, Kathleen," she said. She smiled at Andrew and offered her right hand. There was a mischievous gleam in her eye. "Hello, I'm Mary Lowe," she said. "And you are?"

Tiny and gray-haired, Mary looked like she should be in the kitchen baking apple pies—which she did like to do. She was also the state kickboxing champion for her age and weight class. She may have looked like a sweet little grandmother, but she also had what she called her don't-give-a-flying-fig-newton side.

Andrew shook her hand and introduced himself. I went up the steps, unlocked the main doors and turned off the alarm.

He stepped through the second set of doors and stopped. I watched him take in the wide wooden trim, the stained-glass windows and the mosaic tile floor. "Oh, Kath, this is nice work. Very nice work," he said, nodding his head as he continued to look around.

I grinned as though I'd actually been the one to repair the mosaic floor tiles and sand the gleaming woodwork.

"This is one of the Carnegie libraries."

Mary nodded, shifting her quilted tote bag from one hand to the other. "It was built a hundred years ago."

Andrew gestured toward the curve of windows in the computer area overlooking the water. "All that trim can't be original."

"It's not." You could hear the pride in Mary's voice and see it in her smile.

"Someone did some excellent work in here."

"That would be Oren Kenyon," I said.

"And Kathleen," Mary added, beaming at me. "None of this would have happened without her." She turned her attention back to Andrew. "You like old buildings."

He nodded. "Yes, I do."

"Mary, would you do me a favor?" I asked.

"Of course," she said at once. "What is it?"

"Could you put together a little walking tour of town for Andrew and give him directions?"

"I'd love to."

"I don't want to put you out," he said.

"Nonsense." She waved away his objection with her free hand. "In fact, I think Susan put a few of those new walking maps of the downtown out here." She moved behind the circulation desk to take a look.

Andrew walked over to me. He propped one arm on my right shoulder. "Very nice, but you can't get rid of me that easily," he whispered.

I smiled sweetly and gave a noncommittal shrug, which also managed to dislodge his arm.

"Found them," Mary said. She beckoned to Andrew. "Since you like old buildings, I think the place to start is the Stratton Theater."

I picked up my briefcase. "Enjoy your tour," I said to Andrew.

"I will," he said. Then he raised his voice a little. "And don't worry, I'll be back in plenty of time for us to go to the food tasting. You said one o'clock, right?"

His gaze met mine and I could see the challenge in his green eyes, daring me to say no.

"One thirty," I said tightly, narrowing my own gaze back at him.

"The food tasting is going to be splendid," Mary said. She patted Andrew's arm. "I think you got here at just the perfect time."

His eyes slid away from me and he grinned at her, giving her the full-on charming-boy-next-door smile. "You know," he said, "I think you're right."

3

Everett Henderson called at exactly one minute after nine. Susan had arrived and was working the circulation desk. "I'll take it in my office," I told her.

"What did you do with that tasty treat you had breakfast with?" she asked after she'd told Everett I'd be right with him and put him on hold.

"That what?" I said, staring at her.

"The guy you had breakfast with. That's what Claire called him, and from her description I'm guessing it wasn't your dad or your brother." She propped an elbow on the desktop and leaned her chin on her hand. "So who was it? A husband you never told us you had? Your Internet love from Mismatch.com? The guy who had a crush on you in first grade and never forgot you so he hired a private detective to track you down?"

My sling meant I couldn't cross my arms and give her my best stern-librarian look, so I settled for folding my free arm over my chest and wrinkling my nose at her. "No more old-movie marathons for you," I said. "They make your imagination go into overdrive." I started for the stairs. "I'm going to take Everett's call."

"I'm not letting this go," Susan called after me.

"I didn't think you would," I said, waving over my shoulder in case she hadn't heard me. Upstairs I unlocked my office door and immediately reached for the phone. I didn't want to keep Everett waiting.

"Good morning, Everett," I said, pulling the phone closer and sinking down onto the corner of the desk. "I was just about to call you."

"I take it you've talked to Abigail." He had a deep, strong voice and a clipped way of speaking that made him sound younger than his seventy-odd years.

"I have."

"Good. Then I don't have to give you all the details." I could hear papers being moved and I guessed that he was in his office just up the hill from Maggie's studio in the River Arts Center. "I've talked to everyone and the library board is fully behind using the building and the grounds to help make this festival a success. Wouldn't hurt to bring some tourist dollars to town this time of year."

"I'll help in any way I can," I said, picking gray cat hair off my gray trousers, proof that Owen had been sitting in the bedroom chair on top of the pants while I'd been brushing my teeth.

"I knew I could count on you, Kathleen. Thank you."

"You're welcome," I said. "Abigail's already talking about using the new gazebo as a stage."

He laughed. "That idea came from Rebecca."

I really wasn't surprised. Rebecca, my backyard neighbor and Everett's soon-to-be wife, was a very creative person and she was usually involved in whatever was happening around town in one way or the other.

"How are the wedding plans coming?" I asked.

"I think we have a date . . . maybe."

"You could always run off to Las Vegas and get married by an Elvis impersonator."

Everett laughed. "You've been talking to Rebecca. She's the only woman I've ever come across who's getting married but doesn't care about the details."

"All Rebecca wants is to be married to you." The edge of my desk wasn't made for sitting on in any kind of comfort so I stood up and turned to look out the window. The clouds were clearing away. It was going to be a nice afternoon.

"I want that, too," he said. "I've wanted it for a long time."

"I'll see if I can put in a good word for you," I said.

"I appreciate that." His tone turned serious. "Kathleen, with Abigail working on the theater festival for the next couple of weeks, you're going to be stretched a little thin. Why don't we put off our conversation about your future here until it's over?"

"That's fine with me, Everett," I said. He reminded me, as he always did, to call Lita if I needed anything and we said good-bye. I hung up the phone and went to sit in my desk chair.

Having a couple of extra weeks to decide whether I was going to stay in Mayville Heights was just what I needed. It gave me time to figure things out with Marcus.

I reached for the photo that Lise had taken when I'd been back in Boston over the summer, the day that Andrew had seen us in the park. My mother was laughing, leaning back against Dad's shoulder. When they were working on a play together they tended to get a little too caught up in their characters, which meant things could get decidedly odd around the house, but they were crazy about each other, even when they drove each other crazy. Always had been, which was why they'd been married twice—to each other.

Marcus made me crazy sometimes. I liked him—a lot more than I'd been willing to admit to anyone, especially myself. Well, Owen and Hercules appeared to have figured it out. But we always seemed to bang heads over his cases. Being a police officer was more than Marcus's job; it was part of who he was. Just the way wanting to help the people I cared about was part of who I was. Were we crazy enough about each other to work through the things that made us crazy? I wasn't sure.

I rubbed the space between my eyebrows with the heel of my hand. What had Maggie said to me?

What's meant to be always finds a way to be. Maybe what I needed to do was take a step back and let whatever was meant to be just happen. I just wasn't very good at that.

It was late morning and I had my head in the book drop—literally—trying to figure out why it kept jamming when it was half full of books, when I heard a group of people come into the library. I straightened up to find a tall man dressed all in black—leather jacket, jeans and tee—smiling at me.

"Kathleen Paulson, what on earth are you doing here?" he said.

"I work here," I said, beaming back at him. "Are you part of the theater festival?"

He nodded. "I'm the artistic director. When Abigail Pierce said the librarian's name was Kathleen, I had no idea it was going to be you."

I hadn't seen Ben Saroyan in years. He'd directed my parents in several productions and he'd given my mother her first directing job. He looked exactly the same, very tall and thin with a lined, craggy face, dark eyes and short, iron gray hair that seemed to grow straight up from his head.

"How are Thea and John?" he asked. Ben had a deep, booming voice that seemed a bit at odds with his long, lanky frame.

"Dad is in rehearsals for *Noises Off* and Mom's in Los Angeles working on *Wild and Wonderful*." The soap happened to be one of Maggie's favorite shows.

He slid his round wire-rimmed glasses up his

nose and laughed. "I seem to remember Thea saying she was never doing a soap again after the last time. How did they change her mind?"

There were bits of paper stuck to the front of my shirt. I brushed them away with my free hand. "It's a short-term contract," I said. "And the executive producer sent her a chocolate cheesecake every day for a week until she said yes." I laughed at the memory. "Mom was ready to sign by the second day, but she held out for an entire week for all the cheesecake."

Ben laughed, the sound bouncing off the library walls. "That sounds like Thea." He seemed to realize then that he hadn't introduced the man and woman who had come in with him. "I'm sorry, Kathleen," he said. "This is Hugh Davis. He's my other director, and Hannah Walker, who's one of our actors." He smiled at me. "Kathleen is Thea and John Paulson's daughter."

Hugh Davis held out his hand. He was a couple of inches shorter than Ben. His brown hair was on the longish side, streaked with white at the temples. And there was some gray in his close-cropped goatee. "I saw your mother years ago in *A Midsummer Night's Dream*," he said. "She's very talented."

"Thank you." I shook his hand. I could hear just a hint of a British accent in his voice, which made me wonder if he'd worked or studied in Great Britain. I didn't recognize his face or his name, but I knew my mother would. She knew everyone in the theater world.

I did recognize Hannah Walker, though. I'd seen her in a couple of commercials, and I was fairly certain she'd had a role on an episode of *Law & Order*.

"Hi, Kathleen. It's nice to meet you," she said with a smile.

"You too," I said. Hannah was somewhere in her twenties, with dark, wavy hair to her shoulders and deep blue eyes. There was something instantly likable about her. Maybe it was the genuine warmth in her smile and the interest in her gaze.

Ben had one hand in his jacket pocket, jiggling his keys or something. I remembered then that he wasn't a very patient person.

"You didn't come here just to see me, Ben," I said. "What can I do for you?"

"Abigail said there's a gazebo here that we could use for one of the outdoor performances."

I nodded. "It's at the back, overlooking the water."

Hugh Davis made a sour face. "The acoustics are going to be deplorable," he said to Ben.

I shook my head. "Not necessarily. The river actually curves at this point." I gestured toward the back of the library. "We're sheltered from both the wind and the street noise."

"Good," Ben said, as though the issue had been settled.

Hugh still looked unhappy. "How much space is there? Where are people going to sit? I'm not convinced that this is the best way to showcase our productions."

I was starting to be irritated by the man already, and he'd been in the building for only a few minutes. He didn't seem to know much about the theater world's history of taking performances to the street. The Romans had celebrated festival performances of street theater. During the Middle Ages professional theater companies were traveling and performing all over England.

I opened my mouth to say something, changed my mind and closed it again, glancing at Hannah as I did so. Her body language suggested she didn't like Hugh very much. She'd folded her arms across her chest and she was leaning just slightly away from him.

I took a deep breath, exhaled and pasted on my best polite-librarian smile. "The gazebo is probably bigger than you're expecting." I pointed again toward the tall bank of windows that rimmed the computer area. "There's lots of lawn out there and we have folding chairs you're welcome to use. Why don't I take you around and let you see for yourself?"

Ben rolled his left arm over to look at his watch. "I have about five minutes," he said. He turned to Hugh. "Let's take a look."

Hugh shrugged. "Fine."

I stepped sideways so I could see Susan at the desk. "We're just going out to take a look at the gazebo."

She nodded.

As I turned back around I caught sight of Marcus coming through the front doors. His face lit up with a smile as he looked in our direction and I felt my heart start to pound like a rock band drum solo. Without really thinking about it, I took a couple of steps toward him—and then stopped.

Because Hannah had already beaten me to him. She threw herself into Marcus's arms and he wrapped her in a bear hug, leaning down to kiss the top of her head.

They knew each other. Obviously very well.

She broke out of the hug, still grinning from ear to ear at him. Her arm went around his waist and with his arm across her shoulders they walked over to us.

Marcus's eyes darted to my face. I wasn't sure what I was seeing in his expression—embarrassment or uncertainty, or maybe a bit of both.

Hannah leaned against him with the familiarity of someone who'd known him a long time. And looking at them I got it, just as she started to speak.

"Everyone, this is my big brother, Marcus." She introduced Ben and Hugh and then turned to me. "Kathleen, you probably already know each other."

"Yes, we do," I said, rubbing the top of my left shoulder, which had suddenly started to ache again.

Hannah didn't know anything about me. Which in an odd way made sense, since I didn't know anything about her. I'd known that Marcus had a sister, but I didn't know her name or that she was an actress. He was a very private person, but the fact that I didn't even know his sister's name was more than a little odd.

My mouth was suddenly dry and I had to swallow before I spoke. "Marcus, I need to take Ben and Hugh outside to look at the gazebo. You could take Hannah over to the chairs by the windows and catch up."

"Sure," he said. His hair was a shade darker than his sister's, but they had the same blue eyes.

Before he could say anything else, I touched Ben's arm. "Let's go," I said. I could feel Marcus's eyes on me as we moved toward the door, warming my back as though I were standing in a beam of sunlight. Or maybe it was my imagination. I didn't turn around to find out.

Ben seemed happy with the gazebo and the wide expanse of lawn around it. The trees and the rock wall acted as a natural sound barrier and to me it seemed like a perfect place to stage a short play. Even Hugh couldn't find real fault with the space, although he did try.

When we walked back around the building I saw Hannah waiting beside a silver SUV in the parking lot.

"Abigail will be in touch about the schedule and what we need for chairs and space and"—Ben flung his hands into the air—"everything."

"Don't worry," I said. "We'll work it all out."

"Give my best to your mother and father." He pulled a set of keys out of his jacket pocket. "If Thea weren't in Los Angeles, I'd get a cheesecake and try to lure her here."

"It would probably work," I said with a laugh.

They walked in the direction of the parking lot and I headed for the main doors. Marcus was waiting at the bottom of the stairs.

"Kathleen, do you have a couple of minutes?" he asked.

"Of course," I said. I pointed toward the stone path that curved around the building. "Do you want to walk?"

He nodded. "Your arm hurts," he said as we started along the walkway.

I'd been rubbing my shoulder again and didn't even realize it. "I'm all right," I said.

He continued to look at me but didn't say anything.

"Okay, so it aches, but just a little. I swear."

"Don't overdo it, please," he said.

"I'm not . . . I won't."

We followed the path back to the gazebo and over to the rock wall. Farther along the shoreline I could see the large warehouses, built from stone cut at Wild Rose Bluff, that had stored lumber for shipping downriver back in Mayville Heights's heyday as a lumber town.

"Thank you for my chair," I said, watching a seagull floating on the surface dip his head below the water. "You did a beautiful job."

Out of the corner of my eye I saw a small smile on

his face. "You're welcome. Thank you for the cupcakes. I was the most popular person in the building for a while."

I'd sent a dozen chocolate peanut butter cupcakes over to the police station as a thank-you for the chair. And maybe as a small please-forgive-me.

"I like Hannah," I said, tipping my head back to look up at him.

"Everyone does."

"Why does she use Walker instead of Gordon?"

"Walker was our grandmother's name. She and Hannah were close." He hesitated. "I should have told you more about her."

I looked away and then back at him before I spoke. "I wish you'd told me something. You said you had a sister, but I only know her name because she came into the library today. You mentioned your father, but I don't know if he's alive or dead. Or your mother." I cleared my throat. "Last night you said I didn't trust you, but now I realize I don't know anything about you. Are you sure you trust me?"

I could feel his body tense.

He swiped a hand over the back of his neck. "My mother and father are both alive and well."

I waited for him to say something about them. "My father's a Supreme Court justice," or "He grows organic soybeans on a commune in Oregon and my mother is a circus contortionist." But he didn't offer anything else.

My chest felt heavy, as though an elephant had

decided to use it as a footstool. "Marcus, I'm sorry about last night," I said. I held up my hand before he could say anything. "I'm sorry that what I did made you feel like I didn't have faith in you, or trust you. I think you're a very good police officer. And a good person." I took a breath and let it out. "I like you. And I think you like me, but we seem to be at an impasse."

For a long moment he just stared out over the water. I waited until he looked at me. "Can we be friends?" he asked.

I didn't want to be friends with Marcus. I wanted to be . . . something else. I wasn't exactly sure what the something else was, or maybe I just didn't want to admit it to myself. But right now, maybe friends was all we could manage.

"I hope so," I said. The sun was shining and what few clouds there were seemed to be floating in the sky, but all of a sudden I felt cold. "I need to get back to work," I said. "I'll . . . see you."

I went back along the path and some small part of me hoped that he'd come after me or at least call my name, but he didn't.

Susan returned from lunch at the food-tasting tents just before one thirty, smelling like caramel, with a dab of whipped cream on her nose and another on her ear.

"I don't even want to know how you got whipped cream on your ear," I said, as Abigail came through the front door, talking on her cell phone and carrying

what looked like a canvas army satchel, bulging
with papers.

"That would be Eric," Susan said with a grin. She
swiped at her ear and licked the bit of cream off her
finger. "He was getting pudding cake ready to serve,
but he got a little sidetracked." She wiggled her eyebrows at me.

"Way, way more information than I needed," I
said, holding up my good hand.

That just made her laugh. Then she cocked her
head to one side and peered at me over the top of her
cat-eye glasses. "Speaking of information, I'm going
to need way, way more about Andrew." She did the
eyebrow thing again and started for the stairs.

"Kathleen, I'm sorry I'm late," Abigail said as she
tucked her phone in her pocket. She set her bag on
the circulation desk.

"You're not late." I glanced at the clock. "How are
things going with the festival?"

She shook her head. "Kathleen, are you familiar
with the play *Yesterday's Children*?"

"Uh-huh."

"So you know some people think it's . . . cursed,
or jinxed?"

"I know," I said. "The theater burned down on the
day before the very first production. A lighting tech
broke his leg and I think one of the actors was in a
car accident."

"*Yesterday's Children* was originally on the schedule for the festival."

I nodded. "Doesn't surprise me. Ben's not that superstitious, as far as I know."

Abigail shifted her bag on the counter, tucking a couple of loose papers inside. "There was some kind of problem with the rights and the play was dropped, but . . ." She let the end of the sentence trail off.

I gave her a wry smile. "Let me guess. People are saying the fire in Red Wing was because of the so-called jinx."

"Exactly. Some of the actors are a little skittish. And it doesn't help that this would have been the fourth year for the festival in Red Wing. Several of the tech people and a couple of the actors have done the festival before. People on the festival committee in Red Wing know them. I don't know a single person involved and neither does anyone else here. It makes it that much harder for all of us." She glanced quickly at her watch. "Has Ben Saroyan been in yet?"

I nodded. "I know Ben. He's worked with my mother. You'll find him easy to get along with. He seems to think the gazebo will work fine, and I think there are enough chairs here so you won't have to bring any down from the Stratton. And I got the okay from Everett, by the way."

"Thank you, Kathleen. You're a godsend," Abigail said. "I suppose Hugh wasn't happy with the gazebo."

"He doesn't seem that enthusiastic about having performances outside."

Her fingers played with the strap of the canvas satchel. "He's still a control freak, I've discovered."

"Is there anything else I can do?" I said.

She shook her head. "The biggest problem I have at the moment is that Young Harry took Elizabeth home to her other family. He won't be back until next weekend."

Elizabeth was the daughter of my friend Harry Taylor Senior. She was the result of a relationship he'd had when his wife was dying. They'd just found each other in the past few months.

"Why is that a problem? Oren's around, isn't he?" I glanced over at the wooden sunburst that Oren Kenyon had built, hanging above the library doors. It was a tribute to the library's history as a Carnegie library.

Abigail put a hand on top of her bulging bag. "He is, but I also have a long list of things I need him to do. I don't suppose you know how to build a small octagonal stage, do you?"

"Sorry. It's not one of my skills."

"It's one of mine," a voice behind me said. I hadn't seen Andrew come in and walk over to us. He looked at Abigail. "Seriously, I can do it. I'm a building contractor."

She gave him a long, appraising look. "An octagonal stage? Eight sides? You could build it?"

He shrugged. "A stage is easy. I could build an octagonal house if you wanted one."

"By the end of the week?"

"The stage, sure; the house, probably not." He looked at me and made a gesture toward Abigail with one hand. "Tell her."

"I've never seen this man before in my life," I said solemnly.

Andrew glared at me with mock annoyance. "Very funny, Kath."

I grinned at him and turned to Abigail. "He could build pretty much any shape stage you wanted. He could build one in the shape of a nonagon if that's what you wanted and do it almost as well as Harry."

"Hang on." Andrew held up one hand. "What the heck is a nonagon?"

"A nine-sided polygon," Abigail and I said at the same time. We looked at each other and laughed.

Andrew rolled his eyes. "Great. I have Encyclopedia Brown times two." He turned to Abigail. "So do I have the job?"

"I'm not sure," she said. "For all I know you could start building the stage and then disappear."

"I could," he agreed, stuffing his hands in the pockets of his jeans, "but I won't. Tell me what size you want the stage to be and I'll draw a plan tonight. If you're happy with it, I'll get you a list of materials tomorrow. As soon as you can get everything delivered, I can start. I'd take care of the supplies myself, but since I don't know any of the building supply stores around here, it would probably be faster if someone else does that. As for my time, I'll donate that."

Abigail looked at him suspiciously. "Why?"

"Because I'm a nice guy?" He phrased it as a question.

She leaned against the counter and thought about his words for a moment. "No," she said with a small shake of her head. "I don't think that's it."

Andrew's gaze shot to me. He shrugged. "Okay, the truth is, I'm wooing Kathleen."

Abigail's eyebrows went up, more from amusement than surprise. "Really?"

He nodded. "I was stupid enough to let her get away before, but I came to my senses and I plan to spend the next two weeks changing her mind about me. If I help you, that will make me look good to her and heaven knows I need all the help I can get in that department."

Abigail turned toward me. "Is this all true?"

"Yes, it is," I said, pulling at the top edge of the nylon sling, which was rubbing against the inside of my arm. "Andrew and I used to be a couple, before I came to Mayville Heights. We had a . . . falling-out."

Her eyes immediately went to Andrew. "I sort of . . . accidentally married someone else," he said, at least having the good grace to look a little shame-faced.

"Yeah, I hate it when that happens," Abigail said dryly.

"He has the idea that he can convince me to go back to Boston with him when my contract here expires," I said.

"Can he?"

"I don't think so." I glanced at my watch. Andrew and I needed to get on our way if we were going to have time to walk through both tents.

Abigail reached for her bag and swung the strap over her shoulder. "It seems to me that you and I may be working at cross-purposes," she said to Andrew, "because I want Kathleen to stay here. On the other hand, I've never been one to say no to free labor and I think watching you—as you put it—woo Kathleen is probably going to be fairly entertaining. So, thank you. I accept your offer."

She grabbed a piece of paper and a pencil off the desk, scribbled something on the paper and handed it to him. "I need a stage that's twelve feet wide and between four and six inches off the ground. Bring whatever plan you come up with to the Stratton Theater tomorrow morning about eight and we'll go from there." She smiled at me. "Have fun at the food tasting," she said, and then she headed for the second floor.

Andrew didn't say a word until we were on the way to the Riverwalk. "Are you mad because I told your friend about us?" he asked.

"No," I said.

"Are you impressed that I offered to build the stage?" He nudged me with his shoulder.

"No," I repeated.

He bumped me again. It was like I was walking

down the street with a big, bouncy dog. "Not even a tiny bit?" he asked, his mouth close to my face.

It was hard to keep a serious expression with his warm, teasing voice in my ear.

"If I say yes, will you stop asking me about going back to Boston and will you stop talking about wooing me, as though we were characters in some kind of bodice-ripper novel?"

"So I am making progress!" he crowed.

"Only in driving me crazy," I said, but I couldn't keep from smiling, which pretty much negated the effect of my words. I would rather have been walking down Main Street with Marcus, but I wasn't. On the other hand, the sun was shining, the sky was blue and we were on our way to get a bowl of Eric's chocolate pudding cake.

Andrew was still grinning at me and I gave up and smiled back. "Don't get any ideas."

He held up two fingers like a peace sign. "Two weeks, Kathleen," he said softly. "Who knows what could happen in two weeks?"

"Nothing's going to happen," I said.

Of course I was wrong.

4

The next week passed in a blur of preparations for the festival. Andrew built not one but two portable stages for Abigail, and helped Oren with a new ramp at the Stratton. He was ingratiating himself all over town, dispensing charm and that killer grin. His self-deprecating story of how he'd ruined things with me by getting drunk and marrying a waitress from a fifties diner somehow had the effect of making people like him even more. More than once I found myself remembering how much fun we used to have together.

Only Owen and Hercules seemed to be immune to that charm. It wasn't as though they didn't like Andrew. They just ignored him completely. The two times he'd been at the house, both cats acted as though he weren't even in the room.

On Friday morning I decided to walk down to Eric's Place for a breakfast sandwich and coffee. Maggie and I had spent the previous evening after tai chi class painting the stages Andrew had built.

Hannah had brought us hot chocolate and cinnamon rolls, which made the work go a little faster, but I was still tired when I woke up. And by the time I gave Hercules and Owen their breakfast I didn't feel like making my own.

Marcus was waiting at the counter. I walked over and touched his arm. He turned, smiling when he saw it was me. That smile made my chest tighten for a moment.

"Hi," I said. "Are you here getting breakfast, too?"

He nodded. "I have a pile of paperwork on my desk and I thought it might go a little better with one of Eric's breakfast sandwiches and a decent cup of coffee."

"Everything goes better with a decent cup of coffee," I said. A lock of his dark hair had fallen onto his forehead and I had to put my hands in my pockets to stop myself from reaching up and brushing it back.

"Yeah, I seem to remember that," he said.

More than once I'd taken coffee to Marcus when he was working on a case. At least once I'd had to resist an urge to pour it on his shoes.

He gestured to my left arm. "How's your shoulder?"

"It's better," I said. I could see the skepticism in his gaze. Marcus knew how much I disliked hospitals and doctors. "I swear." I held out both hands. "The sling came off yesterday and I've been checked by Roma and my own doctor.'

"Good to know," he said.

Claire came from the kitchen then with a brown paper take-out bag. She handed it to Marcus and then took my order. After she'd relayed it to Eric, she got me my own cup of coffee. I took a big sip and sighed with pleasure.

"How late were you and Maggie painting?" Marcus asked.

"Too late," I said. I looked at him over the rim of the cup. "How did you know?"

"I picked Hannah up after her rehearsal. She's staying with me." He set the take-out bag on the counter and pulled out his wallet. "I should get to the station," he said. "It was good to see you, Kathleen."

"You too, Marcus," I said.

He turned toward the cash register.

"Thank you for the hot chocolate and cinnamon rolls last night," I said.

He stopped and turned halfway around, his face reddening. "You knew?"

I set my briefcase down on one of the stools at the counter. "I didn't until just now when you said you picked Hannah up. She brought them in to us and I thought she'd just made a lucky guess."

"It was Hannah's idea to get you something," he said. "I just stopped at Eric's. I remembered how much you like his cinnamon rolls and I didn't think you'd want coffee so late."

"Well . . . thank you."

His hand moved as though he was going to touch

my arm and then he jammed it in his pocket instead. "I'll, uh, I'll see you, Kathleen," he said.

I nodded without speaking and watched him walk over to pay Claire for his food. A moment later Eric stuck his head around the swinging door. "Hey, Kathleen," he said. "Thank you for recommending me to Ben Saroyan to cater the opening reception for the theater festival."

"Does that mean you got the job?"

He grinned. "Yes, it does."

I grinned back at him and took the paper sack he held out to me. "I'm so glad," I said. "Remember, if you need to test any recipes, all of us at the library are willing to act as your tasters."

Eric laughed. "I'll keep that in mind," he said and disappeared back into the kitchen.

I walked over to Claire at the cash register.

"Detective Gordon already paid for your order," she said.

"Oh . . . um . . . oh," I said stupidly. It was the second time Marcus had done that recently.

Claire gave me a look of sympathy. Everyone seemed to know that whatever had been going on between Marcus and me wasn't going on any longer. I wished her a good day and headed for the library.

Ben called just before lunch. "Good morning, Kathleen." His big voice boomed through the receiver. "Is your wi-fi working over there?"

"I think so," I said. "Let me check." I reached for my laptop. "It's working," I said after a moment.

He exhaled loudly. "I need a favor."

"Of course. What is it?"

"I'm at the theater and our wi-fi keeps cutting out. They're sending someone to check it, but Hugh needs a place to work for the rest of the afternoon. Any chance you could find some space for him over there?"

I thought for a moment. The library's workroom could be available if I moved the boxes of programs that were being stored there into my office. The room had a big table and I could give him one of the chairs from the computer area. There'd be coffee in the staff room, too. "I think we can make it work," I said.

"Thank you." I could hear the smile in his voice.

"Send him over," I said. "We'll get things ready."

He thanked me again and hung up. I went downstairs and got Susan to give me a hand. We shifted the boxes into my office, cleared the table and managed to carry a chair up from downstairs.

"This should be perfect," I said to her, smiling with satisfaction over how quickly we'd gotten the space ready.

It wasn't.

Hugh Davis stood in the doorway of the workroom and made a face. "This won't work," he said, shaking his head. "I need a desk." He looked over at me. "Don't you have an office?"

"Yes, I do," I said, "but I need it."

"Well," he said. He didn't finish the sentence but the disparaging tone in his voice told me he didn't like my answer.

Susan touched my arm. "Kathleen, what about the antique library desk?" She spoke in a low voice, but her eyes darted in Hugh's direction and I knew she'd intended for him to hear what she said.

The problem was I had absolutely no idea what she was talking about.

"I don't know," I said slowly. Heaven knew, that was the truth.

Hugh looked at us, his eyes narrowed in curiosity. "Excuse me—do you have a desk I could use or not?"

Susan made a face. "We do have a writing desk, but, well, it's very old. I can't even begin to tell you what it's worth. This building is a hundred years old, so you can understand the desk isn't something that gets used on a day-to-day basis."

I still had no clue what desk she was referring to.

Susan let her gaze slide away from Hugh's face as though she was uncertain about what she was going to say next. "You know that F. Scott Fitzgerald was born in St. Paul?" she blurted.

Whatever she was up to was going too far. "Susan," I said warningly.

She nudged her cat-eye glasses up her nose. "I'm sorry, Kathleen," she said. "I know I'm not supposed to talk about that."

"If you have a desk somewhere here in the building, then let me see it," Hugh demanded.

Susan looked at me.

I nodded. "Show him." I was curious to see this "antique writing desk" myself.

Susan led the way downstairs and through the building to the larger of our two meeting rooms. "Do you have your keys?" she said to me.

I pulled them out of my pocket and handed them to her. She unlocked the door and as she did I suddenly figured out what she was up to.

There was no way it was going to work. But there was no stopping Susan now. For the first time I had a sense of where her twins got their fearless spirit.

She walked across the room and opened the door to a large storage closet. Packed carefully beside a pile of boxes there was in fact a small desk, wrapped in padded mover's blankets.

It could have been an antique, although I doubted it. Harry Taylor Junior's brother, Larry, had found the desk in the back corner of the basement. Susan wasn't lying when she said that she had no idea of its value. What I did know was that no one had been willing to pay five dollars for the thing when we'd had the library's yard sale.

Susan carefully removed the coverings. The old desk had been varnished at one time but more than half the finish had worn off. It had intricate turned legs, a small writing surface and a back that went up about two and a half feet. There were two rows of tiny drawers on the back unit and two small doors in the center.

The desk was dinged and battered and it wobbled, but Susan unwrapped the thing like it was a treasure.

Hugh Davis laid a hand on the worn desktop. "F. Scott Fitzgerald?" he said.

"I can't in all good conscience tell you that I have proof that he used this desk," Susan said. She ran one finger along the side of the banged-up writing surface and smiled. "But . . ." She let the end of the sentence trail off.

Hugh turned to me. "This will work." He gestured at the desk. "We should get this upstairs. I've already wasted too much time today."

Hugh's "we" actually meant Susan and me. The desk may have been banged up, but it was likely made of black walnut, according to Larry Taylor, and it was heavy. Still, we managed to get it up the stairs and set it down in the center of the workroom.

Hugh pulled his chair over and sat down. He looked up at me. "My briefcase is in the hall."

It took me a moment to realize he expected me to go out and get it.

His briefcase turned out to be a huge black leather pilot's flight case. I set it beside his chair and realized that his chair was actually my office chair.

Hugh followed my gaze. "I had to switch chairs with you," he said, with an offhand gesture. "The other one didn't have the right support for my back."

I took a deep breath, imagining my frustration filling a balloon coming out of the top of my head. It was a technique my mother used with her acting students.

Hugh leaned over to open his case. "I'm going to

need that table in here," he said without looking up. "I need to spread out my papers and I guess that's going to have to do."

I looked at Susan and inclined my head in the direction of the hallway. Once we were out there I flicked at the imaginary balloon with my finger and pictured it spiraling down the wide wooden steps to the main floor. The thought made me smile.

"What are you grinning at?" Susan asked, grabbing one end of the table. It was a lot lighter than the desk.

"Your ability to spin a line of you-know-what," I said, taking hold of the other end of the table.

"I wasn't spinning anything," she said, squaring her shoulders. "Everything I said was the truth. The library is a hundred years old, F. Scott Fitzgerald was born in St. Paul, and we certainly have no idea what that old desk is worth. It could be a valuable antique."

"And I could be a talking duck," I countered, backing toward the door with my end of the table.

Susan wrinkled her nose at me. "I don't think you're a duck. Your feet aren't big enough."

We moved the folding table about an inch to the left and then forward and back until Hugh was happy with where it sat. Susan got him a cup of coffee—with cream and exactly half a packet of sweetener. I adjusted the blind at the window so there was no direct sunlight shining on his workspace. Then we left him alone.

Susan shook her head. "How do people work with him? He's so picky."

"He's not that bad," I said. "He's just . . . creative."

She slid her glasses down her nose with one finger, frowned at me over the top of them and then pushed them back up again. "Honestly, Kathleen, you'd try to find something nice to say about Attila the Hun."

"All right, he might be a bit of a challenge."

She gave a snort of derision and went back downstairs.

A group of kids from the after-school program came in around four to pick out some books and videos. By then I was so tired of being Hugh's personal minion that I was entertaining the idea of taking my limited computer skills over to the Stratton and trying to fix the wi-fi myself.

He came down the stairs just as I was about to show the kids our newest DVDs. I sighed, a little louder than I'd intended to.

Susan smirked at me. "Remember, he's creative."

"What's creative?" a little girl with brown pigtails and red-framed glasses asked me. She was probably about seven.

"'Creative' means you have a good imagination," I said.

Hugh spotted us and walked over. The little girl looked at him, frowning. "Do you really have a good imagination?" She pointed at me. "*She* said you did."

"Yes, I do," he said, his expression serious.

She twisted her mouth to one side. "You're kind of old."

Hugh smiled then. "Old people can have good imaginations."

The child shook her head. "You're older than my dad, and my mom says he has no imagination."

I struggled to keep a straight face. Hugh suddenly dropped down onto all fours, arched his back and stretched.

The little girl grinned with delight. "You're a cat!" she said.

Hugh nodded. "Very good. I was using my imagination. Now you try it."

She got down on her hands and knees and meowed at us. With some gentle nudges, Hugh soon had her stretching just the way Owen and Hercules did.

"Great," Susan said against my ear. "Kind of makes it hard to dislike the guy when he's good with kids."

Hugh stood up and brushed bits of lint off his pants. The little girl—whose name was Ivy—went back to the rest of her group.

"You were great with her," I said.

He ran a hand over his beard. "I like kids. They're more enjoyable to spend time with than most adults." He held up the sheaf of papers in his hands. "These need to be stapled."

I smiled at him. "Mary has a stapler at the circulation desk."

He nodded. "Good." He handed me the papers and went back upstairs.

Susan smirked at me. "I was wrong," she said, shaking her head so her topknot, secured with a red plastic pitchfork, bobbed at me. "It's really not that hard to dislike him after all."

Hugh left for an early supper about half an hour later. I made sure that he knew what time we closed and I crossed my fingers that the wi-fi would be working at the theater in the morning.

Andrew came in about six thirty, just as I was going to warm up some chicken soup in the staff room. There was a day's worth of stubble on his face, but he was one of those men who look good with a bit of scruff. "Hey, Kathleen," he said, "you think I could borrow your truck for half an hour? I have to move a piece of staging. Oren's gone somewhere with his truck and I have no idea where Abigail is. She's not answering her cell."

"Sure," I said. "Where are you taking it?"

"The marina." He looked around. "It's that way, right?" he asked, pointing upriver.

"No. That way," I said, indicating a hundred and eighty degrees in the opposite direction.

He sighed loudly. "Explain to me the difference between Main Street and Old Main Street. I can't keep the two of them straight. I take it Old Main Street is the original street and Main Street is some kind of extension."

I shook my head. "Nope. Main Street is the original."

He frowned. "That makes no sense."

"It does when you know the history of the names. Old Main Street used to be Olde Street, with an E at the end. It was the main route from the lumber camps to where the marina is now. Over time it turned into Old Main Street."

"Okay, so how do I get there?"

"Just turn left and go straight until you see the sign for the marina." I pulled my keys out of my pocket. "No, wait a minute," I said. "You can't do that. There was a water main break right in front of the hotel. The street's dug up. You'll have to go around."

He groaned. "Kathleen, please don't make me drive around town in circles."

I held up a hand. "Hang on. Let me see if Mary can stay a little longer and I'll just come with you."

"Thanks," he said. "I can't believe how easy it is to get turned around in such a small place."

Mary was happy to stay later. I grabbed my sweater and purse and Andrew and I went out to the truck.

"I'll drive," he said, holding out his hand for the keys. "You can direct me."

"Or, since I know where we're going, I can just drive." I made a shooing motion and reached around him to unlock the driver's-side door.

We drove back to the Stratton and I helped Andrew get the extra section of staging into the back of the truck. Luckily it wasn't that heavy. We drove across town to the marina, managing to avoid most of the detoured traffic.

"Where are you putting this thing?" I asked as I turned into the marina driveway.

"Right down there at the far end of the parking lot." Andrew pointed to a grassy space just beyond the pavement. "Just by those stairs. You can't see them, but the other pieces are already there."

I backed the truck up to the edge of the grass so we didn't have far to carry the load. The view over the river was beautiful as the sun sank in the evening sky. Three sailboats bobbed in the water, their masts bathed in amber light.

I knew that Burtis Chapman and two of his sons would be at the marina the next morning with the crane to lift the boats out of the water. Abigail had persuaded Burtis to do the job a week early so it wouldn't interfere with any of the festival performances.

Andrew came to stand beside me. "It is a pretty spot. I'll give you that," he said.

"What? No speech about the sunsets over Boston Harbor?" I asked.

He shook his head. "Nope. But they are pretty spectacular."

I poked him in the ribs with my elbow, but he just laughed.

"Where do they go?" he asked, pointing at the stairs.

"They'll take you up to the first lookout."

"C'mon," he said. "Let's climb up and watch the sunset."

I shook my head. "I have to get back to the library."

"Don't be a stick in the mud, Kathleen," he said. "Come with me. Watch the sunset. See the pretty colors." He reached for my hand. "Please?"

He was extremely annoying, but I knew the sunset would be gorgeous from the lookout and there really was no big hurry to get back to the library. Friday was almost always our quietest night.

"Fine," I said.

Andrew gave me a self-satisfied smile and pulled me toward the steps. It felt odd, holding his hand again, and I let go of it to grab the railing.

"You getting soft?" he teased. "Do you need to hold on to pull yourself up?"

I stopped a step below him. "Who are you calling soft?" I challenged. Andrew had always brought out my competitive side. "Seems to me I heard a lot of heavy breathing while we were unloading that piece of staging."

He leaned forward, raising one eyebrow in a leer. "That heavy breathing was just because I was so close to you."

I rolled my eyes. "What a load of . . . lumber," I said. Then before he knew what was happening, I faked left, darted around him on the right and tore up the steps.

"Hey!" he yelled.

I took the stairs two at a time, glad that I had long legs because I could hear him gaining on me, his feet pounding on the weathered wooden treads.

I lunged for the top step, sticking my arm out to the right so he couldn't dart past me the way I'd done with him. When I looked back over my shoulder, he was maybe a couple of steps behind me, laughing and breathing hard. I reached blindly for the top of the railing that ran along the edge of the lookout and stumbled over something I couldn't see clearly in the waning light. Instead of landing on wood, weathered smooth by rain and snow, my hand landed on something soft.

Hair. Skin.

I jerked away and Andrew banged into my back, grabbing my shoulders to steady himself.

"Whoa! You okay?" he said.

I nodded, and took a second to catch my breath.

Then Andrew saw what I'd fallen over. "Is that . . . ?" He didn't finish the sentence.

I nodded. "Yes."

It was Hugh Davis.

It was pretty clear that he was dead.

5

Andrew swore under his breath and fumbled for his cell phone. "We need an ambulance."

I caught his arm. "No, we don't," I said. "We just . . ." I swallowed. "We just need the police."

The color drained from his face. "Is he dead?"

I nodded. "Yes."

Andrew was already punching in 911 on his phone.

"Tell them we're at the first lookout on Spruce Bluff," I said.

He swallowed and put the phone to his ear. "Okay."

I looked at the body—Hugh's body—again. It was half sitting, slumped sideways against the lookout railing at the top of the stairs, almost as though his legs had given out after climbing up and he'd had to sit down fast. His eyes were closed and I could see what looked like blood on the collar of his jacket. There was some kind of ragged open wound just below his left ear.

I leaned over for a closer look. Was it a bullet hole?

My stomach clenched and I could taste something sour in the back of my throat.

Had Hugh been shot? He'd left the library no more than about three hours before. What could have happened in that amount of time that had ended with him up here with a bullet hole in the side of his head? I shivered.

Andrew put a hand on my shoulder. "They're coming."

We moved a few steps away from the body. "Do you know who it is?" he asked.

"It's Hugh Davis," I said.

He frowned. "You mean that director from the theater festival?"

I nodded.

"He seemed like a bit of a control freak. He must have come over to check out the stage. You think he had a heart attack or something?"

I could hear the sirens wailing in the distance. I shook my head. "I . . . No."

"So? What? You think he fell?" Andrew stared up at the jagged rock face of the bluff rising above us.

"I think someone might have shot him," I said quietly.

"Shot him?" His grip on my shoulder tightened.

I dug my fingers into the knots of muscle in my neck. "I . . . uh. It looks like there's a bullet hole just behind his ear."

"Let's go." His hand moved to my back and he pushed me toward the stairs.

"The police will be here in a couple of minutes," I said. "I don't think we should just leave the body."

Andrew shook his head, his mouth pulled into a thin line. "Kathleen, if he was shot, whoever did it could still be around. I'm sorry, but we can't help him. It'll be safer down in the parking lot."

I knew he was right. Still, it felt wrong to leave Hugh's body slumped against the lookout railing. I took one last look over my shoulder for any sign of another person or any clue to what had happened and then I went down the steps.

We stood against the side of the bluff at the bottom of the stairs. The automatic streetlights had come on, washing the parking lot in a weird pinkish-orange light. I remembered Maggie saying the odd-colored bulbs saved energy.

The paramedics arrived first, but Officer Derek Craig was right behind them in his squad car. "Stay here," Andrew said.

I ignored him and started toward the police car.

He stepped in front of me. "Kathleen, I can take care of this. Just wait."

"I'm not going to have an attack of the vapors," I said, shaking off his hand. "This isn't the first dead body I've seen, and I know these people. You don't." I stopped, realizing how abrupt my voice sounded. I took a deep breath. "It's okay, Andrew. I can do this."

After a moment he nodded.

I recognized one of the paramedics coming toward us. He'd taken care of me when an embankment out at Wisteria Hill had collapsed after days and days of rain this past spring. Ric nodded at me and I pointed back over my shoulder. "The top of the stairs." I knew Hugh Davis was past any help Ric and his partner could give him.

Derek Craig walked around the front of his police car. "What happened?" he asked as I reached him.

"We—my friend Andrew and I—brought a piece of staging over in my truck for the theater festival. Then we decided to walk up to the lookout. The body was at the top of the steps." I stopped to clear my throat. "It's . . . His name is Hugh Davis."

He nodded as he made notes in a small ring-bound notebook, then looked up at me. "Did either of you touch anything?"

I nodded slowly. "I did. I almost fell over hi—the body. My hand touched the top of his head."

Derek tucked the notebook back in his shirt pocket. "I'll be right back. I need you and your friend to wait here." He gave me a half smile. "You know how this works."

I did.

I walked back to Andrew, who stood with his hands in his pockets, looking out over the water.

"We have to wait a little longer," I said.

"How can you stay here?" he asked, not looking at me.

I knew he didn't mean here in the parking lot.

"I like it here," I said. "I have a life here."

He gestured toward the bluff behind us and his green eyes met mine then. "Kathleen, there's a dead person up there. Dead." There were two deep frown lines between his eyes. "This is the last place I would have expected to find someone shot." He swiped a hand over the side of his face. "This is stupid. You need to come home."

I pressed my lips together and took a couple of deep breaths before I answered. "People get shot in Boston."

"I know that," he said, his voice tight. "But when was the last time you fell over a body in Boston?"

"I'm not having this conversation right now," I said. I couldn't keep the edge of anger completely out of my voice. From the corner of my eye I saw a black car I didn't recognize pull in next to Derek Craig's police cruiser. Marcus got out of the driver's side.

"I'll be right back," I said to Andrew. I didn't wait to see if he had anything to say.

A feeling of déjà vu washed over me as I walked up to Marcus. "Hi," I said. "Where's your car?"

He smiled. Not a big smile, but a smile nonetheless. It chased away a little of the anger I was feeling.

"Hi," he said. "Hannah has it, so I'm driving a station car. What happened?"

I gestured over my shoulder. "It's Hugh Davis. Andrew and I found his body at the lookout."

He glanced briefly over at Andrew and then his eyes came back to me. "What were you doing here?"

"Andrew had a piece of staging to bring over. He needed my truck. I drove because of the water main break in front of the hotel."

"Did you see anyone?"

I shook my head and tucked a strand of wind-blown hair behind one ear. "No. We unloaded the section of staging. Then we decided to climb up to the lookout for the view. I didn't see anyone."

"It's okay," he said. "I'm just glad you're all right." His hand moved as though he was going to touch me and then he stopped himself. "I'm going to talk to your friend for a minute. Stay here. Please?"

I nodded. "Okay."

I wrapped my arms around my midsection and watched him walk over to Andrew. They talked for a couple of minutes and then Andrew started toward me. "We can go," he said when he got within earshot.

Marcus was just starting up the wooden steps to the lookout. As though he could feel my eyes on him, he turned and looked over his shoulder. After a moment's hesitation I raised a hand and he did the same.

I fished the keys to the truck out of my pocket. I couldn't believe Hugh Davis was dead. I thought about him showing the little girl at the library how to be a cat just a few hours ago. What was he doing up on the lookout? Why would anyone have wanted to shoot him? He had been a bit of a diva, but that wasn't really a reason to kill someone.

I had a lot of questions and no answers. I couldn't help glancing back toward the bluff one more time as I unlocked the truck.

"He's the reason you're thinking of staying, isn't he?" Andrew said.

I stared at him across the bed of the truck. "What?"

"The detective. He's why you're thinking about not coming home."

I sighed, tipped my head back and looked up at the stars just winking on overhead. I was thinking about not going back to Boston because of Maggie. And because of Roma. And Rebecca and Susan and every other friend I'd made in Mayville Heights. Because of all the work I'd put into the library. Because of my little house, and Owen and Hercules. And yes, because of Marcus.

After a moment I dropped my head and looked at Andrew again. "No. There's nothing going on between Marcus and me."

I slid onto the bench seat and leaned across to unlock the passenger door. Andrew got in, fastened his belt and then shifted sideways a little to look at me.

"There was something, though," he said. He held up a hand. "And don't say no, because even if I hadn't heard a few things around town, I'd be able to tell just watching the two of you." He rested one hand, palm down on the dashboard. "Why didn't you tell me?"

"Because there's nothing to tell. Marcus and I are friends. We went out a few times, but that's it."

I didn't want to talk about Marcus with Andrew.
I didn't really want to talk about him with anyone—not Maggie, not Roma. Even Owen and Hercules seemed to have an opinion. I didn't want to
hear that we could work things out. Because we
couldn't.

Andrew didn't say anything else until I pulled out
of the lot. "So what went wrong?" he asked. "Don't
tell me he got drunk and married a waitress he'd just
met?" I knew he was trying to lighten the mood. It
was something he always did when things got tense
or angry.

"No, you're the only person I know who's done
that." I shot him a quick glance. "Marcus and I just
don't look at life the same way, that's all."

Out of the corner of my eye I saw him nod his
head. "I'd take it back if I could," he said after another silence.

I slowed down to let a car turn in front of us. "I
believe you," I said, this time keeping my eyes fixed
on the road.

"Then give me another chance. I swear I won't
screw it up again."

"It's not that simple."

"It can be," he said, his voice low and intense.
"Just think about it. You and I were happy once. And
we could be again. Come home. And I'm not saying
that because we found a dead body. Come home for
us. Maybe he doesn't appreciate you, but I do."

"A year and a half is a long time, Andrew," I said,

turning my blinker on. "I'm not the person I used to be."

He took his hand away. "You're not as different as you think you are, Kathleen. Think about what I said, okay? Just think about it."

I dropped Andrew at the theater and went back to the library. Mary was at the checkout desk getting the requests ready to be put on the pick-up shelf. "I'm sorry we took so long," I said, pulling off my sweater.

"Don't worry about it," she said. "I think we've had maybe half a dozen people in all evening. Even for a Friday it's been quiet." She held out a yellow message slip. "Abigail called."

I rubbed the top of my left shoulder. It was still a little stiff. "I'll go call her," I said.

Mary shook her gray curls. "She said she'll call you in the morning. She's having problems with her phone."

Abigail was going to have a lot on her plate once news got out that Hugh Davis was dead. Marcus hadn't asked me to keep that information to myself, but I knew that's what he'd want. I made a mental note to check in with Abigail in the morning if I didn't hear from her.

It was almost time to close up for the night. "Where's Susan?" I asked.

"Shelving over in cookbooks," Mary said, waving a hand in the direction of the nonfiction section.

I threaded my way around the magazines, stopping to put a couple of back issues of *National Geographic* into their slot. Susan came toward me, pushing an empty book cart.

I tapped my watch. "It's almost time to close."

"Want me to shut down the computers?" she asked. Her glasses were stuck on the top of her head and her topknot was listing to one side.

"Please," I said. All of a sudden I was tired. It had been a long day and I just remembered that I hadn't had any supper. I rolled my neck from one side to the other.

Susan frowned. "You okay, Kathleen?" she asked.

"Just tired," I said. "I think I'll go home, fill the tub full of bubbles and eat brownies while I soak."

"Take me with you," she said. "I have to go home and put the boys in the tub. No bubbles."

"They figure they're too old for that stuff now?" I asked.

She made a face. "Not exactly."

I folded my arms over my chest. "What did they do? Fill the bathroom with bubbles?"

"The washing machine. And the laundry room. And half the basement." She pulled her glasses down onto her nose. "Trust me, don't say 'bubbles' to Eric." She rolled her eyes and set out for the circulation desk with her cart.

Upstairs, Hugh Davis's things were still in the workroom. The door was locked, so I decided I'd just leave things the way they were and call Marcus once I was home.

Hercules was in the backyard when I came around the side of the house, but I didn't see him at first. I was unlocking the door when he meowed from somewhere behind me. I looked around and discovered he was sitting on the wooden bench under the maple tree. If it hadn't been for the white fur on his face and chest he would have blended into the darkness.

"Are you coming in?" I asked. Because of his wall-walking ability, he came and went as he pleased.

He looked up into the branches over his head. The war between Herc and a particularly brazen grackle had been heating up over the past few weeks. Hercules had apparently snagged one of the bird's tail feathers and the grackle—which I'd named Professor Moriarty—had come this close to getting a tuft of hair from the cat's head. For Hercules the bigger affront was his nemesis stealing two sardine cat crackers that he'd been about to eat.

"I think Professor Moriarty has probably turned in for the night," I said. "Why don't you come inside?"

A bat zipped by, probably coming from the bat house in the Justasons' backyard, one house above me on the hill. Hercules whipped his head in my direction. I couldn't see the glare in his green eyes, but I knew it was there.

"No, that wasn't Professor Moriarty. That was a bat."

"Meow?" he said. Was I just imagining the question in that meow?

"Yes, I'm sure," I said.

I waited on the top step while he looked all around one last time, then jumped down and came across the grass.

There was no sign of Owen in the kitchen. "I'm home," I called.

Nothing.

"Are you hungry?" I said to Hercules.

The cat meowed softly again and stretched, almost as though he was saying, "I could eat."

I put away my sweater and briefcase, washed my hands and looked in the fridge for something quick and easy for a late supper. I felt a cat rub against my leg.

"Hi, Owen," I said, reaching for the eggs and cheese.

"Merow," he said.

"You hungry?"

That got another meow, with a slightly pitiful tone to it. I grabbed the little dish of sardines, too.

I scrambled a couple of eggs with some cheese and a bit of an orange pepper. While the eggs cooked, I toasted the last piece of Mary's orange-raisin bread and put a sardine in each cat's dish. Owen immediately began sniffing the oily little fish, the way he did with everything he ate. Hercules, on the other hand, cocked his head to one side and looked inquisitively at me almost as though he was wondering why I'd given them each a treat without suggesting they might be a little spoiled.

"Haven't you ever heard the expression 'Don't look a gift sardine in the mouth'?" I asked.

For a moment he seemed to be considering my words. Then he started to eat.

I sat at the table with my feet propped on another chair and picked up my fork. Owen had decided there was nothing "fishy" about his sardine and was blissfully eating it. Hercules was doing the same, although he kept shooting me little glances from time to time. Somehow he knew something was off. I'd finished about half my eggs when he came over to the table. Without waiting for an invitation, he jumped onto my lap, put his white-tipped paws on my chest and looked unblinkingly at me. I knew that look. It meant *What's going on?*

I stroked the soft black fur on the top of his head. "Do you remember me telling you about Hugh Davis?" I asked.

Hercules seemed to think for a moment, then he murped what I decided to believe was a *yes.*

"He's dead," I said, putting my fork down so I could rub the side of my head.

The cat's green eyes stayed locked on my face.

I let out a breath. "Andrew and I found the body at the Spruce Point lookout."

I wondered if Marcus was still at the marina. Did Ben or Abigail know what had happened yet? What would this do to the New Horizons Theatre Festival?

Hercules walked his front paws up my chest and bumped my chin with the top of his head. Either he was after more details or he wanted a bite of my scrambled eggs. I decided to go with the idea that he was looking for more information, since I knew Roma would frown on me feeding him eggs with cheese and peppers.

I picked up my fork and in between bites told the boys what had happened at the library, how Andrew and I had ended up in the marina parking lot, and how I'd raced him up the stairs and then almost fallen over Hugh Davis's body.

Hercules turned his head to look at the schedule for feeding the cats at Wisteria Hill.

"Yes, Marcus was there," I said.

Owen had finished his sardine and was licking the remaining fish oil out of his dish. At the sound of Marcus's name his head whipped around like it was on a swivel and he and his brother locked eyes. Some kind of unspoken message seemed to pass between the two cats. Then Owen dropped his head again and Hercules brought his attention back to me. It seemed a little . . . well . . . crazy to think the two of them could somehow communicate without making a sound, but considering their other talents, it wasn't really that far-fetched. Was it?

Hercules gave me another head butt.

I slid down in the chair and scratched the place just above his nose where the white fur of his face met the black fur on the top of his head. "And yes, I talked to him," I said.

He made a small murp. "Nothing's changed," I said with a sigh. "Except I seem to be mixed up in one of his cases. Again."

Owen had come to sit by my feet. He gave an enthusiastic meow.

"No, that's not a good thing," I said testily. More than once in the past couple of weeks I'd almost gotten the sense that the cats wanted Marcus and me to get back together. The rocking chair had been in the living room for more than a week now, but as far as I could tell neither cat had tried to sit in it, although they'd tried to herd me—deliberately, it seemed—to sit in it a couple of times.

I looked at one cat and then the other. "I'm not talking about Marcus," I said firmly.

Owen stared at me for a minute, then turned to look expectantly at the back door. A second passed, and then another and then I heard a knock.

I stood up and set Hercules on the floor. "How do you do that?" I said, bending down to give Owen a quick scratch behind one ear. All I got for an answer was a twitch of his whiskers. I padded out to the porch door in my sock feet. Andrew didn't give up easily. I rolled my head from one shoulder to the other and then opened the door.

It wasn't Andrew standing there. It was Marcus.

6

"Oh, hi," I said stupidly.

"Do you have a few minutes?" he asked. "I have a couple more questions." His hair was windblown and in the light I could see he needed a shave.

"Sure," I said. "C'mon in."

He followed me into the kitchen. Owen and Hercules were sitting by the refrigerator.

I gestured at the table. "Have a seat. I was about to make some hot chocolate. Would you like some? Or I could make coffee."

"Hot chocolate's fine. Thank you," he said. Then he leaned forward, hands between his knees. "Hello," he said to the cats.

"Meow," Owen said. Hercules was content to just dip his head in acknowledgment.

I put milk in the microwave to warm and got two mugs and my stash of marshmallows out of the cupboard. Then I leaned against the counter. "You have questions."

He nodded. "Tell me again how you found Hugh Davis's body."

I repeated the story while I waited for the milk to heat, leaving out how I'd tried to race Andrew to the top of the stairs.

"And you didn't see anybody up on the lookout?" Marcus asked as I set a steaming mug in front of him.

"No. But it was starting to get dark." I dropped a couple of marshmallows into my cup. The scent of vanilla mixed with the cocoa. I pushed the container across the table to him. "Would you like a marshmallow?"

Marcus squinted into the little china bowl. "They don't look like marshmallows," he said.

"That's because they're homemade."

"You made marshmallows?" He still had that skeptical look on his face.

"I didn't make them," I said. "Maggie got them for me at the farmers' market. The Jam Lady makes them."

"What do they taste like?"

I laughed. "You're as bad as Owen. Try one." At the sound of his name, Owen, who had been washing his tail, lifted his head.

Marcus picked up the dish. "Well, what do you think?" he asked the cat.

Owen tipped his head to one side and his whiskers twitched as he sniffed the air.

Marcus held out the bowl. "They do smell pretty good."

"Don't do—"

Owen swiped one gray paw over the top of the small bowl and a plump marshmallow landed on the floor at his feet.

"—that," I finished.

The cat immediately began to sniff his treasure.

"You better not put a paw on that marshmallow," I warned, pushing back my chair and standing up.

Wrong thing to say.

Owen's eyes flicked in my direction and then he dipped his head and licked the top of the marshmallow. He looked up at me, defiance in his gold eyes.

Marcus started to laugh as a look passed between man and cat.

"You better not have done that on purpose," I said, glaring at Marcus. He picked up two marshmallows for himself and dropped them into his mug. "I didn't. I swear," he said, holding up a hand.

I reached for the marshmallow on the floor. Owen yowled his objections and raised a paw.

"Oh, c'mon, Kathleen," Marcus said. "Let him have it."

"You're just as bad as Maggie," I said. "Roma will have my head if she finds out I let Owen have marshmallows."

He reached for his hot chocolate. "Well, I'm not going to tell her," he said. He leaned sideways to look at the gray tabby, still guarding his prize, one paw ready to swat anyone (me) who tried to take it away.

"Marshmallows are not good for cats. They're going to stick to his teeth. Are you planning on hanging around to brush them?"

Marcus's expression turned thoughtful. "Maybe you could make a trade."

Owen's gaze had been shifting between Marcus and me. Now he meowed softly.

"Fine," I said. "I'll trade half a sardine for that marshmallow."

"One sardine," Marcus countered.

"He already had one sardine. One half."

"One. Fish is brain food." Marcus leaned back in the chair and folded his arms over his chest. "You're the one who pointed out that he's going to have marshmallow stuck to his teeth if he eats it. Do you want to floss his teeth tonight?"

He glanced at Owen, who somehow seemed to be following the conversation and chose the perfect moment to lean down and lick the marshmallow again.

I knew when I was beaten, but I made them wait just a few moments longer before I gave in. "One sardine," I said, holding up a finger. "One." I leaned forward and snatched the marshmallow off the floor before the two of them tried to up the ante. Then I got Owen his sardine and another for Hercules, who had sat silently, watching and listening to the "negotiations" with a bemused expression on his black-and-white face.

I sat back down at the table and Marcus smiled at

me. "You're right," he said. "These marshmallows are good."

I made a face at him and reached for my own cup.

His expression grew serious. "Did you touch anything?" he said. I knew he meant when I'd stumbled over Hugh Davis's body.

"The top of his head, when I put my hand out to steady myself. And the collar of his jacket, when I felt for a pulse."

"What about Andrew?"

I shook my head. "No."

"Then what did you do?"

I explained about Andrew calling 911 and how we'd waited at the bottom of the stairs. Both cats had finished eating and were judiciously washing their paws. I knew by the way their ears were moving that they were also listening to everything I was saying.

Marcus traced a finger around the inside of the handle of his mug. "Did you see anyone? In the parking lot, maybe, or over by the marina?"

"No. I didn't see anyone."

"What about cars in the parking lot?"

I closed my eyes for a moment and pictured the almost deserted parking lot in my head. "There were two trucks that belong to the marina in the far corner of the lot, a little silver-colored car and a van. I think it was white. That's it." I opened my eyes. "Wait a minute. There were no other cars in the parking lot. How did Hugh get there?"

He gave a slight shrug. "That's a good question."

He drained the last of his hot chocolate and stood up. "I have to get down to the station. Thank you for the hot chocolate."

"Anytime," I said. I got to my feet and came around the table. For a moment we just stood there, an awkward silence stretching between us.

"If you think of anything . . ." Marcus began.

I remembered the papers in the workroom. "I don't know if it matters, but Hugh was working at the library this afternoon," I said. "There was something wrong with the wi-fi at the Stratton. He left his briefcase and a bunch of papers in the workroom."

"I'll send someone over to get them first thing in the morning. Thanks."

I walked him to the back door. "Have you talked to Abigail, or Ben Saroyan?" I asked.

"That's where I'm going."

"This doesn't make any sense," I said. "Hugh Davis has only been here for a week. Why would anybody want to kill him?"

Marcus pulled his keys out of his jacket pocket. "That's what I'm trying to find out."

It wasn't until he was gone that I realized he hadn't corrected me when I'd said someone had killed Hugh Davis.

Someone had killed Hugh Davis. Shot him on purpose.

Who?

Why?

I made another cup of hot chocolate and settled at

the table with it. "What is this going to do to the festival?" I said aloud. Neither of the cats seemed to know. I didn't see how Ben could continue without another director. There was one more week of rehearsals and he couldn't be everywhere.

Owen stretched and launched himself onto my lap. "Hello," I said. He was too busy sniffing my mug— probably hoping to snag another marshmallow—to pay any attention to me.

I reached for the cup, lifting it over his head and out of reach of his paws. "Get your nose out of that."

He made an annoyed murp.

"Forget it," I said. "You've had all the marshmallows and sardines you're getting tonight." I stroked his fur with my free hand and after a few moments of stubbornly looking the other way he leaned against my chest with a soft sigh.

His warm, purring body was comforting. I barely knew Hugh Davis, but I still felt unsettled by his death.

"'Any man's death diminishes me, because I am involved in mankind,'" I said softly. At my feet, Hercules, who had been carefully washing his tail, lifted his head and looked at me. "John Donne," I said. "He was a British poet."

The cat seemed to think about that for a moment, as though he was storing the information in his kitty brain, and then went back to working the knots out of his tail.

I felt bad for Abigail, too. She'd put in so much

effort on the festival over the past week. Now I didn't see how it could continue. She'd told me that she wasn't trying to steal the event from Red Wing, but she had hoped that if things went well, maybe the festival would expand and the two towns could share the performances—and the tourist dollars.

Abigail and Ben had hit it off and I knew he would have put in a good word for Mayville Heights. It mattered to Ben that things got done when they were promised, and Abigail didn't make promises she didn't keep. He had an excellent reputation in the theater community, so his word would carry weight with New Horizon's producers.

"I wonder what Hugh would have said about Mayville Heights," I said to Owen. He wrinkled his nose as he thought about it. Or maybe he was plotting world domination. It was hard to tell.

What had Abigail said about Hugh that day of the food tasting when Andrew had volunteered to build the stages for her? I closed my eyes for a moment and replayed the conversation in my head. *He's still a control freak, I've discovered.*

Owen nudged my hand with his head because I'd stopped scratching behind his left ear.

"She said 'still.'"

He looked at me blankly.

"Abigail said Hugh was 'still a control freak.' *Still.* But how could she know that? How on earth could she know something like that?"

Owen looked at me. Thoughtfully, it seemed to me.

"They knew each other," I said slowly, as pieces clicked together in a way I didn't like. A knot tightened in my stomach. "Abigail and Hugh knew each other. So why did she say she didn't know anyone involved with the festival?"

The cat didn't have an answer to that question, either.

"It has to be a coincidence," I told the small gray cat. "I know Abigail. She didn't have anything to do with Hugh's death." The knot twisted in my stomach.

Up to now I would have said that Abigail wouldn't lie, either. But it looked as if she had. Why? Why would she have lied about knowing Hugh? It didn't make any sense.

Owen sat up, yawned, and then looked pointedly at the refrigerator again. I knew he wasn't hinting for a treat.

"No, I'm not calling Marcus," I said.

A look passed between the boys and then Hercules meowed softly. *Why?*

"Because Marcus is a good police officer. If—*if* there was some kind of connection between Abigail and Hugh Davis, he'll find it." I got up and carried my dishes over to the sink. "I'm staying out of this— I'm staying out of all of Marcus's cases."

I looked over my shoulder to find two furry faces cocked to one side and two sets of unblinking eyes staring at me. "I'm serious," I said, feeling a little silly explaining myself to a couple of cat skeptics.

Neither cat moved. How could they go so long without blinking? No wonder they won every staring contest I was foolish enough to get involved in with them.

"Will you two please look somewhere else?" I said. After a moment, Hercules dropped his head and studied the speckled pattern on the kitchen floor. Owen yawned again and stretched his neck up to stare at the ceiling.

"Thank you," I said, turning back to the sink and putting the plug in the drain so I could wash the dishes by hand—the other way, aside from talking to the cats, that I worked things out in my head.

I knew the two of them didn't believe I would really stay out of Marcus's case. But I would, I told myself as the sink filled with hot water and bubbles. I ignored the little voice in the back of my head that was asking who was I trying to convince. Owen and Hercules?

Or myself?

7

Abigail came into the library just after we opened in the morning. There were dark circles, like smudges of charcoal, under her eyes, and her usually smiling face was serious. Ben was with her.

"Kathleen, do you have a couple of minutes?" she asked.

"Of course," I said. I gave Ben a small smile. "Hi."

"You know about Hugh Davis, don't you?" Abigail said, pushing the strap of her messenger bag up on her shoulder.

I nodded. "Yes, I do."

Three women came in the front door and made a beeline for the cookbook section. They were followed by a teenage girl, her platinum and black hair sticking up all over her head, carrying a pile of books stacked so high she could rest her chin on top—and did—yawning as she carried them to the desk.

"Come up to my office. It's a little quieter there," I said, gesturing toward the stairs.

Ben and Abigail took the two chairs in front of my

desk, while I leaned back against it. "I'm sorry about Hugh," I said. "Is there anything I can do?"

"Yes," Ben said. He was sitting on the edge of his seat, elbows propped on his knees. "Call Thea and ask her to come fill in for Hugh."

"Please," Abigail added.

I ran one hand along the edge of the dark wood of the desk. "Like I told you, Mom's in Los Angeles, doing *Wild and Wonderful*."

Ben leaned forward. "We got lucky. I talked to a friend out there. The show's going to be dark for the next ten days—some kind of renovations to the studio. She'll come if you ask her."

He was right. I just wasn't sure if I wanted to ask.

I loved my family. When I'd gone home to visit during the summer I'd realized just how much I missed them. All four of them—Mom, Dad, Sara, and Ethan—were exuberant and melodramatic and sometimes it felt as though they sucked all the air out of the room. Mayville Heights was the first place I'd ever lived where I was Kathleen first, not Ethan's big sister or Thea's daughter.

My mother was a force of nature. No one ever forgot her. I had a mental picture of her holding court at Eric's, teaching a stunt-fighting class on the Riverwalk or, heaven forbid, getting onstage with Mary for amateur night at the Brick, strutting her stuff in a feathered corset to Bon Jovi or Beyoncé. She was capable of doing all that and then some.

On the other hand, she was a good director and

an even better actor, and if she came, the festival could continue.

And I missed her.

I took a deep breath and let it out slowly. Abigail looked tired, the expression in her eyes almost pleading. Whatever relationship she'd had before the festival with Hugh Davis was none of my business. I'd learned how to size people up from my mother. And I knew Abigail. She hadn't had anything to do with Hugh's death. Mayville Heights was my home now. I wanted the New Horizons festival to be successful as much as anyone else in town did.

"Yes," I said. "I'll ask her."

Abigail closed her eyes for a second and I saw some of the tension ease in her shoulders.

Ben's face relaxed into a smile. His eyes darted to the phone. "Why don't you call her right now?" he said.

I laughed. "It's quarter after seven in Los Angeles, Ben."

My dad insisted Mom had been a raccoon in a past life. She liked shiny things and roaming around at night. She didn't like mornings. When she had to be up early, she did it with more of her usual dramatic flare.

Ben leaned back in the chair. "She's probably had a lot earlier wake-up call for the past couple of weeks."

"And it's Saturday. I promise I'll call her after lunch, but unless you want to hear 'menj el à máj' growled at you, you won't call her now."

"Menj el what?" Ben said.

"Menj el à máj," I said. "It loosely translates to 'go away or I'll eat your liver.' It's Hungarian. I think."

"Your mother speaks Hungarian?" Abigail asked, reaching for her bag.

"Let's just say my mom knows a lot of 'colorful' expressions in a lot of different languages."

"I think I'm going to like her," she said, pulling a dark green folder out of the canvas satchel.

I nodded. "Yes, you are."

I really wanted her to come, I realized. My mother wasn't the conventional bake-cookies/remind-you-to-wear-clean-underwear kind of mom. The only things she could make with any degree of success were baking powder biscuits, lemonade and toast. And the toast was iffy. And the only advice she'd ever given me pertaining to underwear was to tell me not to get my knickers in a knot over something. But she loved Ethan and Sara and me with the fierceness of a mama grizzly bear, and I could use a little of that right now.

Abigail handed me the green folder and stood up. "That's the tentative schedule for the next week. As soon as she says yes, I'll arrange the plane tickets and everything else."

"I'll call you as soon as I talk to her," I said.

She threw her arms around me, whispering, "I owe you" in my ear.

Ben got to his feet, patted his pockets and pulled out a pen. He took the green folder from me and scrawled a phone number across its front. "That's my cell. Tell Thea she can call me when it's good for her." He squeezed my arm. "And thank you."

I smiled at him. "You're welcome."

I walked them to the top of the stairs, then got myself a cup of coffee from the staff room and went back to my office to tackle the pile of paperwork next to my computer. About quarter after ten I went downstairs again to relieve Susan and Mary so they could take their breaks.

Mary was at the circulation desk checking out books for a teacher from one of the neighborhood day-care centers. Susan was pushing a cart full of books toward the stacks. Mia was in the children's department, her neon blue hair pulled back from her face with a wide zebra-print headband. She had a small bucket and a cloth and she was washing the tables.

I walked over to Susan. "I can't wait to meet your mom," she said.

"Abigail told you," I said.

"Actually Abigail told Mary. Mary told me."

I shook my head. "Of course. I forgot how information moves around here."

"Faster than a speeding bullet," Susan said with a grin. She tipped her head in Mia's direction. "For the record, best student intern ever."

"She picked up the computer system like that," I said, snapping my fingers.

"The story-time kids love her hair. They were all

clamoring to sit around her." Susan pointed to the round table in the children's department. Mia was scraping gum from under the bottom edge. "Nobody asked her to clean those tables. She volunteered."

"You think I should offer her the part-time job when she's done with her work-study?"

Susan nodded. "Yeah, I do. You said at the last staff meeting that we needed more help around here. Why not Mia?"

"Okay," I said. "I'll think about it." I looked at my watch. "Do you want to take your break first?"

She shook her head. "I'd rather get these shelved before I do. It's the last cart. Anyway, I think Mary should go first. She doesn't exactly seem like herself today."

The day-care teacher was heading out the door and Mary was on the phone.

"What do you mean, she doesn't seem like herself?" I said.

Susan poked the crochet hook holding her topknot a little tighter into her hair. Either she was trying to keep it away from the twins so they didn't put someone's eye out or Abigail was still trying to teach her how to crochet.

"I don't know. She seems kind of preoccupied about something. She went to put the coffee on and then came back down without doing it. And she forgot to lock the book drop after we emptied it." She held up a hand. "That reminds me. Oren put a new strip of metal on the top edge where it was eating magazines. He said to let him know how it works."

I nodded and made a mental note to make a written one so I wouldn't forget.

Mary was just hanging up the phone when I walked over to the desk. "You can take your break now," I said.

She looked blankly at me for a moment, then shook her head. "Sorry, Kathleen. I was somewhere else."

"Is everything all right?" I asked.

"Yes," she said, tugging at the bottom of her cream-colored cardigan. The sweater had slipped down on her right shoulder, and the totem pole of scarecrows that decorated that side looked as though it was about to topple over. She sighed. "No, everything's not all right."

"Could I help?"

"Maybe you could. Obviously you know that Hugh Davis is dead."

I nodded.

"Well, yesterday morning I walked over to the Stratton to see if I could help Abigail with anything. It was early and the only car in the lot was hers. I just assumed she was there by herself." She gave me a wry smile. "At my age you'd think I'd know not to assume anything."

I knew better than to try to rush Mary. She would get to the point in her own time.

"I thought that Abigail would be in the office at that time of day, so I went in the front."

"She wasn't there?"

Mary shook her head. "The auditorium doors were locked, so I decided to just go back outside and use the stage door." She fingered a button on her sweater. "She was actually standing in the parking lot. I think she was getting boxes out of her car. I was about halfway around the building when I saw her."

"Mary, did you and Abigail have some kind of an argument?" I asked.

"We didn't," she said. "But Abigail and Hugh Davis did."

"People argue," I said, choosing my words carefully. "You saw what Hugh was like when he was here yesterday. He couldn't have been easy to work with. So they had a disagreement. It doesn't mean anything." I realized I was trying to convince myself as much as I was trying to convince Mary.

Abigail had lied about knowing Hugh. Mary had heard them arguing. And now he was dead. Big coincidence. On the other hand, I knew Abigail couldn't kill anyone. Stuff someone in her rain barrel? Maybe. Shoot them? Never.

Mary shook her head slowly. "You don't understand, Kathleen," she said, lowering her voice. "This was a lot more than a disagreement. You know how Abigail is. She doesn't lose her temper. She doesn't raise her voice. In the last year and a half have you ever seen her get angry?"

"No, I haven't," I said.

She picked up a scrap piece of paper from the

desk and dropped it into the recycling bin. "Well, I've known Abigail a lot longer than that and I've never seen her really lose her temper—that is, not before yesterday."

"So what were they fighting about?"

"I don't know. I didn't even realize it was the two of them at first. I could hear the tone of their voices, but I couldn't really make out the words. Then when I saw who it was . . ." She looked away for a moment. "They didn't see me, so I just backtracked to the sidewalk and left."

"And then you found out Hugh was dead."

There were tiny pinched lines around her mouth. "I don't mean that I think Abigail had anything to do with that," she said hastily. Then she sighed. "Kathleen, Abigail and Hugh Davis had some kind of past, but they were both pretending they'd never met."

"Why do you say that?" I hoped that what I was feeling didn't show on my face.

"Because of the one thing I did hear her say to him before I got out of there. She said, 'If I'd killed you the first time you messed up my life, I'd be out of prison by now.'"

8

I called Mom about twelve thirty. She answered the phone on the ninth ring with a sound that was more like a growl than a hello. Her smoky voice was even huskier than usual.

"Katydid, you better be on fire if you're calling me at this ungodly hour," she rasped.

"It's lunchtime here," I said, grinning and swinging around in my chair so I could see the clouds drifting in over the water.

"How nice for you. Why did you call me, assuming you're *not* on fire at the moment?"

I relayed Ben's offer.

"Hugh Davis is dead?" She sounded a little more awake. "The man was a toad, but still."

"You knew him?"

"Mostly by reputation, sweetie. What happened?"

"I'm not exactly sure," I replied, hedging. "What do you mean he was a toad?"

"Long story, Katydid," she said with a yawn. "I'll tell you all about it when I see you."

"So you'll come?"

"Of course I'll come," she said. "I haven't worked with Ben in years and how could I pass up the opportunity to spend time with you?"

I told her Abigail would be in touch with all the details and promised I'd have her favorite tea and we'd hung up.

When we closed at one o'clock, I walked over to the co-op store to see if Maggie was available for lunch. I couldn't get what Mary had told me out of my head. I hadn't been wrong. Abigail and Hugh Davis had known each other. So why did they pretend they didn't? Could that somehow have something to do with his death? I wanted someone else's perspective—someone other than the cats. I'd left a message for Mags, but I hadn't heard back from her so I was guessing it had been a busy morning at the store.

There were four people browsing in the small space. Maggie and Ruby Blackthorne were behind the counter looking after a fifth customer. Ruby was nesting a small earth goddess statue in a box filled with packing peanuts that looked like white cheese curls. They were made out of cornstarch and I remembered how happy Maggie had been to find them on a trip we'd made to Minneapolis with Roma . . . at a business Abigail had suggested she check out.

I needed to talk to Maggie. I needed her to tell me I was seeing connections where there really weren't any.

She looked up from the cash register, smiled and held up one finger, which meant "Give me a minute."

I nodded.

Marcus's sister, Hannah, was in the far corner of the room looking at wind chimes. I walked over and tapped her on the shoulder.

She turned around, smiling when she saw it was me. "Hi, Kathleen," she said.

Her dark hair was pulled back in a messy bun and what makeup she wore had been expertly applied, but it couldn't completely disguise the fact that she hadn't had enough sleep. Her skin was pale and tiny lines pulled at the corners of her eyes.

"Hi," I said.

She looked around. "This place is wonderful."

I nodded. "Yes, it is."

The artists' co-op had had its problems in the past. The basement had flooded after days of steady rain in the spring. Even worse, the body of mask-maker Jaeger Merrill had been found floating down there the same day he'd had an angry confrontation with the co-op board. But Maggie, as chairman of the board, had kept the store running and now it was showing a decent and consistent profit.

"I'm sorry about Hugh," I said.

Hannah shrugged. "Me too. I didn't know him that well, but nobody should die like that." She brushed a tendril of hair away from her face. "Ben says your mom is coming to step in, though."

"Yes, she is."

"What's your mother like?" Hannah was wearing a couple of vivid multicolored fabric bracelets on her right arm and she twisted them around her wrist with her other hand.

"Dramatic," I said with a smile.

"What director isn't?"

"She's very good at finding that one little detail that helps an actor figure out who their character is—at least according to my dad."

"Your parents work together?" She looked surprised.

I nodded. "They both teach at a private school. And they've been performing together since before I was born. *And* they've been married twice and divorced once."

Hannah smiled. "I bet it was interesting growing up in your family."

That made me laugh. "I never knew when I came home from school if my parents would be Lord and Lady Macbeth or Bonnie and Clyde." Out of the corner of my eye I could see that Maggie was still busy at the counter with her customer. "Seriously, though, I think you'll like working with my mother."

"I'm just happy she agreed to come." Hannah was still twisting the bracelets around her arm. "I went to Red Wing after rehearsal and spent a couple of hours going through the bags and boxes of stuff that had been in the theater, hoping I could salvage something from the fire. When I got back and found out what had happened to Hugh, I assumed everything would be canceled." She shook her head. "It seemed like all the talk about jinxes might be coming true. First it was the fire. Then when I got to Red Wing so much of what had been saved was a mess." She sighed and looked down at the floor for a minute. "Pretty much everything either had water damage or smelled like smoke. When Ben called last night, it just seemed like too much."

"I hope the worst is over now," I said.

She nodded. "Me too."

Maggie joined us then, stretching her arms up over her head. "Yes, I would like to go to Eric's for lunch," she said to me. "I'm sorry I didn't call you back, but every time I tried to someone wanted to buy something." She smiled at Hannah. "Can you join us?"

"Yes. Can you?" I said.

Hannah shook her head. "Thanks, but I can't. Ben's going to take us through a quick rehearsal"— she looked at her watch—"in about half an hour. I should get going."

She turned to Maggie. "Could you put that mug aside for me?" She pointed to a large cream-colored coffee cup with a line drawing of a cat's face etched on one side. "I don't have my wallet, but I'll come back for it after rehearsal." She looked at me. "You think Marcus will like it?"

I nodded. "It looks like it'll hold a lot of coffee. He'll like it."

Maggie lifted the cup off the shelf. "Ruby will have it behind the counter for you."

"Thanks," Hannah said. "It was good to see you, Kathleen."

"You too," I said.

She left and I followed Maggie over to the counter, where she gave Ruby the pottery coffee mug and explained that Hannah would be back for it. "I just have to get my jacket and purse from my office and I'll be right back," Maggie said to me.

I nodded. "Okay."

Ruby smiled at me. "I was going to call you," she said. Her hair, which was red and blue this week, was pulled back in a low, stubby ponytail since she was growing it out, and she was wearing wire-framed glasses instead of her usual contacts. "The painting of Hercules is pretty much finished. Would you like to see it?"

"Yes, I would," I said. Ruby was doing a couple of paintings of Hercules and Owen to be auctioned off to benefit a cat rescue organization.

She tipped her head to one side. "Would it be weird to say you could bring Hercules if you wanted to?"

"I don't think so," I said. I didn't say that I was pretty sure Hercules would love to see the finished painting. *That* would have been weird.

"Would first thing Monday morning be okay?" Ruby asked.

"That's fine."

She gave me a sly smile. "Tell Hercules I have some of those fish crackers left."

"You're going to be his new best friend, you know."

"Works for me."

I grinned. "I'll remind you of that the next time your new best friend has to go to Roma for a shot."

She laughed.

"You have paint under your chin," I said, pointing at a streak of indigo just under her jawline.

She made a face and swiped at her chin with the sleeve of her psychedelic green T-shirt. "I was painting a backdrop for Abigail this morning and I didn't have time to get cleaned up before I had to come over here. I was supposed to do it last night, but Abigail's phone died. I tried her three times but I couldn't get her." She rolled her eyes. "Sometimes technology makes me crazy."

I nodded. "Me too."

Maggie came up behind me. "Ready to go?" she asked.

I turned around to face her. "Yes. I'm getting hungry."

Maggie looked at Ruby. "Could I bring you back anything?"

Ruby thought for a moment. "A large chai tea would be good. And if a cinnamon roll jumped in the bag, well, I wouldn't be rude and reject it."

"That's very . . . kind of you," Maggie said with a smile. "I'll be about an hour."

"And I'll see you Monday morning," I said. "Call me if anything changes."

Maggie put the strap of her purse over her head and we started up the sidewalk toward Eric's Place.

"Busy morning?" I asked.

"Uh-huh, but that's a good thing." She shifted the small denim purse onto her hip. "Andrew told me about Hugh Davis. Are you okay?"

I frowned at her. "Andrew told you?"

She nodded. "Uh-huh. I went to Eric's for some tea before I opened the store. Andrew showed up at the same time. We had breakfast."

"He's trying to win you over to his side, you know."

"I know," she said. She rubbed her palms together and studied me. "So you're all right?"

"I'm fine," I said. "But there is something I wanted to ask you about."

"Anything. What is it?"

We stopped at the corner, looked both ways and crossed the street. Eric's was just ahead. "It's Abigail. I think she knew Hugh, I mean I think she knew him before the festival ended up here."

Maggie frowned. "Are you sure?"

I shook my head. "Not really. It's just something she said to me and something else Mary overheard."

"You don't think Abigail had something to do with Hugh Davis's death, do you?"

"No. But I think she's hiding something, which isn't like Abigail. And he is dead."

"Which is an awfully big coincidence—not that coincidences don't happen."

We were at the café. I followed Maggie in. A tall man I didn't recognize was behind the counter. He smiled at Maggie. She gestured toward an empty table in the window, raising her eyebrows. He nodded and she smiled back and started for the table.

"Who's that?" I asked, shrugging off my jacket.

"That's Nicolas," Maggie said "He's about to be the newest member of the co-op. He's a found-metal artist."

"What's a found-metal artist?"

She hung her purse on the back of her chair and peeled off her jacket. "He recycles all kind of metal— forks, knives, gears, screws—into sculptures. He's working on a series of birds right now that are just incredible."

Nicolas was on his way over with hot water and tea bags for Maggie and the coffeepot. "Hi, Maggie," he said, setting the metal carafe of hot water and a small stoneware teapot in front of her.

He was about medium height, built like a hockey goalie with a smooth, shaved head, light brown skin and deep brown eyes.

"Coffee?" he asked me.

"Please." I pushed my cup closer.

"Nic, this is my friend Kathleen," Maggie said.

"Nice to meet you," I said.

He smiled as he filled my cup. "You as well."

Maggie leaned forward and looked in the direction of the kitchen. She reminded me of Owen when I was making kitty crackers. "Do I smell pea soup?" she asked.

He nodded. "With corn bread. It's today's special."

Maggie's gaze shifted to me. "Yes?"

"Yes," I said with a smile.

"It'll just be a few minutes," he said and headed back to the kitchen.

I added cream and sugar to my coffee. "He's nice."

"He is," Maggie said, dropping a tea bag into the pot and reaching for the hot water. "I think he'll be a good addition to the co-op."

I leaned back in my chair and watched the little ritual she went through when she made her tea. Finally she picked up the cup and stretched her long legs under the table.

"Okay, tell me why you think Abigail knew Hugh before the festival," she said.

"This stays between us."

"Of course."

I ran my finger around the top edge of my coffee mug. "It was what she said after Ben Saroyan and Hugh had come to take a look at the gazebo, although I didn't pay attention to it at the time. Hugh wasn't happy with the idea of using it as a stage. Abigail said, 'He's still a control freak, I've discovered.' "

Maggie's eyebrows went up. " 'Still'?"

I nodded.

"And you said Mary overheard something."

"Mary went over to the Stratton yesterday morning, early, to talk to Abigail and overheard her in the parking lot, arguing with Hugh."

Maggie shrugged. "People argue. It doesn't always mean they know each other that well."

Nicolas was coming our way with a tray. The aroma of smoked ham and onions drifted in our direction.

"It's not the fact that they were arguing that bothers me," I said. "It's what Mary heard Abigail say."

"Which was?"

"'If I'd killed you the first time you messed up my life I'd be out of prison by now.'" I looked at Maggie across the table. "No one says that to someone they just met."

She sighed. "True."

Nic had reached the table. He slipped fragrant, steaming bowls of thick soup in front of us and set a napkin-lined basket of corn bread in the middle of the table. "I'll be right back with the coffeepot," he said with a smile.

I didn't say anything else until my cup had been topped up and I'd buttered a slab of corn bread, still warm from the oven. "It's not like Abigail," I said. "Do you remember when she found that box of old books at the library? The one with the first edition of *Alice in Wonderland*?"

"I remember," Maggie said, gesturing with her

spoon. "That was how you bought all the books for the children's section, wasn't it? Just from auctioning that one book."

I dunked a chunk of corn bread in my soup and took a bite before I answered. "It was. Abigail found those books in the storage room stuffed in a box that had been donated to the library, and the first thing she did was bring them to me. Everyone had forgotten they were even there. She could have taken that first edition and the rest of the books and no one would have known."

Maggie dipped a piece of the corn bread in her own bowl, took a bite and gave a little groan of happiness. "Abigail's not a deceitful person," she said.

"I know," I said. "So her lying about this doesn't make any sense. And it's not like she can keep it up. Marcus is a good detective. He'll figure it out."

"So tell her that."

"I'm trying not to get mixed up in another one of Marcus's cases." I glanced out the window, wondering where Marcus was right now.

Maggie leaned forward, resting one elbow on the table. "Kath, I didn't ask you a lot of questions about why things didn't work out with Marcus because that's none of my business, but I think I have a pretty good idea. All I'm going to say is it's not wrong to care about your friends."

I nodded. "Thanks." I'd told Marcus more than once that I couldn't turn away if someone I cared about was in trouble. It helped to hear Maggie say that wasn't wrong.

I picked up my spoon again. "There's something else that bothers me about this whole thing."

Maggie sipped her tea and then added a little more honey. "What?" she asked.

"Abigail was lying about knowing Hugh," I said. "But why was he lying about knowing her?"

9

"And he did act like they didn't know each other, didn't he?" Maggie said thoughtfully. "When we were painting the stage the other night Hugh came in looking for Abigail. Remember? He called her Ms. Pierce."

"I remember," I said.

She shrugged. "Maybe it was as simple as they had a thing and were embarrassed about it."

"A thing?"

"You know Abigail loves the theater." Maggie gestured with her cup, almost spilling her tea. "She went on that tour to New York in the spring. Maybe she met Hugh, they had a wild and torrid affair over a long weekend, and then they were both mortified at what they'd done so they agreed to pretend it never happened."

I tried to get a mental picture of Abigail having a torrid affair with Hugh—and couldn't. I shook my head. "If we were talking about Mary, maybe," I said. "But I just can't picture Abigail doing something so impulsive."

"No one could picture you leaving Boston for the wilds of Minnesota, but you did."

Because I'd been hurt over Andrew's drunken marriage and tired of always being practical and sensible. Maybe Maggie was right. Maybe the same thing had happened to Abigail, minus someone marrying a waitress they'd just met. Maybe I was seeing mysterious connections where there weren't any.

"Point taken," I said with a smile. "I'm going to ask her what's going on. Thanks, Mags."

She smiled back at me. "Anytime."

We finished lunch without talking anymore about Abigail or Hugh. Maggie got a take-out cup of chai tea for Ruby, along with a cinnamon roll still warm from the oven.

"Why don't you come for supper tomorrow night?" she said once we were outside on the sidewalk. "I feel like pizza."

Maggie made wonderful pizza. Every pot, pan and dish in her apartment would be dirty, but the result would be delicious. "Umm, yes," I said. "What can I bring?"

"I wouldn't say no to brownies."

"When have you ever said no to brownies?"

She grinned. "Consistency is the key to a happy life."

I wiggled one finger at her. "Emerson said 'A foolish consistency is the hobgoblin of little minds.'"

Maggie laughed. "The man obviously wasn't eating enough brownies." She hugged me. "I'll see you tomorrow night. I'll call Roma too and see if she can come."

Andrew's red rental car was just circling the parking lot as I came up the sidewalk in front of the library. I walked over to my truck and he pulled into the empty space beside me and got out.

He was wearing jeans and a blue henley shirt with the sleeves pushed back. His hair was damp and he looked like a sheepish little boy. "Hi," he said. "I was looking for you."

"You found me," I said, fishing out my keys. "What do you need?"

"To say I'm sorry for acting like a caveman last night."

He really did look contrite, standing there with his feet apart and his hands jammed in his pockets. "You were more of a jerk than a caveman," I said. "It's not like you threw me over your shoulder and carried me back to your cave."

"I thought about it for a minute," he said, the start of a smile stretching across his face.

It was hard not to smile back. "I really can take care of myself, Andrew."

"I do know that." His expression grew serious again. "It's just . . . someone shot that man, Hugh Davis. Shot him, Kath."

"And I know that," I said.

"Have you heard if the police have any suspects?"

"No, I haven't."

"Maybe he was just in the wrong place at the wrong time. Although it's hard to think of this little place as being any kind of hotbed of criminal activity."

I shifted my keys from one hand to the other. "Did you notice anything . . . odd last night?"

He kicked a rock and sent it skittering across the pavement. "Not really."

Something in his voice made me frown at him. "What do you mean, not really?"

"I didn't see anyone in the parking lot or up on the lookout."

I pushed back the sleeves of my sweater. "But you did see someone somewhere else."

"It wasn't a person." He shifted from one foot to the other. "But I did see a car, a navy blue SUV, with roof racks actually. It drove past out on the road a couple of times while we were unloading."

I tried to picture the parking lot at the marina and the road that curved around the bluff just above it. It was well lit by streetlights all around the curve. "I don't remember seeing any SUV," I said. My heart was suddenly pounding in my chest, but I didn't think Andrew could tell.

"That's because you were in the bed of the truck pushing the staging out to me. Your back was to the road." He narrowed his gaze. "C'mon, Kath, you don't think that SUV had anything to do with that Davis guy, do you?"

"Most people use the highway if they're heading east," I said with a shrug. "But there's still a fair amount of traffic on that road. People around here actually use it as a shortcut."

"Whoever it was, she probably just forgot something at home and went back to get whatever it was," Andrew said.

The laces on my left boot were untied and I bent down to fix them. "Probably," I agreed, pulling the laces tight and knotting them carefully before I stood up again.

He smiled. "Have dinner with me tonight?"

I needed to make the bed in my spare bedroom, do some laundry and vacuum up the cat hair before my mother arrived. Not to mention find out exactly when she would be arriving. But mostly, I just needed to go. I needed to think.

I shook my head. "I can't. My mother's coming."

"Seriously?" Andrew said. "Thea's coming here?"

I nodded. "She's going to step in for Hugh Davis." I was glad to have the subject changed.

"I haven't seen her for a while." He shot me an inquiring look. "Does she know I'm here?"

"I was asking her to give up her time off to come here and step into a directing job at the last minute. I wasn't sure how I could work in the fact that you were here trying to charm me back into your arms, so, no, she doesn't."

He laughed. "Don't worry. I'll remember to duck and move in a zigzag pattern when I see her."

"C'mon, she always liked you," I said.

"I don't know about that," he said, with a slight eye roll. "I think she blames me a little for you coming here." He gave me a sly sideways look. "Of course, if you came home with me I'd be back on her good side."

I shook my head. "You don't give up, do you?"

"When it comes to you, never." He wiggled his eyebrows at me. "Since you won't have dinner with me, how about breakfast tomorrow morning?"

I hesitated.

"C'mon, Kathleen. It's breakfast, not a lifetime commitment. At least not right now."

I waffled for another half a minute. If we had breakfast maybe I'd be able to find out a little more about that SUV he'd seen, because I really needed to know how certain he was about it. We settled on a time and I didn't even argue when he said he'd pick me up.

I got in the truck and drove up the hill. Andrew had said he noticed a navy blue SUV drive back and forth along the road above the marina. Navy blue with roof racks. Maybe he was wrong, although I didn't see how he could be. Andrew was the kind of guy who noticed cars and that stretch of road was certainly lit well enough for him to be able to tell a navy SUV from a black one. Or whether the driver was a man or a woman. I'd noticed he'd used "she" when he talked about the driver.

I took a deep breath and exhaled slowly, but it

didn't make me feel any better. A lot of people in Mayville Heights drove half-ton trucks, like I did. There were actually a couple of trucks identical to mine in town—Ruby had one. They'd originally been part of a special order that had ended up being sold off by a local car dealer a few years ago. But I knew only one person in town who drove a navy blue SUV with roof racks.

Marcus.

Marcus, who had loaned his SUV to Hannah, who had made a point of telling me she'd been in Red Wing when Hugh Davis had been killed. But clearly hadn't been.

"Tell me I'm wrong," I said to Hercules. I was sitting in the big chair in the living room. He was sprawled on my lap, while Owen lay across my legs.

Hercules suddenly became very busy washing the splash of white fur on his chest. I looked at Owen. His golden eyes were closed and he was pretending to be asleep, although I knew from the way his whiskers were twitching that he was very much awake.

I scratched the top of Hercules's head and he began to purr. "Maybe Andrew was mistaken," I said. "Maybe the SUV was a different color. Or there weren't any roof racks. And just because he said 'she' doesn't mean the driver was a woman."

He made a rumbly sound that made me think he didn't agree. At least that's what I decided it meant.

I sighed. "It's possible he was wrong, but it's not that likely. If I'd dyed my hair purple it would have taken a week for him to notice, but he could tell the difference between a gray car and a silver one from the opposite end of a parking lot. That's just the way Andrew is."

The cat batted a strand of my hair with one paw and tipped his black-and-white head back to look up at me. "No, I didn't actually dye my hair purple," I said because he seemed to be wondering.

The phone rang then. Owen jumped at the sound and almost ended up on the floor. He shook himself, then sent a daggers look at the phone. "Don't laugh," I whispered to Hercules, who was leaning forward to look at his brother as I reached for the receiver.

It was Ben Saroyan. "Kathleen, you said if there was any way you could help, to let you know," he said, his voice rumbling against my ear. "I'm calling to take you up on your offer. I could use your help with a couple of things."

"Of course," I said, shifting slightly in the chair, which netted me a disgruntled look from Owen. "What do you need?"

"Hannah brought back some boxes and bags from the theater in Red Wing and we've started going through them. I have a couple more I actually salvaged the night of the fire. Hugh was meticulous about keeping notes on a production and I'd like to overnight some of them to Thea so she can look at them before she gets here on Tuesday, but I haven't been able to find very much so far."

"And you'd like some help looking through the boxes."

"I would," he said. "If I dropped off those two I have in my rental car, could you sort through them? You know the sort of thing your mother would find useful."

Owen decided then that he had other things to do. He jumped down and made a beeline for the stairs. Either he was going to look for a Fred the Funky Chicken—Rebecca was always finding an excuse to buy him one of the neon yellow catnip chickens that he loved—or he was planning to prowl around in my closet.

"Of course I could," I said. "Would it help if I came and got them?"

I heard Ben exhale. "Honestly? Yes."

"I'll be there in a few minutes then." He thanked me and I hung up. I gave Hercules one last scratch and set him on the floor, where he stretched and yawned. "So what are your plans for the afternoon?" I asked.

He cocked his head to one side as though he was considering his options.

"Lie in the sunshine by the front door, maybe? Hide a funky chicken from Owen?"

The cat gave me a blank look.

"Yes, I know you do that," I said.

He ducked his head and looked a little sheepish. At least as sheepish as a little tuxedo cat could look.

"You could go take a little nap in Rebecca's gazebo."

He lifted a paw and gave it a shake. Hercules was a total wuss about wet feet.

"Yes, I know I said it's going to rain, but not until later," I told him. "There's still a lot of blue sky out there."

His whiskers twitched as though he was considering the nap.

"Or you could go out and look for Professor Moriarty."

His green eyes narrowed. Even though their little war had escalated during the past couple of weeks, I was beginning to think both the cat and the bird were enjoying the battle. Hercules could be pretty fast on his paws when he wanted to be and I'd seen the grackle fly over literally inches above the cat's head, but they were both, for the most part, unscathed from their encounters. I had discovered Hercules with one of the bird's tail feathers recently, but that didn't mean it was a prize of war, so to speak.

Now he was headed for the kitchen like a cat with a purpose. Clearly, the game was afoot. Or in this case, maybe apaw. I turned to head upstairs and it hit me. I'd invited my mother to stay here, for a week, with me . . . and Hercules and Owen. She wouldn't think it was odd that I talked to them or that Hercules liked Barry Manilow and Owen didn't—although I knew she'd be firmly in Owen's camp on that. But I was pretty sure she wouldn't understand if Hercules walked through the porch door or Owen suddenly became invisible.

"Hercules," I said.

He had one paw on the kitchen floor and he stopped and looked back over his shoulder at me.

"Come back here for a minute," I said.

He sat down and gave me an expectant look. I knew that meant *you come over here.* So I did, because I didn't have a lot of time.

I crouched down beside him. "My mother's coming to stay with us for a few days," I said.

"Merow," he said. Translation: *I know.*

"I need you not to walk through any walls or doors or anything like that while she's here."

I felt a little foolish. I knew the cats understood a lot more words than the average house cat, which made a certain sense because they weren't average house cats. On the other hand, I had no idea if Hercules could comprehend anything I'd just said. For all I knew, what he'd heard was *la, la, la doors.*

He gave me a green-eyed blink and started for the porch again. I got the feeling that he had understood every single word. Of course, even if he'd understood what I said, that didn't mean he would actually *do* what I said.

I went upstairs to get my sweater. Owen's back end was sticking out of the half-open closet door. It struck me that I wouldn't mind taking some furry company with me. I pulled the door open a little farther. He seemed to be studying my clothes and he looked at me with a slightly miffed expression at the interruption.

"What do you do when you just stand here staring into the closet?" I asked. "Is this some kitty version of *What Not to Wear*?"

That got me a look that was pure disdain. Then he went back to eyeing my wardrobe as though I weren't there.

I reached down and stroked the gray fur on the side of his face, just above his neck. After a moment he leaned into my hand. All was forgiven.

"My mother's coming on Tuesday," I said. The only response that I got was a small rumble from the back of his throat. I was pretty sure that was enthusiasm for the scratch he was getting and not because we were having a visitor. The one visitor he got excited about was Maggie, whom he adored. "Could you please hold off on the whole invisibility thing while she's here?"

He shook his furry head, swatted my hand away and took a couple of steps farther into the closet. Then he just winked out of sight.

I sighed and straightened up. Cats might not get sarcasm when it was directed at them, but they were pretty good at dishing it out.

"Okay," I said. "I have to go down to the Stratton to pick up a couple of boxes." I grabbed my sweater off the bed and started for the door. "I'm going to see if your brother wants to come with me." I counted silently in my head, *two . . . three . . . four*.

Owen appeared in front of me on *four*.

"Oh, would you like to come with me?" I asked.

He turned in the direction of the stairs, flicking his tail at me, probably because he didn't have fingers.

I found Ben in the theater office at the Stratton. There were two desks squeezed into the small room and a coffee machine on a little round table by the door, along with a plate of cupcakes I was guessing had come from Georgia Tepper's business, Sweet Thing.

Ben had just poured coffee for himself. "Hi, Kathleen," he said. "Would you like a cup?"

I shook my head. "Is Abigail around, by any chance?"

He took a long drink from his oversize mug, then set it on the metal desk just behind him. "Rehearsal ran long. Some of the cast went for a late lunch and Abigail went with them. Why?"

"It's not important. I'll talk to her later," I said. "Where are the boxes?"

"In the trunk of my rental. It's just outside." He pointed toward the main parking lot, where I'd left the truck.

"Thank you again for asking Thea to come," Ben said as we walked around the side of the old stone building.

"I'm happy to get a chance to see her," I said. "She's been so busy."

"I'm just glad *Wild and Wonderful* is going dark for the next ten days so she could come. The timing couldn't be better." He shrugged. "Otherwise New Horizons would have had to be canceled. You probably know some people think the festival is jinxed?"

"I heard."

He sent me a sideways glance. "He tried to text me, you know."

"Hugh?"

Ben nodded. "Before he died. It was around six thirty and we were still rehearsing, so I didn't have my phone with me."

My stomach did a little flip-flop. "What did the text say?"

"I don't know. It didn't go through and the police wouldn't tell me." He exhaled loudly. "He didn't deserve this."

"What was Hugh like as a director?" I asked, mostly to change the subject.

Ben gave a snort of laughter. "Hughie could be a royal pain in the ass. He was meticulous, bordering on obsessive. He had this way of breaking down actors so they could get inside the characters. It was ugly, but it seemed to work for him."

My mother was nothing like that. She nudged and coaxed and pushed her actors, sometimes gently, sometimes loudly. She didn't believe in breaking anyone down.

Ben stopped beside his silver SUV. "I know that's not Thea's style," he said.

"Dad says her style is 'hovering mother.' She stands over you until she gets what she wants." I laughed. "That's pretty much how she got me through calculus in high school."

"That's her strength, you know," Ben said.

"Hovering?"

"Making the actors feel like she believes in them."

I nodded without saying anything. It was also my mom's strength as a mother. Growing up, my life had been far from conventional and sometimes I'd felt like I was the most responsible person in the house—probably because a lot of the time I was—but I'd never once doubted my mother's faith in me. She really did believe that Sara and Ethan and I could do anything. I remembered all those weeks that I struggled with calculus. Her certainty that I would eventually master it had been unshakable. Every night she told me, "Every day, in every way, you're getting better and better."

It had annoyed the heck out of me then. Now all I could think was that it really was going to be good to see her on Tuesday.

I saw Ben sneak a look at his watch. "Are the boxes in the back?" I asked.

"They are." He pulled a set of keys out of his jeans pocket and popped the hatch. He grabbed one of the cardboard cartons and I got the other.

I dipped my head in the direction of the truck, parked half a dozen spaces away. I could see Owen watching out the driver's-side window. "That's my truck," I said.

"And I assume that's your cat," Ben said as we crossed the pavement.

I smiled. "That's Owen."

My keys were in my sweater pocket. I set the box on the hood of the truck and fished them out.

Owen stayed where he was, watching with curiosity as I set one carton on the floor and the other on the seat.

"Is it okay to pet him?" Ben asked, leaning around the door frame to look at the cat.

"Only if you want to pet the Tasmanian devil," I said. "Owen was feral. He doesn't like being touched by pretty much anyone else but me."

"Okay." He straightened up. "How did you end up with a feral cat?"

"Two feral cats, actually. Would you believe they followed me home?"

He laughed. "I would. You're a lot like your mother, although she was always rescuing two-legged strays." He gestured at the cartons. "Thanks for going through those boxes for me."

"I don't mind," I said. "I'll sort everything and bring it back tomorrow."

Have a good evening, Kathleen."

"You too," I said.

When we got home I put both boxes on the kitchen

table. Owen immediately jumped up onto one of the chairs. He slid one gray paw under the flap of the closest carton, trying to get the top open.

"You're wasting your time," I said over my shoulder.

"Merow," he said. I knew that meant he wanted me to come and open the boxes for him. Owen loved boxes, mostly because he was incredibly nosy.

I went over to the table, picked him up and set him on the floor. He made a huffy noise and glared at me.

"I'm going to make the brownies first," I told him. "Then you can see what's inside these boxes." We had a brief staring contest and then he decided to see what was happening in the living room.

I waited until the brownies were cooling on a wire rack to start on the boxes. I pulled the first one closer and Owen immediately appeared in the doorway. "C'mon," I said.

He trotted over, jumped up on the chair next to me and gave me an expectant look.

"You can look, but keep your paws off the papers," I warned. That got me a wide-eyed who-me? look of innocence.

I opened the flaps of the first box with Owen at my elbow craning his neck for a look inside. The heavy smell of smoke, like an ashtray full of wet cigarette butts, had settled inside the carton. Owen made a face and shook his gray head.

I pulled out a handful of papers and started going

through them. "Hugh has—had—very small, angular handwriting," Ben had told me. Anything that looked like it might have been written by the dead director I put in one pile so I could take a better look at it later; everything else I tried to sort by general category. Owen watched, sniffing at everything and poking the odd pile with one paw.

The stack of pages in Hugh's scratchy script began piling up at my elbow. How could one man generate so much paper? I couldn't believe that he'd kept all his notes and thoughts on paper. A laptop or a tablet would have been a lot more efficient.

I should have realized that Owen would get bored pretty quickly. He started sniffing the second box. Then he put one paw on the table and the other on the top edge of the carton. The small difference in weight was enough to shift the box's center of gravity. It toppled sideways off the table as the cat jumped back, almost falling off the chair.

The box landed on its side, the contents spreading out across the floor like a fan.

"Owen!" I said sharply. He ducked his furry head as I moved around the table to pick up the scattered papers. One page had floated over by the back door. Owen jumped down and poked his head in the upended carton.

"Get out of there!" I snapped, bending down to grab the stray piece of paper.

He jumped at the sound of my voice and I heard his head bump the top of the box. Then he backed out, sliding a piece of paper onto the floor with his right paw. He shook his head, looked at me, and meowed loudly.

I knelt on the floor next to him. "I think you're okay," I said. "Let me see." He bent his head and I felt the top of it. He was fine. He didn't even have a bump. It was just a cardboard box that he'd made contact with, and a saggy one at that. I leaned over and kissed the top of his head. "You'll live," I said.

He licked my chin, then pawed at the piece of paper he'd pulled out of the overturned carton.

"What is that?" I asked, putting my hands on the floor and leaning in for a closer look.

A newspaper clipping was stuck to the top of a page of Hugh's cramped writing. The clipping, from a New York paper dated ten days before, was a brief article about casting for an upcoming off-Broadway play. But it wasn't the clipping itself that held my attention. It was the words written across it with thick black marker in large, square letters: DROP DEAD. I got that roller-coaster-racing-around-a-curve feeling in my stomach as I realized that the boxy printing looked familiar. I was pretty sure it was Hannah's.

10

Owen put one gray paw on my knee and looked up at me, curiosity in his golden eyes.

"I think that's Hannah's handwriting," I said. "She helped pack programs last week and she wrote on the tops of all the boxes. I need to call Marcus."

But I didn't get up. I stayed there on the floor, staring at the bold, square letters scrawled across the newsprint. How could I call Marcus if Hannah had written the words? How could I not call him? It was his case. On the other hand, Hannah was his sister.

The cat murped softly at me. "I know," I said. I reached for my purse, hanging on the back of the chair behind me, and pulled out my cell phone.

Marcus's phone rang six times before he answered. I explained that I was sorting papers from the Red Wing theater and that I'd found something that might be related to Hugh Davis's death. I didn't saying anything about Hannah.

"I'll be there in about fifteen minutes," he said.

I was glad he hadn't asked me what I'd found. I

set the piece of paper with the attached clipping on the table and got to my feet. "I'm going to make coffee," I said to Owen. "Would you please go watch for Marcus?"

He looked at me for a moment, then turned and headed for the porch. About ten minutes later I heard a loud meow. I stuck my head into the porch in time to see Marcus come around the side of the house. Owen was on the bench by the window. "Thank you," I said to him as I went to open the door.

Marcus was wearing khakis and his leather jacket over a long-sleeved green T-shirt. The ends of his hair were slightly damp as though he'd just gotten out of the shower.

Okay, Marcus getting out of the shower was not something I should've been thinking about. "Come in," I said, dragging my imagination back from places it shouldn't have been going.

He followed me to the kitchen. For the moment Owen decided to stay where he was.

"What did you find?" Marcus asked.

"This," I said, sliding the page of notes with the clipping stuck to the top over to the edge of the table.

I saw the muscles along his jawline tighten. He swallowed and looked at me. "Where exactly did you find this?"

I pointed at the box, which was sitting on a chair now. "I was sorting through these couple of boxes that came from the theater in Red Wing, to help Ben.

It's all papers he managed to grab the night of the fire there. Owen knocked that box on the floor. The newspaper clipping was mixed in with the other papers."

"What is all this stuff?" he asked.

"Mostly Hugh Davis's notes, mock-ups of the program and sketches for costumes. Apparently he kept all his notes on paper instead of on a computer."

Marcus looked at the clipping again.

I laced my fingers together. "That's Hannah's handwriting, isn't it?" I asked.

He didn't hedge and he really didn't look surprised that I knew. "Yes," he said.

"I don't think this really has anything to do with Hugh's death."

"It doesn't." He didn't look at me.

I hesitated and then I put my hand on his arm, hoping he could somehow feel the warmth through his jacket.

"I'll call the station," he said. "Somebody else should deal with this." He touched my hand for just a moment, then stepped away from the table and took out his phone.

I didn't know Hannah very well, but I liked her. I would have liked her even if she hadn't been Marcus's sister. I couldn't imagine her shooting anyone. But why was a clipping with *drop dead* written on it in her handwriting stuck to a page of Hugh Davis's notes? And why had she driven back and forth in front of the marina the night he was killed? I'd been trying not to think about that, but if Andrew had seen Marcus's SUV Friday night, then it had to have been Hannah driving it. I glanced at Marcus. I needed to talk to Andrew again before I said anything about the car.

Marcus put his phone back in his jacket pocket and turned around. "Someone's on the way," he said. "It should only be a few minutes."

"How about a cup of coffee?" I asked.

"Maybe I should just go wait out front," he said, shifting from one foot to the other.

"You can wait in the porch," I said.

He exhaled slowly. "Okay, and yes, I'll have a cup of coffee."

I poured a mug for each of us and we went out to the porch. Owen jumped down from the bench and went to stand by the door. Marcus opened it for him and the cat went outside, meowing his thanks.

"You don't have to wait out here with me," he said.

I nodded. "I know." I brushed a bit of gray cat hair off the bench and sat down.

"How many cups of coffee have we had together?" he asked as he sat down next to me.

"A lot."

Marcus and I had met when I discovered the body of Gregor Easton at the Stratton Theater. He'd come to question me later at the library and I'd made coffee for him. Somehow I'd ended up making or getting coffee for him on every case he'd had since.

"I just made brownies. Would you like one?"

He shook his head.

"There's a fresh batch of stinky crackers, too."

That almost coaxed a smile out of him. "Tempting, but thank you, no."

Maybe someone who didn't know him as well as I did wouldn't have noticed it, but I could tell he was worried. His blue eyes were guarded and he was squeezing the mug tightly with one hand. He glanced out the window, then looked at me again. "Kathleen, how exactly did you get those boxes?" he asked.

"I went down to the Stratton and got them from Ben." I laced my fingers around my cup.

"You didn't see Hannah, did you?"

I shook my head. "No, but Ben said rehearsal ran late and some of the actors had gone out for a late lunch. Maybe that's where she is. They're all probably at Eric's."

"Probably," he said. "I'll try her later."

I didn't know what else to say. He was going to find out what Andrew had seen, but I couldn't do that to him now. So I didn't say anything. I just sat there, and the silence was just fine. After a few minutes I could see he was getting antsy. I set my cup on the floor at my feet.

"Let's go wait out front," I said.

He looked at me for a long moment, then set his mug on the bench. "All right," he said.

We walked around to the driveway and stood next to the black Caprice. Marcus watched the road and after a few more minutes a small blue car came up the hill.

He turned to me. "Thank you for keeping me company, Kathleen."

"Anytime," I said.

The car pulled into the driveway and the driver got out, carrying a stainless-steel coffee mug. Detective Hope Lind probably drank more coffee than I did. She was all business in black trousers, a cranberry red shirt and a cropped black leather jacket, her dark curly hair a little shorter than the last time I'd seen her.

"Hi, Kathleen," she said with a smile. She turned to Marcus. "So what's going on?"

I stood there silently while he explained and Hope sipped her coffee. She was a good foot shorter than Marcus, but I knew her size was misleading. Hope ran marathons in her spare time. For fun. She'd been on a leave of absence from the Mayville Heights police force for the last year, finishing her degree in criminology with a minor in Spanish.

She turned to me. "So why do you have these boxes, Kathleen?" she asked.

I told her about Ben's phone call and how Owen had upended the carton onto the kitchen floor.

"You recognized the handwriting, too?"

"Hannah and I were putting the programs together for the festival a couple of days ago at the library. She has a very distinctive way of making her letters."

Hope's gaze darted momentarily to Marcus. "Do you know where your sister is?" she asked.

His hands were stuffed in his pockets. "I'm not sure. Probably at the theater."

Hope set her coffee mug on the roof of Marcus's car. "Show me what you found," she said to me. She glanced at Marcus. "Probably better if you wait here."

He nodded. "All right."

I led her around to the back door. She was wearing black ankle boots a lot like the pair I owned. Their chunky heels put her height closer to mine.

Hercules was sitting by the porch door.

"Nice cat," Hope said.

"This is Hercules," I said. "Owen is . . . somewhere."

I took Hope into the kitchen. She pulled on a pair of gloves before she picked up the sheet of paper.

"You're sure this is Hugh Davis's handwriting?" she asked.

I nodded and pointed at the pile of notes. "Those are all his notes. It's the same writing."

She gave me a long, appraising look. "Kathleen, rumor has it that you and Detective Gordon are . . . involved."

She was clearly out of the loop.

"Not anymore," I said.

She searched my face and I wondered what she

was looking for. "I don't know how things are be-tween the two of you—" She held up a hand. "None of my business—but I can see you care about him, so are you absolutely sure that clipping was attached to those notes?"

I swallowed and pulled a hand across the back of my neck. "Yes," I said.

She took out her cell phone, glanced at the screen and put it back in her jacket pocket. "I'm going to take all of this," she said. "I'll notify Mr. Saroyan."

I took a step forward to start putting all the papers back in the boxes and then stopped, realizing that she wasn't going to want me to do that. I folded my arms across my chest.

"Kathleen, you seem to have a knack for getting involved in police business," Hope said. "If you come across anything—anything else—that has to do with this case, you call me." She fished a business card out of her pants pocket and handed it to me.

I thought about telling her that I was fairly certain Hannah had been near the marina the previous eve-ning. And that there was a good chance that Hugh and Abigail had known each other. *Fairly certain and a good chance aren't one hundred percent certain*, I told myself.

I nodded. "I will," I said. *Just not right now,* I added silently.

Hope quickly gathered up all the papers and packed them into the two boxes. She stacked one on top of the other and picked them both up.

"I'll get the door," I said. I followed her back to the driveway. Marcus was leaning against the driver's-side fender of his car. He straightened up when he saw us.

"I'll see you at the station," Hope said to him. She glanced at me. "Thank you, Kathleen." She took the boxes and put them on the backseat of her car.

Neither Marcus nor I said anything until she'd pulled into the street and started down the hill.

"I better go," he said then.

I took a deep breath and let it out. "Okay," I said. "I'll . . . see you around."

He nodded.

As I turned to go, he suddenly caught my hand and gave it a squeeze. "Thanks, Kathleen," he said softly.

"You're welcome," I said.

Hercules was on the bench in the porch. I gathered the mugs and went into the kitchen. He followed. "Merow?" he said.

It seemed to me there was a question in the sound.

"That was Detective Lind," I said as I put the mugs in the sink and ran some water to wash them.

He tipped his black-and-white head to one side and gave me a quizzical look. Either he wanted to know if there were any more stinky crackers or he was wondering why he hadn't seen Hope Lind before. I decided to go with the latter.

"She's been away finishing her degree."

He murped and sat down beside me while I washed the cups and dried all the dishes.

I thought about what I would do if I were in Marcus's place, if Sara or Ethan had a connection to a murder. I wouldn't be able to do nothing.

I glanced down at the cat. "Marcus is going to try to talk to Hannah before anyone else does."

Hercules made a noncommittal sound.

"It's not really any of my business," I said.

No response. I wasn't sure if that meant that he agreed or disagreed. It probably meant he wasn't even listening.

"Marcus won't be allowed to stay on the case, not as long as Hannah's connected to it in any way. And she is connected. I'm going to have to tell Detective Lind about Andrew seeing Marcus's car. I should have told her already." I was twisting the dish towel so tightly in my hands that the skin was stretched white over my knuckles.

Marcus wouldn't just step away from an investigation, especially one his sister was mixed up in. The first moment I'd seen them together I'd realized how close they were, even though he'd never talked about her to me.

"He's not going to back off," I said. I could feel Hercules's unblinking gaze before I looked down to see him staring up at me. I did see the irony of what I was saying. How many times had Marcus told me to stay out of one of his cases? Now I was the one who thought he should stay out of things.

"It's not the same thing."

Hercules made little muttering sounds and stared up at the ceiling.

"How can I just do nothing?" I said.

The last time I'd said those words—just a couple of weeks ago—things hadn't ended so well. But this really was different; at least that's what I told myself.

"Marcus and I are friends. I don't want him to do something that might put his job at risk. I'd do the same thing for Maggie or Roma."

The cat made a noise that could best be described as a snort. I ignored it. I grabbed my purse and started for the door with the cat on my heels. There was no point in trying to make him stay in the house. He would just walk through the door.

I found a place to park on one of the side streets that ran up the hill from Eric's. I wasn't certain that was where Hannah was, but I knew it was a pretty good guess. "I won't be very long," I told Hercules, who had ridden shotgun down the hill, his green eyes seemingly watching the street all the way. "Then we'll go home and have some sardines."

He walked across the bench seat to the driver's door and pawed the air near my jacket pocket. I narrowed my eyes at him. "How did you know there were crackers in that pocket?" I asked, pulling out the bag.

He wrinkled his nose at me. He would have been able to smell those crackers if they'd been in a lead-lined bag.

I put the remaining treats on the seat. "I'll be back," I said. "Stay in the truck and stay out of trouble."

He shot me a look and murped as he dropped his head over the crackers. I didn't have to speak cat to know that meant *You too*.

11

As I rounded the corner, Hannah was just coming out of Eric's—and Marcus was standing outside waiting for her. Neither of them noticed me until I literally stepped between them.

"Umm, hi, Kathleen," Hannah said. She was confused, her eyes darting from me to her big brother.

"What are you doing here?" Marcus asked, his mouth pulled into a tight line.

"Same thing as you," I said. "I came for some coffee." I turned to Hannah. "By the way, Detective Lind is looking for you."

"Me? Why?" She was a very good actress. Nothing showed in her face. On the other hand, I could feel the tension coming off of Marcus's body like mist rising from the river.

There was no point in dancing around it. "I was going through Hugh's papers, looking for some of his notes for Ben. There was a clipping stuck to a piece of paper. You wrote 'Drop dead' across the front of it."

She laughed. "Yeah, I did." She tightened the scarf at her neck. "I don't know if you noticed, but the clipping was about a new play that's going to be produced. I'm on the short list for a part. They lost their director and Hugh was at me to suggest him as a replacement." She held up her hand. "I told him that I didn't want to get involved in anything political like that and ruin my chances at the part. He wouldn't let it go. He kept bugging me about it. It was a couple of days before the fire at the theater in Red Wing and I'd had enough. I picked up a marker from his desk and wrote 'Drop dead' right across that clipping. Then I stalked off." She rolled her eyes. "It was very dramatic."

I smiled. "Then you just need to tell Detective Lind that."

Hannah shrugged. "All right."

"And you probably should have a lawyer."

"Because I wrote 'Drop dead' on an article from a newspaper? You can't be serious?"

"Kathleen's right, Hannah," Marcus said behind me. "That's how the system works."

"Where am I supposed to find a lawyer?" she said. "I guess I could open up the phone book and play one potato, two potato." She crossed her arms over her chest and gave both of us a slightly annoyed look.

"I can get you a lawyer," I said. "Marcus is right. Let the system work the way it's designed to work."

Hannah held up both hands in surrender. "Okay. Find me a lawyer then."

"It won't take very long," I said. I took a couple of steps away from them, pulled out my cell and dialed Lita Clarke's home number. Everett's assistant answered on the third ring. "Hi, Lita," I said. "It's Kathleen."

"Hi, Kathleen," she said. I could hear her smile through the phone. "What can I do for you?"

"I'm looking for a lawyer."

"Criminal or civil?"

"Criminal."

"Brady Chapman," she said at once.

"Chapman?" I said. "Any relation to Burtis?"

"His youngest."

Burtis Chapman, the town bootlegger, had a son who was a lawyer? Why didn't I know that? I glanced over at Hannah and Marcus. They were talking quietly about something.

"Lita, it's Saturday. Do you have a number for Brady Chapman other than his office?" I asked.

"I have his cell." She rattled off a phone number and I repeated it to myself so I wouldn't forget it. "Give me a couple of minutes and I'll call Brady," she said, "and give him a heads-up that he'll be hearing from you."

It occurred to me that Lita was just about the only person I knew who, if I said I needed a lawyer, wouldn't ask me why. "Thanks, Lita," I said. "I owe you for this."

"Oh, you're welcome," she said. "I'm glad I could help."

I ended the call and looked at my watch. I watched the second hand make three circuits of the dial and then I punched in the number that Lita had given me.

"I just talked to Lita," Brady Chapman said after I'd explained who I was. He sounded a little like his father. "She said you need a lawyer. What's the problem?"

I explained about Hannah and the clipping.

"Where are you?" he asked.

"Eric's Place," I said.

"Stay put. I can be there in about ten minutes."

I put my phone in my purse and walked back to Hannah and Marcus. "You have a lawyer," I said to Hannah. "Brady Chapman. He'll be here in about ten minutes."

Marcus nodded. "He's good." His blue eyes flicked to me. "Thanks."

I nodded.

"Yes, thank you, Kathleen," Hannah said. She looked around. "So should we just wait here?"

I pushed my bangs back off my face. "Why don't we go have coffee while we wait?"

"All right," she said.

We went inside. Eric raised a hand in hello from the counter. I pointed to a table along the end wall and he nodded. I held up three fingers, figuring he would know I meant three coffees.

Nicolas came over in a moment with the pot and filled our mugs. "Can I get you anything else?" he asked.

Marcus shook his head. "Not right now, thank you."

"Just let me know when you need a refill," he said and moved toward another table.

Hannah put both hands flat on the table. "I'm sorry," she said. "I shouldn't have written that on the newspaper clipping. It was childish, but I was just so frustrated in the moment." She glanced at her brother. "I forgot all about it. If I'd remembered, I would have told you."

"It's okay," Marcus said. "Once Chapman gets here you can talk to Detective Lind and get this whole thing straightened out."

I knew I needed to say something about the SUV Andrew had seen before Brady Chapman arrived. I traced the curve of my spoon handle with one finger. "Hannah, what time did you get back from Red Wing last night?"

She shrugged. "I don't know. I didn't look at the clock. It was late. Eleven thirty, maybe?" She nudged Marcus with her arm. "Do you remember?"

"Quarter to twelve, I think," he said. "I'd only been home myself about ten minutes." He stretched his long legs under the table.

"Okay, about quarter to twelve then," Hannah said. "Why did you want to know?"

"Did you by any chance drive past the marina on your way to Red Wing?" I asked.

"No." She pointed over her shoulder. "Red Wing is that way."

"Why are you asking?" Marcus said. His hand had tightened around his cup. It was the only sign that he had slipped into police detective mode.

I took a sip of my coffee before I answered. "I talked to Andrew this afternoon. He remembers seeing a dark-colored SUV drive past the marina a couple of times while we were unloading the piece of the stage."

"Why didn't he tell me that last night?"

I shifted in my chair, eyeing the door and hoping that Brady Chapman would show up soon. "He probably forgot. And he didn't even realize it was important."

"Marcus, it doesn't matter," Hannah said. "It wasn't me. I drove to Red Wing right after rehearsal and I spent hours going through everything that had been salvaged from the fire. There were boxes and bags of stuff and it all smelled like it had been barbecued." She looked at me across the table. "Anyway, there has to be more than one dark-colored SUV like yours around here."

She was a very good liar. She didn't flush. She didn't fidget. She remembered to look me in the eye. Her body seemed relaxed. But I was certain she was lying. She met my gaze just a little too much. She shared more details than she needed to and her explanations were a little too practiced.

Just then Brady Chapman walked in and looked around. I knew it had to be him—he looked so much like his father, a large man with broad shoulders and a square jaw. Burtis wore heavy work pants and flannel shirts, but Brady was dressed in an olive green fleece jacket over a black T-shirt and jeans.

I got to my feet. He caught sight of me and walked over.

"Kathleen?" he asked.

I nodded and held out my hand. He had a strong, firm grip, again like his father.

"I've discovered that you know my father," he said with a smile. He had pale blue eyes—I'd once seen a husky with the same eye color—and salt-and-pepper hair.

"Yes, I do," I said, smiling back at him. Burtis could be intimidating but I liked him. He wasn't above playing the hick from Wild Rose Bluff when it suited him, but he was, in reality, a whip-smart, very well-read man. I didn't remember ever seeing Brady in the library.

"I was at the house when Lita called. Dad gave me orders to make sure I helped you any way I can."

"That's very kind of him." I made a mental note to thank Burtis next time I saw him.

Marcus had gotten to his feet.

"Good to see you, Detective," Brady said. The two men shook hands and then Marcus introduced him to Hannah.

Brady took the chair where I'd been sitting and I slid into the seat opposite Marcus. He pulled a small notebook and a mechanical pencil from his pocket. "Okay, tell me what happened."

I explained how I'd found the newspaper clipping in the box of papers and recognized Hannah's handwriting. Brady held up his hand. "Not one word," he said to Hannah. He looked at Marcus and me. "We're going to move to another table and you two are going to stay here."

"I already explained things to them," Hannah said.

Brady shook his head. "Doesn't change anything," he said. He got to his feet. After a moment's hesitation Hannah followed him.

We sat in silence for at least a couple of minutes. Marcus watched his sister and Brady and I drank my coffee. Finally Brady pulled out his cell phone and made a brief call.

Hannah got up and came over to us. "We're set," she said. "Detective Lind is at the police station. We're going to talk to her."

"I'll come with you," Marcus said, getting to his feet again.

She shook her head. "No, you won't. I agreed to a lawyer, but I'm not taking you with me. I'm not six, Marcus."

"I'm a police officer," he said. "I know how things work."

She gestured toward Brady. "And he's a lawyer. I'm guessing he knows how things work as well." She took a step back from the table. "I'll see you later." She turned to me. "Thank you, Kathleen, for all your help."

"You're welcome," I said.

Marcus stood there without speaking until they were gone. "I'll take care of the check and I'll walk you out," he said.

"I'll get it," I said, zipping up my hoodie, but he was already on his way to the counter.

I waited and we walked outside together.

"And thank you for calling Brady Chapman," he said once we were on the sidewalk in front of the restaurant.

"Thank Lita next time you see her."

He nodded. "I will."

I checked my watch. I had just enough time to go home, have a shower and go to Maggie's—after I gave Hercules the sardines I'd promised him.

"Hannah shouldn't be very long," I said to Marcus.

"Why didn't you tell me what your friend saw?" he asked.

I should have seen that conversational detour coming. "I didn't exactly have a chance," I said. "I didn't realize Andrew had seen anything until a few hours ago. He didn't know that what he'd noticed was important."

Marcus jammed his hands in the pockets of his jacket. "You could have called me."

I tipped my head to one side and looked up at him. "I could have, but I was hoping somehow that I was wrong."

"Hannah said it wasn't her."

I exhaled slowly. "I think she's lying. I don't know why and I wish she wasn't, but I think she is." I tucked a strand of hair behind one ear. "I didn't want to put you in a difficult position because your sister was in the wrong place at the wrong time."

"You really think it was her who drove past the marina last night?"

"How many navy blue SUVs with roof racks are there in this town, Marcus? Most people drive cars or half-tons."

He looked past me out toward the water. "You don't know that for sure," he said.

"It was Hannah, Marcus," I said. "You think it was, too."

It took another long moment before he looked at me again.

"So now you know what I'm thinking?"

I tipped my head back for a moment and stared up at the clouds coming in from the river. When I looked at him again I tried to keep the frustration out of my voice. "No. I never know what you're thinking. But I noticed you said, 'Hannah said it wasn't her,' not 'it wasn't her.'" I swallowed the lump in my throat. This was what we always did and it always ended the same way. "Maybe I was trying to protect you, Marcus. Did you think of that?"

He opened his mouth as though he was going to say something and then closed it again.

His cases were always going to come between us.

How could we be friends? How could we be anything? For the first time I wondered if maybe I should go back to Boston with Andrew.

"I'm sorry," I said, then turned and walked away down the sidewalk.

"Kathleen, hang on," he called after me.

"My cat's waiting for me," I said.

I didn't look back over my shoulder and, as usual, he didn't come after me.

12

Hercules was asleep on the passenger side of the truck, with his head on one paw and the other curled around his nose. He lifted his head and gave a curious "Merow" when I got in.

"Marcus is a dipwad," I said darkly.

He put his head back down on the blanket that covered the front seat. Clearly that wasn't news to him.

There was no sign of Owen when we got home. I got Hercules half a sardine as payment for keeping me company and put out fresh water for both cats. Upstairs I grabbed my robe and headed into the bathroom for a quick shower. I gave a squeak of surprise when I discovered Herc had followed me and was sitting on the top of the toilet tank.

When I started he jumped, almost losing his footing.

"What are you doing in here?" I asked, hanging my robe on the hook on the back of the door.

His response was to look around at the pale cream walls as though he was thinking about redecorating.

"I'm going to have a shower." I put the shower curtain inside the claw-foot tub. "You can stay if you want to."

I figured Hercules would leave as soon as the water started, but he was perched in the same place when I got out. Looking at him sitting there, I remembered Ruby's invitation to see his portrait. "Ruby finished your picture," I said. "She's going to show it to me on Monday."

He jumped down, making a wide circuit around any possible damp spots on the floor, sat in front of me—albeit far enough away that no stray drops of water would get on him—and meowed loudly.

"Do you want to go with me?"

He looked over his shoulder at the door.

"You'll have to spend the morning at the library."

He licked his lips.

"No," I said firmly, shaking my head for emphasis. "I'm not buying you a breakfast sandwich from Eric's."

His shoulders sagged and he hung his head. He was the picture of cat dejection, except that I'd witnessed this little act before. Plus I could see one green eye watching me.

"It's not working," I said, pushing past him to go back into the bedroom.

After a moment he followed, rubbing against my leg as I put on my favorite purple sweater. Since the woebegone-kitty approach hadn't worked, he'd decided to try sucking up. He hadn't considered the body lotion Maggie had made for my dry skin. The rich cream was infused with lavender.

Hercules screwed up his face as he got a noseful of the scent. He sneezed and jumped because he always scared himself when he did that. He sneezed three more times in rapid succession, starting at the sound each time.

I made a shooing motion with one hand. "Go downstairs and get a drink."

He glared at me and stalked out of the room. I heard him sneeze one more time on his way down the stairs.

When I went down to the kitchen, he was sitting by the refrigerator, washing his face with more vigor than usual.

"I'll see you later," I said. "I won't be late."

No acknowledgment. I'd been put on Ignore.

I found Owen on the porch bench, looking out into the backyard. I sat down beside him. "I'm leaving," I said. "Time to go inside."

He climbed onto my lap and nuzzled my neck.

"I love you, too," I said, scratching the top of his head. "But I need to get going. Maggie's waiting." The moment the words came out I realized what a mistake I'd just made. Owen jumped down from my lap and went to sit by the back door.

I stood up and brushed a clump of gray cat fur off my sweater. "You're not coming with me," I said.

He didn't even twitch a whisker. I knew what was coming next. I swooped down and scooped him up before he could wink out of sight. He yowled and tried to wriggle out of my arms.

"I'm sorry," I said. I set him just inside the kitchen door and closed it in his face. He yowled again in angry protest.

I went out to the truck. Now all the men in my life were mad at me.

"C'mon up," Maggie called when I knocked on her apartment door. The aroma of sausage and onions floated down the stairs to meet me. She was at the counter, tearing a ball of mozzarella into small pieces. And Roma was sitting on the sofa.

"I was hoping you'd be here," I said, dropping down next to her on the couch.

"I bribed her," Maggie said. There was a blob of sauce on the end of her nose and a dusting of flour in her hair. And there wasn't a bare bit of counter space for me to put the brownies down. I set the square plastic container on the chair next to the sofa.

Roma smiled. "She did. She promised me half a pizza to take home."

"You get the other half," Maggie said to me.

"Good." I took off my heavy blue cable knit sweater and tossed it over the back of the chair. "I can use it to bribe my way back into Owen's good graces."

Maggie frowned. "What did you do to Owen?"

"I didn't do anything. He wanted to come with me and I said no." I kicked off my shoes, pulled a foot up underneath me and settled in one corner of the couch.

"You could have brought him," she said. She frowned and looked around the cluttered kitchen.

"No, I could not have brought him. It would have set a precedent and I swear to you Owen would know that."

"Please tell me you're not really going to feed Owen pizza," Roma said. "He's a cat. He's not supposed to eat people food."

"You tell him that," I said.

"I have."

"So that explains why the cats don't like you," Maggie said with a grin, bending down to peer into the oven.

"I won't give Owen any pizza," I said. "I promise."

Roma smiled. "Thank you."

I'd been guilty in the past of letting the cats eat all kinds of people food. Roma had been horrified when she found out. Owen and Hercules weren't typical cats by any standards and I didn't think they had a typical cat's digestive system, but I was still trying to stick to cat food and not people food.

Neither Owen nor Hercules was very happy about the change in their eating habits. If they'd known that Roma was behind it they would have had even more reason to be cool to her. Roma wasn't one of their favorite people, probably because whenever they saw her at the clinic they were invariably on the business end of a needle and she was the one doing the poking.

"How's Eddie?" I asked.

Roma's boyfriend, Eddie Sweeney, played for the Minnesota Wild in the NHL. Plus he could cook, and he handled a hammer about as well as he did a hockey stick. And he was as gorgeous as a *GQ* cover model.

She fingered the antique rose gold locket Eddie had given her and the smile got a little wider. "He's great. They have a preseason game tonight in St. Louis." Her expression grew serious. "Maggie told me about you and Andrew finding that director, Hugh Davis. You all right?"

I nodded. "I'm okay, thanks. It was worse for Andrew, I think." I gave her a wry smile. "It wasn't my first dead body."

She leaned back against the sofa cushions. "Did you see Marcus?"

"I did."

She reached across the back of the sofa and patted my arm. "I'm sorry things turned out the way they did."

"You and me both," I said.

Maggie was scraping dishes and loading them into the dishwasher.

Roma leaned sideways to see what she was doing. "Could we help?" she asked.

"You could set the table," Maggie said. "Place mats are in the second drawer." She gestured with one elbow.

"What could I do?" I asked.

"Come scratch my nose. Please."

I got up and went over to her. She tipped her head to one side and I scratched the bridge of her nose.

"Up a little bit more," she urged. She sighed when I hit the itchy spot. "Ahh, that's better. Thank you."

"You sound like Hercules," I said. I stuck the plug in the sink and started running some hot water so I could wipe the counter.

"That reminds me," Maggie said, waving a plate at me. "I forgot to tell you. Ruby showed me the painting she did of him last night. It's fantastic."

"Good," I said. "She's going to show it to me Monday morning."

"I thought you had a planning meeting for Winterfest last night," Roma said as she folded napkins to put at each place.

Maggie was on the organizing committee for the Mayville Heights winter festival.

"It was canceled because of the water-main break down in front of the James—excuse me—the St. James Hotel." Maggie made a face. "I'm never going to get used to the new name."

The St. James Hotel, formerly the James Hotel, had undergone a major refurbishment in the late spring and early summer, and the owners had decided to go back to the name the hotel originally had when it opened in 1902: the St. James. Most people in town still called it the James. It had to be confusing for tourists.

"Andrew and I had to go the long way around to get to the marina." I added soap to the water in the sink.

"So did I," Maggie said, putting two large bowls in the dishwasher. "I mean, to get to my studio. They even had the sidewalk closed. I was carrying one of those big rolls of bubble wrap and the darn thing kept unrolling." She held out her arms like she was going to hug me. "I ended up having to carry it like this and peer around the side of it."

"Oh, Mags, I'm sorry," I said. "I wish I'd seen you. I would have given you a ride."

She smiled. "It wasn't that far." She peeked at the pizza through the oven window and seemed to be happy with what she saw. "Did Abigail go out to the marina with you and Andrew?" she asked as she straightened up.

"No." I rinsed a cloth and started wiping the counter to the left of the sink. "Why?"

"I saw her when I was walking. She came from that direction and she was driving Burtis's old truck."

"Abigail was driving Burtis Chapman's truck?" Roma said. She frowned at the place mat she'd put in the middle of the table and turned it a hundred and eighty degrees.

Maggie nodded. "Uh-huh. I cut across Jefferson because it was faster. It's a one-way street now and Abigail was actually going the wrong way. Of course, so was Marcus's sister. When you said you and

Andrew had gone out to the marina I just assumed Abigail had gone to help you."

I scrubbed at a bit of dried dough stuck to the granite countertop. "What do you mean, so was Marcus's sister?" I asked, trying to keep my tone casual.

"I mean she was going the wrong way, too," Maggie said, peering at the pizza again.

She was almost as obsessive about her pizza as she was about her artwork. That was probably why they were both so good.

"I was just about to head down the hill when I saw her. At first I thought it was Marcus, because it was his car and I thought *Why is he going the wrong way?* and then I saw that it was Hannah. She probably didn't even realize she was on a one-way street. I think Abigail was just in a hurry and wasn't really paying attention."

I kept my head down over the counter. Maggie had seen Hannah, which meant it definitely had been her that Andrew had noticed driving past the marina when we were unloading the staging. Hannah was lying when she'd said she was in Red Wing all evening. Somewhere in the back of my mind I'd been hoping it was someone else—anyone else— that Andrew had seen.

So why had she lied? I didn't want to think about the obvious reason. There had to be another explanation. But right now wasn't the time to figure it out.

Mags squinted through the glass and reached for

her oven mitts. "I think they're done," she said. She flapped a hand at me. "Kath, would you get the plates, please?"

The pizza was wonderful—sausage, caramelized onions and long strings of chewy mozzarella on a crisp, fragrant crust. The promise I'd made to myself to have just one slice evaporated.

We moved into the living room for dessert.

"I think I have chocolate overload." Roma groaned, licking icing off her thumb after her second brownie.

"There's no such thing," Maggie countered, stretching her long legs onto the footstool. She looked at Roma. "Did I hear you say you're going to see Eddie next weekend?"

"I am," Roma said, a huge smile lighting up her face. It happened every time Eddie's name came up.

Maggie folded her hands over her stomach. "Does he have any cute hockey player friends? They don't have to be Eddie cute, just, you know, ordinary-human-being cute."

"What happened to Liam?" I asked. Maggie had been casually dating the bartender-slash–grad student for a couple of months.

She sighed. "After everything that happened with Legacy and the tour proposal, he decided to go back to Minneapolis and work on his thesis this term."

Liam had been part of a group pitching Mayville Heights as a fall tourist destination to Legacy Tours from Chicago. The proposal had fallen apart when Mike Glazer, one of the three partners in the tour company, had been found dead down on the River-walk.

"I'd just like to go out with someone who's fun," she said. "No drama, no dead bodies."

I leaned against the back of the sofa and tucked both feet underneath me. "That sounds good," I said. "Could you see if Eddie has two friends?"

"You really can't work things out with Marcus?" Roma asked. She liked Marcus. He'd been her first recruit when she'd decided to put together a group of volunteers to care for the feral cat colony at Wisteria Hill.

"No. We keep . . ." I took a deep breath. "It's like running into a stone wall. We have different ideas about loyalty and friendship."

I stopped to swallow down the lump that had suddenly settled in my throat. "It's not going to work."

Maggie flashed me a look of sympathy.

Roma reached over and gave my arm a squeeze.

"Too much negative energy," Maggie said, shifting upright a little in her chair. "Let's talk about something else." She turned to Roma. "Tell us what's happening at Wisteria Hill."

Roma had bought the old Henderson estate a few weeks before.

"Is Oren going to do the work for you?" I asked.

Roma held up a finger. "I just need to call and check on a patient and then I'll you what we've figured out." She smiled at me. "And yes, Oren's going to do the work." She got up from the couch and took her cell phone out of her pocket.

I leaned forward toward Maggie. "Mags, are you sure it was Hannah you saw last night?"

She frowned. "You mean going the wrong way on Jefferson? Yes, I'm sure. It wasn't Marcus, if that's what you were wondering."

"Okay, thanks," I said.

Maggie continued to study my face, her eyes narrowed with curiosity. "Why do you ask?"

I played with the knotted fringe on one of the pillows. "It's complicated."

"It has something to do with Marcus, doesn't it?"

I nodded. "I'll tell you about it—I promise. I need to figure a couple of things out first."

"Okay," she said. "If you need someone who isn't furry and four-legged to bounce anything off of, I'm here."

"Thanks," I said.

Roma came back over to us.

"How's your patient?" Maggie asked.

"Alive and barking," she said with a grin, wiggling her eyebrows at us.

Maggie threw her head back and groaned. I patted the sofa cushion beside me. "Now that you've dazzled us with your wit, dazzle us with your ideas for Wisteria Hill."

We spent the next hour talking about the work Roma had planned for the old farmhouse and the grounds. It was impossible not to get caught up in her enthusiasm.

Finally she looked at her watch. "It's getting late, and as much as I like you two, I'm tired." She stretched. "I have to drive to Minneapolis to consult on a surgery with a guy I went to veterinary school with and it's my morning to feed the cats."

"Couldn't whoever you're on the schedule with go without you for one morning?" Maggie asked.

Roma shook her head. "I'm on the schedule with Harry and he's still out of town."

"Roma, I'll go," I said. "I have food and a couple of water jugs at home."

"Are you sure?" she said. "It really would help if I didn't have to go out there first thing."

"Yes, I'm sure."

She leaned over to hug me. "Thanks," she said.

Maggie had half of the second pizza wrapped up for Roma to take with her and I gave her half of the remaining brownies. "I'll talk to you both soon," she said before she disappeared down the stairs.

I stretched my arms up over my head. "I should go, too," I said to Maggie. "But I'll help you clean up first."

She shook her head. "No, you won't. All I have to do is put the rest of the dishes in the dishwasher. Don't forget your pizza."

"There's no chance of that happening," I said. "That's lunch tomorrow."

"Not breakfast?" Maggie teased as I pulled on my long blue sweater.

"I'm having breakfast with Andrew."

Her eyebrows went up, but she didn't say anything.

"You had breakfast with him," I said.

"He's not trying to woo me away to Boston with him," she said. "At least as far as I know."

I smiled at her. "He can woo all he wants. We're not getting back together."

"Does he know that?"

"I've told him enough times in the last week," I said, taking the container of pizza she handed me.

"As long as you don't tell him you'll go back to Boston," she said.

I hugged her. "You can't get rid of me that easily."

"Seems to me you can't get rid of Marcus that easily, either," she said, smiling at me. "Maybe the universe is trying to tell you something."

I thought about that as I drove home. *If the universe is trying to send me a message about Marcus, what the heck is it?*

13

Early Sunday morning, I was bouncing my way up the rutted driveway at Wisteria Hill just as the sun was coming over the horizon. It felt strange to be feeding the cats without Marcus along.

I carried the two water jugs around to the side door of the carriage house and then walked back to the truck to get the clean dishes and the day's supply of cat food. Roma had a new wet food that the cats seemed to like a lot. Luckily it came in flip-top cans.

I slammed the truck door with my hip and as I turned around I heard the sound of tires crunching their way up the driveway. It occurred to me that I was all alone, it was early in the morning, and if I screamed only the cats would hear me.

I tightened up on the handle of the canvas tote bag that held the cans of cat food. If I didn't know the person easing up the driveway, I'd swing the bag like I was a contestant in a Scottish hammer throw and ask questions later.

The car came around the turn at the top of the

driveway and my stomach flip-flopped. It was Marcus. I realized I was smiling and I couldn't seem to make my face stop even though I tried.

He got out of the SUV and I noticed that while he looked surprised he was smiling, too. "What are you doing here?" he said.

I held out the bag with the cat food. "I came to feed the cats. Roma has to go—"

"—to Minneapolis," he finished. He reached into the SUV and pulled out a similar bag of cat food. His blue eyes narrowed. "I suspect a setup."

"Pretty hard to fool you," I said.

"I am a professional detective," he said with mock seriousness.

I walked over to him. "You don't have to stay."

"Would it bother you if I did?" he asked.

Nothing had changed since the previous day, but all I could think about was those gorgeous blue eyes, how strong his hands were, and how warm his mouth had been the first and only time he'd kissed me.

Okay—bad idea to think about those things. I tried to make myself remember all the disagreements we'd had, how he'd accused me of not believing in him, how we had different ideas about loyalty and what it meant to be a friend. The problem was I kept getting distracted by his incredibly strong, broad shoulders and the way a lock of his dark hair fell onto his forehead.

"It wouldn't bother me," I said. It wasn't what I'd intended to say.

For a long moment Marcus just stared at me. Then he gave his head a little shake. "Did you bring water?"

"I put the jugs by the door."

He took the canvas bag of food from my hand and we started walking toward the old carriage house. "Thank you for yesterday," he said. He looked out over the trees. "For calling Brady Chapman and caring about Hannah . . . and me."

I waited for a moment before I said anything, trying to find the right words. "I don't think Hannah killed Hugh Davis," I said.

"She didn't."

"But she's not telling the truth, either. Not about where she was, probably not about that newspaper clipping. Which means she lied to the police."

We were by the side door of the building. Marcus exhaled slowly and looked at me. "I know," he said.

I set the bag of dishes on my feet. "You know?"

He swiped a hand over his face. "When Hannah was six she left her lunch box at the bus stop. It was the third one she'd lost in a month. She knew Dad would be mad, so she said it was stolen by a bear who mistook it for a picnic basket."

"Pretty creative," I said.

"Exactly. Too creative. There was a whole story about how the bear had eaten her orange slices and pita bread and unscrewed her thermos with his teeth so he could get at the tomato soup inside. Way too much detail. Just like her story about that newspaper clipping."

I ran my hand over the weathered wood of the side door to the old building. "There's something else I need to tell you," I said.

"What is it?" he said.

"Remember the water main break Friday night? The traffic was being detoured up and around that whole block."

He nodded.

"The sidewalk was closed as well, so Maggie had to walk from the store over to River Arts. She cut along Jefferson Street."

"And?"

"And she saw Hannah. In fact she was going the wrong way on the street. That's why Maggie noticed her. When she first saw the SUV she thought it was you."

He took a slow, deep breath and let it out. "Driving the wrong way on a one-way street doesn't prove anything," he said.

I put a hand on his arm. "I know that," I said. "But it does prove that she wasn't in Red Wing the way she says she was. She didn't just lie to you; she lied to the police and she lied to her own lawyer. She's hiding something."

He shifted uncomfortably from one foot to the other. "I'll talk to her again." He frowned. "I could fix this if I just knew what the heck was going on."

Fix this?

I swallowed, trying to come up with the right words, words that wouldn't get under his skin. "I think it's a good idea to talk to Hannah, Marcus, but otherwise you need to stay out of this. Just . . . just tell her to be straight with Brady Chapman and then back off."

He looked at me as if I'd suggested he run naked along the Riverwalk. "Kathleen, she's my sister and she's somehow tied up in a murder. I'm not going to 'back off.'"

We'd had this conversation before, too. Only it had always been Marcus warning me to stay out of his investigation and me trying to make him understand that I couldn't do nothing when someone I cared about was caught up in one of his cases.

He'd obviously had the same thought. He reached out as though he was going to touch me and then pulled his hand back. "I get it," he said quietly. "I get why you always tell me you can't help getting involved when it's someone you care about."

I shrugged. "Well, if it makes you feel any better, I understand why you keep telling me to stay out of your cases."

He laughed, but there wasn't a lot of humor in the sound. "This is odd."

I laughed, too. "I guess it is." He pulled a hand back through his hair. He did that a lot when he had something on his mind.

I reached out and gave his arm a squeeze. "How about you just say all the things that you'd ordinarily say to me to yourself and save me a step."

He covered my hand with his own. "I'm sorry I was so rigid."

"It's okay," I said. "I understand a lot better why you were trying to get me to stay out of your cases. I'm sorry that I didn't try harder to see things from your side."

We were only inches apart and there was an energy between us that I was certain I'd be able to feel if I just put my hand up. Then Marcus suddenly moved his own hand and took a step back.

"We should feed the cats," he said.

"Right. We should do that." I took a step backward as well, and almost fell over one of the water jugs.

"I'll get that," Marcus said, reaching for the plastic container at the same time I did.

We almost bumped heads. He smelled like citrus aftershave and Juicy Fruit gum. I wondered what he'd do if I leaned in a little more and kissed him. I wasn't sure enough of the answer to try it.

"Sorry," I said. I pulled back and straightened up. It had suddenly gotten very warm.

Marcus picked up the jugs and pushed open the heavy wooden door. We stepped into the carriage house. It took a moment for my eyes to adjust to the dim light.

I did what I always did first: check out the space. There was no sign of any of the cats and no sign that anything was amiss. We put out the food and water and retreated to the back of the building by the door to wait. I leaned against the wall, arms folded over my chest. Marcus stood behind me, hands stuffed in his pockets.

After a couple of minutes I heard a sound and saw movement in the far corner at the other end of the space. "Lucy," I whispered to Marcus.

The little calico cat came out cautiously, sniffing the air. She looked in our direction, tipping her head to one side.

"Hey, Lucy," I said in a quiet voice.

The cat and I had some kind of connection I couldn't explain. Roma said it was because Lucy was a Wisteria Hill cat just the way Hercules and Owen were. She believed Lucy trusted me for some unknown reason, just the way Owen and Hercules had done the first day I'd come across them up here as tiny, tiny kittens.

I wasn't sure. I sometimes wondered if Lucy, too, like the boys, had some kind of superpower and that was why we connected.

The little calico turned and came toward us. She stopped maybe ten feet away and meowed at us. Then she moved toward the feeding station.

"You're welcome," I called softly after her.

In another moment the rest of the feral cat colony came out to eat. Marcus put his hand on the wide wooden boards and leaned against the wall behind me. Suddenly it got very warm again.

We both checked each cat for any signs that it wasn't healthy.

"They all look good," he whispered under his breath.

After all the cats had eaten—and in Lucy's case,

washed paws and face—they wandered back to their shelters. Marcus and I cleaned up the feeding station and put out more fresh water. We gathered the empty water jugs and everything else and went back outside. When we came around the side of the carriage house I stopped.

"Did you forget something?" Marcus asked.

I shook my head and scanned the overgrown area to the left of the old building. "Roma's seen another cat out here. I'm going to hang around for a few minutes and put some food and water over by the tree and see if maybe it'll come out for something to eat."

"Okay," he said. There was one clean bowl in the bag and he fished it out. "This'll do for water. What are you going to put the food in?"

I'd forgotten to put an extra dish in the bag.

"I guess I'll just use the bag," I said. "You don't have to stay."

"I know," he said. He set the jugs down and managed to jam the empty cans of cat food into the bag with the used dishes. Then he crouched and folded the plastic more or less into a rectangle.

I opened the can of food I'd held back and dumped it in the middle of the makeshift plate. There were a couple of inches of water in the bottom of one of the jugs. Marcus used it to fill the bowl. He handed it to me and carefully picked up the sides of the folded plastic.

"Where do you want this?" he asked, getting to his feet.

"Just on the other side of the tree, I think."

We put the food and water on a flat worn-down patch of grass and moved all the way back to the steps by the side door of the old farmhouse. I sat on the top step and Marcus sat beside me, leaning forward with his hands between his knees.

"What does the cat look like?" he asked, keeping his voice low.

"A bit like Owen, only ginger instead of gray," I said, scanning the high grass and tangle of wild rosebushes for any sign of movement that might signal the little cat was nearby. "Roma calls him Micah."

"Did she put out the cage?"

I shook my head and pushed my bangs off my face. The cage was a humane trap that we used if we had to collect a cat to take it down to Roma's clinic for medical care. They all reacted with fury to being trapped. "Roma was afraid she'd end up catching Lucy or one of the others. She's been trying to figure out some other way to get this one."

Over time all the cats in the colony had been captured and neutered, then brought back out and released. Unlike Owen and Hercules, they were never going to be anyone's pet. In fact Roma believed the boys had probably been abandoned shortly before I found them and had never actually been feral.

Marcus leaned sideways and nudged me with his shoulder. "Look. Right there." He pointed to a tangle of grass. I leaned forward and caught a slight waving of the tall blades.

Neither one of us moved. The grass fluttered again, almost as though it were the wind slipping around the tree, and then I saw the cat. Micah was tiny, the same color as the marmalade Rebecca had made last Christmas. He came forward slowly, looking around cautiously, whiskers twitching at the scent of the food.

He saw us and paused, one paw about an inch off the ground. I thought he would run, but after a long moment he started toward the base of the tree. I let out a breath I hadn't realized I was holding.

The cat ate quickly, looking around after every couple of bites. Marcus and I stayed immobile, like a couple of stone statues on the steps, his arm still against mine. After the cat had eaten, it darted back to the cover of the long grass. I waited another minute before getting up to retrieve the dishes. The food and the water were all gone.

"We have to find a way to get her to eat with the others," Marcus said as we walked to my truck.

"I don't think that'll happen," I said, unlocking the door and setting the bags on the floor on the passenger side. I turned around to look at him. "Wait a minute. You said 'her.'"

He smiled. "Uh-huh. The cat's a she."

I brushed my hands on my jeans. "No. Roma said Micah is a he. She is a vet."

He leaned against the truck's door. "Well, I think I know boy parts when I see them, or when I don't, and Micah is definitely a she."

He glanced down at his watch. "When are you on the schedule again?"

I tried to picture the list on the front of the refrigerator. "Wednesday," I said. "With Thorston, I think. I'm taking some of Harry Junior's shifts."

He nodded. "I'll check and trade with whoever it is."

"Why?" I said, pulling my keys from my pocket.

He gave a half shrug. "Because I know you're going to hang around after and try to feed that cat again. You can't be up here by yourself. You can't even tell a boy cat from a girl cat." He smiled.

"Okay . . . umm, I'll see you Wednesday morning." I hesitated. "Good luck with Hannah. Don't—"

"—do anything stupid."

I smiled. "I was going to say don't do anything I'd do, but I guess that's the same thing."

"Would you tell your friend Andrew to get in touch with Detective Lind and tell her what he saw?"

I studied his face. "Are you sure?"

He nodded. "Yes."

"I will."

He opened his mouth and then closed it.

"What?" I said. "You were going to say something. What was it?"

He shifted from one foot to the other. "I was just going to ask you if you've told Everett whether you're going to stay."

"He said it could wait until the theater festival is over."

Marcus nodded. "That's probably a good idea." I waited for him to tell me to stay, to sweep me into a kiss complete with a dramatic dip, even though Maggie insisted that was bad for the back.

Of course he didn't do either of those things. He just said, "Have a good day," and walked over to his car.

I got into the truck and started it. I'd been watching way too many old movies with Maggie if I thought that Marcus would actually sweep me into his arms and kiss me until I swooned. Not that I was exactly the swooning type.

On the other hand, I couldn't help wondering just exactly what I would have done if he had.

14

I was sitting in one of the Adirondack chairs in the backyard when Andrew arrived. Hercules was perched on the chair's wide arm.

"Hey, Kath," he said when he came around the house and caught sight of me. "Am I late?"

"No," I said. "I was ready early and it was just so nice I decided to wait out here." There were some streaks of cloud across the deepening blue sky and I had a feeling it was going to be warmer than usual for the end of September.

Andrew walked over as I got to my feet. "Hey, cat," he said to Hercules.

The little tuxedo cat gave him a look of disdain that Andrew completely missed. Herc didn't like being called "cat" as a form of address. He glanced at me, green eyes narrowed. I took that to mean I should remind Andrew of his name.

"Hercules," I said.

"After the Greek god, right?" Andrew said, looking around the yard.

Hercules didn't exactly roll his eyes, but he came pretty close.

"Um, Roman, actually," I said. As played by the very yummy Kevin Sorbo in the campy TV series, to be exact, but I didn't see any point in mentioning that.

"Where's the other one?" he asked.

The other one? Hercules looked at Andrew like he was the dust-covered head from one of Owen's funky chickens. He made a huffy sound through his nose, jumped down and headed across the lawn toward Rebecca's backyard, placing each foot down carefully on the damp grass. That he was willing to chance getting his paws wet showed just how annoyed he was.

Hercules and Owen seemed convinced that they were—if not people—then certainly not someone's pets. And they expected to be treated accordingly.

Andrew pointed across the yard. "How old is the gazebo in your neighbor's yard? I've never seen a design quite like it." He walked partway across the lawn to get a better look.

I went over to stand beside him. "I'm not sure," I said. "I could ask Rebecca for you."

"I'd love to know how he worked out the overhang," he said, squinting at the gazebo roof. "I don't suppose there's still a set of plans around anywhere."

I smiled and shook my head. "No. There never were any plans. Harrison Taylor built that gazebo and the only plans he had were in his head."

Andrew turned to look at me. "You're kidding."

I tucked my hands in the pockets of my sweat-shirt. "No, I'm not. I'd take you to meet him, but he's out of town."

He glanced back for another look as we walked toward the driveway. "I'm sorry about that. The guy's good."

I thought about Harry Senior, who always re-minded me of Santa Claus. "Yes, he is," I said.

"So are we going to Eric's?" Andrew asked as we walked around the side of the house.

"I thought I'd take you over to Fern's Diner this morning."

He started for his rental car and I followed instead of arguing that we should take my truck.

"Diner?" he said, raising his eyebrows. "Does that mean old-fashioned diner food?"

"Yes, it does," I said. "Their motto is 'Food just like Mom used to make—Maybe better.'"

He laughed. "Okay. I have to try this place."

"They have a big breakfast like nothing else you've ever had. You probably won't be able to finish it."

He paused, hand on the top of the driver's door. "Is that a challenge?"

I thought about it for a moment. "Yeah, I guess it is," I finally said with a smile.

Andrew grinned. "You're on, then."

Other than the morning I'd had breakfast with Burtis Chapman, the only other times I'd been to the diner was for Meatloaf Tuesday with Roma. Fern's had been part of the landscape of Mayville Heights for a long time. About six years ago it had been restored to its 1950s glory, or as Roma had put it, "Just exactly like it never was."

The building was long and low with a decent-size parking lot in back. It had windows on three sides, and the front glowed with neon after dark. Inside there was the requisite jukebox, a counter with gleaming chrome stools and cozy booths with red vinyl seats.

To my surprise, Burtis Chapman was perched on a stool at the counter, one massive hand wrapped around a coffee cup. The first time I'd ever taken notice of those huge hands it had occurred to me that he could probably squeeze my head between his thumb and index finger and make my brains come squirting out of my ears. I was very glad that he seemed to like me.

We walked over to the counter and Burtis smiled when he caught sight of me. He was a big block of a man and his smile didn't make him look any less intimidating. I remembered that the crocodile had smiled at Captain Hook right before he'd swallowed the pirate's hand.

"Kathleen, girl, it's good to see you," Burtis said. "What in heck are you doing here?"

"Good to see you, too, Burtis," I said. "I came for breakfast. What about you? Isn't it a little past your breakfast time?"

He gave me a sly grin. "Well, for breakfast number one, but not number two."

I turned to Andrew, who had been watching us like he was discovering another culture in a National Geographic special. "Burtis, this is my friend Andrew Reid. He's here from Boston. Andrew, this is Burtis Chapman."

Andrew took the hand Burtis offered and did his best not to wince as they shook.

"So you're the young man who was a big enough asshole to let Kathleen get away," Burtis said. I should have known that if he'd heard the story—and who in town hadn't by now—he'd say something.

Andrew's face reddened but he held the older man's gaze.

"Yes, sir," he said. "I am the asshole who let her go. And now I'm trying to win her back."

"And how's that workin' for you?" Burtis asked.

"Not well," Andrew said with a shake of his head. I saw him surreptitiously clench and unclench the hand Burtis had just shaken. Probably trying to figure out if there were any intact bones left in it.

Burtis laughed. "I gotta give you credit for trying," he said. "But I can't wish you good luck because we want to keep Kathleen here."

Andrew nodded. "Well, then, may the best man win."

"That's what I'm counting on," Burtis said. He winked at me.

I slipped onto the stool beside him and Andrew took the one on the other side of me.

The waitress came out of the kitchen and slid a plate of fried tomatoes and what looked to be sourdough toast in front of Burtis. She was wearing a short-sleeved white shirt with PEGGY SUE embroidered over the pocket, hot pink pedal pushers, and red open-toe wedgies.

She smiled at me. "Hi, hon, what can I get you?"

It probably would have surprised a lot of people to know that Peggy had read every issue of *Scientific American* the library had and all of Stephen Hawking's books on quantum physics.

"The big breakfast for each of us," I said, gesturing at Andrew. "And coffee, please, when you have a minute."

"Sure thing," she said.

"Peggy Sue?" Andrew said softly in my ear.

"It's her real name."

He caught sight of the jukebox at the far end of the diner. "Does that work?"

I nodded. "Do you have quarters?"

He patted his pockets and slid down off the stool. "I do. I'll be right back."

Burtis set his mug on the countertop and looked at me. "Did Brady take care of your friend yesterday?"

"Yes, he did," I said. "I like him."

The sly smile was back. "The boy gets his charm from me."

Peggy put a huge mug of coffee in front of me and I reached for the sugar. "Burtis, I have a feeling that's not all Brady gets from you."

He laughed. "If Brady was here he'd tell me not to say anything that might incriminate myself, so I'll just keep my mouth shut."

I smiled back at him, added cream to my cup and took a long drink. Fern's had excellent coffee.

"Burtis, did you loan your truck to Abigail Pierce the other night?" I asked.

The grin disappeared. "Now who exactly wants to know? You or Detective Marcus Gordon?"

I took another sip of coffee before I answered. "Me," I said. I set the cup down and leaned one elbow on the counter. Andrew was still looking through selections on the jukebox, but I wanted to finish the conversation with Burtis before he came back. "You heard about Hugh Davis, the director from the theater festival Abigail is helping to organize?"

He nodded. "I know who you mean."

"Abigail's my friend. I don't want anything from his death to splash back on her. If you'd rather I ask her, I will."

Burtis shook his head. "No need. Yeah, I loaned her one of my trucks. She had some stuff she needed to move for the festival and I have more than one truck. She picked it up Friday afternoon and brought it back that same night. Didn't look like she'd moved any dead bodies with it, by the way."

"Good to know," I said.

Andrew had finally made his song choice. The first few notes of the music came out of the speakers and I had the urge to pull my shirt up over my head. It was "My Girl" by the Temptations.

"Not exactly subtle, is he?" Burtis said, picking up his fork again.

Peggy returned with our food just as Andrew got back to the counter. She set an oversize oval plate in front of each of us. Andrew looked at his and blinked. I'd already picked up my fork.

There were scrambled eggs, bacon, sausage, fried potatoes with onions, tomato and some fresh rosemary, and two thick slices of raisin toast. I knew from past experience that the eggs would be fluffy, the bacon crisp and the potatoes golden on the outside and fork soft on the inside.

Burtis made short work of the last of his fried tomatoes and drained his coffee. He climbed off his stool and put one hand on my shoulder. "You have a good day, Kathleen," he said.

I smiled. "You too, Burtis," I said.

He nodded at Andrew and walked over to the cash register.

"I no longer have any feeling in my right hand," Andrew said once Burtis was out of earshot.

"Count yourself lucky then," I said, reaching for my coffee. "I'm pretty sure he could break it if he wanted to."

We ate in silence after that until Andrew groaned

and leaned his forearms on the countertop. "Oh, man, that was good," he said. "Do they make that bread here? And where the heck do they get tomatoes that don't taste like Styrofoam?"

There was part of a sausage and half a piece of bread left on his plate. "Yes on the bread and I don't know about the tomatoes."

I leaned sideways, speared the sausage with my fork and ate it. Then I broke the bread in half and ate that, too.

Andrew rolled his eyes. "You win, and where the heck did you put all that?"

I patted my midsection. "I was hungry."

Peggy came back and refilled my cup and after I'd added cream and sugar I swung around so I was facing Andrew.

"I have a question about Friday night," I said.

"Sure," he said, turning his cup in slow circles on the green Formica.

"What else did you see?"

"Aside from that SUV on the highway? Nothing."

"You're sure?"

"I'm sure. Just the dark blue SUV."

"Close your eyes," I said.

Andrew narrowed his gaze at me. "Why?" he asked suspiciously.

"Because it will help you concentrate."

"And I'm concentrating on what, exactly?"

I made a face. "Will you just do it, please?"

He closed his eyes.

"Okay, we're driving toward the water. The marina is coming up on the left side. What do you remember?"

"How good you smelled," he said at once.

"That's not helping."

He shrugged. "You asked what I remembered. That's what I remembered."

I flexed both hands, squeezed them into fists and resisted the urge to slug him.

"We're turning into the driveway. Do you see any cars coming out?"

He shook his head. "No."

I didn't remember any vehicles passing us, either. "What about in the parking lot?"

"Two half-ton trucks with some kind of logo on the door, a white cargo van and a silver sedan. The car had a flat."

I could picture both vehicles, although I hadn't noticed the car had a flat tire. "Anything else?"

"Three sailboats out in the water." He opened his eyes. "I'm sorry, Kathleen. I didn't see anything."

I folded my fingers around the heavy stoneware mug. "It's okay. You should call Detective Lind, though, and tell her about the SUV." I still had Hope Lind's card in my pocket. I pulled it out and handed it to him.

He turned the cardboard rectangle over and frowned at me. "Who's this Detective Lind? I thought your friend was investigating."

"Detective Lind is in charge for now," I said. "Marcus is working on something else."

He shrugged and tucked the card in his shirt pocket.

I drank the last of my coffee and set the mug back on the counter. "Thank you for breakfast," I said, "but I need to get home."

"I was hoping you'd show me around," Andrew said, slipping off his stool.

"I think you've pretty much seen all of Mayville Heights in the last week." I brushed crumbs from my jeans as I stood up.

"I guess I have," he said, dipping his head and giving me that killer smile. "I was hoping to go to the top of the bluff. I heard there're some good hiking trails. And after that I thought we could drive into Minneapolis for a late dinner."

"Thanks, but I can't," I said, pulling my wallet out of my purse.

Andrew held up a hand and shook his head. "No, Kath. I invited you."

I hesitated.

"You may as well say yes," he said with a gleam in his green eyes. "My legs are longer. I can get to the cash register before you can."

"All right. Thank you."

He took a step closer to me. "C'mon, Kath. It's Sunday. Come with me." He held out both hands. "Show me what's so great about this place."

"I already have plans," I said. My plans were to make more sardine crackers for Owen and Hercules and to scrub the kitchen floor, but they were still plans. I twisted my watch around my wrist. "Go home, Andrew," I said. "I mean go home to Boston. I'm glad that you came, but I won't change my mind. It's . . . The time for us has passed."

It sounded like a line from a bad novel, but it was true. We were never, ever getting back together. I think I'd heard that line in a song.

Andrew smiled, a genuine smile, not his I-am-so-damn-cute smile. "I have six more days to change your mind. I'm not going anywhere."

He paid for breakfast and we went out to the car. As he pulled out of the parking lot I saw him glance up the hill.

"Don't," I said quietly.

He looked over at me. "Don't what?"

"Don't head for the bluff instead of taking me home and think I'll be okay with it."

He looked away and shook his head, not even trying to hide the smile. "See? You know me better than anybody."

"It's your big glass head," I said lightly. "It's like a fishbowl. I can see right through you."

His expression grew serious. "That's why we belong together."

I sighed and shook my head. There didn't seem to be any point in saying anything. Andrew didn't want to listen.

"I'll call you later," he said when we got back to the house. "Maybe I'll be able to persuade you to have dinner with me."

"Call Detective Lind," I said as I got out of the car. "It's probably not important, but she still should know what you saw."

"Okay," he said with a shrug. "And I'll talk to you later."

I walked around the side of the house and sat on the back stairs. Hercules came across the grass, stopping every few steps to shake a paw. He sat beside me, a sour look on his face. I used the sleeve of my sweatshirt to wipe the top of his front paws, which seemed to appease him a little.

"I saw Burtis at the diner," I said.

Herc murped softly, which I took to mean "Tell me more."

"Abigail was driving one of his old trucks Friday night. The night she said her phone died. The night nobody knows where she was."

Hercules leaned his head against my arm. "Merow," he said softly.

"I know," I said, reaching over to stroke his fur. "There's no way this is good."

15

I made kitty crackers for the boys and chicken stew with dumplings for myself. When Andrew called after lunch I turned down his offer for dinner. Again.

The cats and I spent most of the afternoon out in the yard, working the compost Harry Junior had dropped off into the cold frame box where I was going to try growing lettuce and kale early in the spring. In midafternoon Rebecca walked over for a visit and we had cranberry scones and tea in her gazebo.

I tried not to think about Hannah or Abigail and their connections to Hugh Davis. There wasn't anything I could do, so I vowed to follow my advice to Marcus and stay out of it.

I was up early the next morning to meet Ruby at River Arts and see her painting of Hercules. When I came downstairs he was sitting underneath the carrier bag.

I folded my arms and looked at him. "What are you doing?"

He looked up at the bag and then over at the back door.

"If you're coming with me you need to have breakfast," I said, picking up his and Owen's water dishes.

He got up and walked over to the back door.

"I told you I'm not buying you a breakfast sandwich. You're a cat. Cats eat cat food."

He walked right through the door into the porch.

"Oh, like that's going to work," I called after him.

Owen came in then and rubbed against my leg.

"Hey, Fuzz Face," I said, bending down to scratch the top of his head.

I got his breakfast and set the dishes in their place by the refrigerator. He looked around the room and checked under the table.

"He's out in the porch," I said.

Owen cocked his head to one side.

I measured coffee into the machine. "He's sulking."

He studied the back door for a moment—thoughtfully, it seemed to me. Then he dropped his head and started sniffing his food.

Once the coffee was ready I poured myself a cup and went out to the porch. Hercules was on the bench, looking into the yard. One ear twitched, but other than that he gave no indication he knew I was in the room.

"Ruby will probably have some of those kitty treats," I said.

He jumped down and headed for his breakfast, pausing only to give me a look best described as patronizing as he passed me. I shook my head and followed him into the kitchen. Nobody had cats like mine. Sometimes they really were like little people in fur suits. Manipulative little people.

Ruby was waiting for me at the back door of the River Arts building. She smiled when she caught sight of the cat bag. "You brought Hercules," she said, her eyes lighting up.

I shrugged. "I know it sounds weird, but I swear he knew I was coming to see you. He was sitting by the carrier when I came down this morning."

"It doesn't sound weird to me." She leaned toward the mesh panel on the top of the bag. "Bonjour, mon petit," she said.

From inside the bag he made a little murp.

Okay, so it appeared Hercules knew how to speak French, too.

Ruby took us up to her studio. The painting was on one of her easels, turned away from the door. I unzipped the carrier and Hercules climbed out, walked to the far side of the table and sat down. He looked expectantly at Ruby.

"Ready?" she asked.

"Yes," I said, just in case she was talking to me, even though I was fairly sure she wasn't.

She swung the easel around and for a moment I was speechless. "Oh, Ruby, it's incredible," I said when I found my voice again. I hugged her and she beamed with pleasure. "I want to jump up and down and squeal," I said, grinning back at her.

She'd painted Hercules in shades of purple from deepest indigo to a pale lavender. He was sitting up, head tipped slightly to one side. It looked just like him—except for the purple.

The cat himself was studying his likeness, squinting and leaning forward. "Well," I asked. "What do you think?"

"Merow!" he said loudly, with much enthusiasm.

"We give it two paws up," I said to Ruby.

Right on cue Hercules held up a paw and looked at me.

Ruby folded her arms over her chest and laughed. "Could I give him a treat?" she asked.

"Would there actually be any point in me saying no?"

She twisted her mouth to one side. "Not really. There are two of us to one of you. I think we could outvote you."

"You have five minutes," I said sternly to Hercules, holding up one hand, fingers spread apart. "Then we have to get to the library."

"You're not going to make him shelve books all morning, are you?" she asked in mock outrage, hands on her hips.

"Don't be silly," I said. "Hercules is too short to shelve books. He's going to update the card catalogue. You should see how fast those little black-and-white paws can move across a keyboard."

Ruby laughed and reached for the bag of cat treats, already approved by Roma. Hercules gave me a look that said I wasn't nearly as funny as I thought I was.

Susan was waiting at the bottom of the steps when I got to the library. She grinned when she saw the cat carrier bag slung over my shoulder. "Is it Bring Your Cat to Work Day already?" she asked. "I'm sorry. I forgot to get you a card."

I made a face at her.

She gestured at the bag. "Owen or Hercules?"

"Hercules," I said. I unlocked the front doors and turned off the alarm. "We were over at River Arts with Ruby."

"How's the painting coming?" Susan asked as we climbed the stairs.

"It's beautiful," I said. "I hope it makes a lot of money for Cat People. They do good work."

"Me too," she said. "That's really nice of Ruby to do the paintings for the auction."

A muffled meow came from the cat carrier.

"And it was nice of you to pose for her, Hercules," Susan said with a grin.

I took the cat to my office, where he jumped up onto my desk, sat down on the budget projections for next year and started to wash his face.

A few minutes after nine a woman came in, stopping just inside the doors. She looked around, smiling at the building. I was about to walk over and say hello when she caught sight of me and smiled even wider. She started toward me, still smiling as though she knew me. I didn't know her, but I felt as though I should. Something about her was very familiar. She was tall and slender with auburn hair brushing her shoulders, and side-swept bangs. She looked to be in her early forties.

"You're Kathleen, aren't you?" she said.

"Yes, I am," I said.

She nodded her head slightly. "You look like your mom, but you have John's smile." She held out her hand. "I'm Chloe Miller. I worked with your dad a couple of times."

Now I knew who she was. Chloe Miller had been on a nighttime drama a few years back called *Vengeance*, playing the main character's mother in flashbacks. I'd stopped at my parents' house unannounced one Wednesday night and found my mother—who claimed she only watched PBS—glued to the TV. I confessed I was recording the show on my DVR at my apartment. A couple of weeks later I discovered that my little brother, Ethan, was a big fan as well.

The three of us started watching the show together every Wednesday night and then speculating about what was going to happen next for the following seven days. My dad and Ethan's twin, Sara, thought we'd taken leave of our senses.

"I was a big fan of *Vengeance*," I said. "I'm glad to meet you."

"When Ben told me you were the librarian here I had to come say hello. I hope that's okay."

"Absolutely," I said with a smile. "Are you here for the New Horizons festival?"

She nodded. "I am. I had another commitment and couldn't get here until last night." She looked around again. "The building is beautiful. How old is it?"

"We celebrated its centennial this past spring." I couldn't keep a touch of pride out of my voice.

"It's a Carnegie library, isn't it?"

I nodded. "Yes, it is."

"I thought so," she said. "I spent a year in Scotland doing theater and I actually got to visit the very first Carnegie library, in Dunfermline."

"I think I'm a little jealous."

"I'm a little jealous that you get to work here every day." She looked toward the stacks. "Would you have a minute to help me find something?" She loosened the black scarf at her neck. "I'm looking for a copy of John Donne's Holy Sonnet 10."

"'Death, be not proud.'"

She smiled again and shook her head. "I should have guessed you'd know it. I heard your dad quote Donne once."

I led her over to the poetry section. "When did you work with Dad?" I asked.

"My very first job," she said. Her cheeks turned red. "Promise you won't laugh?"

I put my hand over my heart. "Librarian's honor."

"It was a cereal commercial."

I shook my head and grinned. "You were in the raisin bran commercial. Were you a raisin or a flake?"

"I was a flake. John was a raisin."

"A dried-up, wizened raisin with no sense of rhythm."

Chloe laughed at the memory. "You know those commercials have a cult following online."

I rolled my eyes. "I'm not surprised. I was at college when the first two aired and that Halloween everyone I knew dressed up as a raisin."

"Now that they've revived the whole campaign, get ready for lots of dried-up raisins running around this Halloween, too."

"What is it about those ads that people like so much?" I asked.

She frowned, narrowing her eyes as she thought about my question. "I don't know. I think it's because they're funny even though they weren't intended to be—at least not the first one." She smiled again. "Ben said your mother's coming to fill in for Hugh."

"She is."

"I'm looking forward to seeing her. We did a benefit reading together a couple of years ago for the Coles Island Theatre. She told a story about doing summer stock, outside in a public park."

"The raccoon story." I scanned the shelves looking for the book of poetry Chloe wanted.

She laughed. "That's it." Her expression grew serious again. "It's really kind of her to offer to come like that, especially at the last minute."

"She's been friends with Ben a long time," I said.

"Ah, there it is." I bent down and pulled the book I'd been looking for from the bottom shelf. "And we get to spend some time together, too," I said, straightening up and handing her the book.

"Thank you," Chloe said, turning it over in her hands. "Ben's having a little . . . remembrance for Hugh this afternoon. I wanted to read 'Death, be not proud,' and I know it sounds silly, but Hugh would have hated it if I'd just printed the poem from somewhere online. He loved books."

There was genuine sadness in her eyes and the set of her mouth.

"You were friends," I said, reaching out to straighten the shelf of books closest to us.

"For a while we were more than friends." She played with her scarf. "My life went in a different direction, but I'm always going to have a soft spot for Hugh." She shook her head. "I wish I could have gotten here sooner. He worked so hard to convince me to take this job and we didn't get to work together in the end."

"Ben has some of Hugh's notes," I said. "They seem to have survived the fire. Once he gets them all sorted out maybe he'd let you read them to get an idea of what Hugh had in mind for your character."

Chloe held the book of poetry against her chest. "That's a good idea. I think I'll do that. I don't mean I won't follow your mom's direction, but I'd like to know what Hugh had been thinking. The play is about star-crossed lovers. Not the kind of part I usually play."

"He must have thought you could handle the part or he wouldn't have pushed you to take it."

"He pushed so hard that I was starting to think maybe he was hoping we could get back together again." She brushed her hair back behind one ear and pasted on a smile. "So thank you for this. It means a lot to me."

"I'm glad I could help."

"How do I check this out?" she asked.

"I'll take you over to the desk and Susan will get you a temporary card," I said.

We walked to the checkout desk and I introduced Chloe to Susan. "It was good to meet you, Chloe," I said.

"You too, Kathleen," she said. "I hope I'll see you again."

I nodded. "Me too."

Abigail came in early for her shift. I went down to the staff room for a cup of coffee before I started in on the budget figures and found her leaning against the counter with a mug in one hand. She was rubbing the back of her neck with the other hand. She looked tired. There were dark circles, like smudges of soot, underneath her eyes.

"Hi, Kathleen," she said. "I forgot to tell you— Ben is going to pick up your mom at the airport tomorrow."

"Are you sure?" I asked, reaching for the coffee-pot. "I can rearrange the schedule and get her myself."

"Thanks, but I think Ben wants to use the time to bring her up to speed."

"How are things going?"

"The police took four boxes of Hugh's notes, but they let us keep the costumes. And somehow Ben managed to organize a rehearsal for every one of the plays without resorting to cloning himself. And he's planned a memorial for Hugh this afternoon." She handed me the sugar, which was on the counter beside her. "I don't know when he sleeps."

"That sounds like Ben," I said, adding milk and sugar to my cup. "What about you? Is everything okay?"

She smiled and I thought it looked a little forced. "I could use a bit more sleep and probably a lot less coffee, but I'm okay."

"You sure?"

She nodded, but her smile wavered just a little.

"Abigail, what was going on between you and Hugh?" I said quietly.

It wasn't a surprise to see her face flood with color.

She took a deep breath and let it out. "We were married."

But that was.

16

I stared at her. "Married?"

"Yes."

"You were married to Hugh Davis?" Of all the things Abigail could have said, this was the last thing I would have expected. "When? How? *How?*"

She pulled out a chair and sat down at the small table in the middle of the room, and I did the same because I had a feeling this was going to take a while.

"We were married when we were in college. It's a lot of years ago."

"You never said anything."

Abigail stared into her cup. "It wasn't my best moment."

I waited until finally she met my gaze. "I was nineteen. We met on a Friday night in a script-writing workshop. Sunday afternoon when the workshop was over I moved my things into his apartment."

"Love at first sight."

She gave me a wry smile. "Or something like that."

"So what happened?"

Abigail shook her head. "I guess you could say real life happened. Practicality intruded." She laid both hands flat on the table. "I was already committed to doing a semester abroad in England. Hugh asked me to marry him before I left. By then my father had found out about the two of us. He said that if I married Hugh he'd take away his financial support. I would have had to drop out."

"That was an awful choice to have to make."

She nodded. "It would have been better if I'd actually made a choice."

"What do you mean?"

"I didn't want to lose Hugh and I knew my father would follow through on his threat. So I found a minister who wasn't licensed to marry us and then I left for London."

"What happened?"

She shrugged. "The whole thing blew up in my face. My father found out that I had gotten 'married.' So I confessed it was a sham. He said I was too immature for college and stopped paying my tuition."

"What about Hugh?"

"He was furious. And he was hurt. He wouldn't listen to anything I said and I can't blame him for that." She sighed. "He stopped answering the phone. I flew back from London and the apartment was empty. I dropped out, got a job fitting bras in a department store, and spent the next six years finishing my degree a course at a time."

My stomach hurt for the nineteen-year-old young woman Abigail had been. And I wanted to shake her father and Hugh for bailing on her. "I'm so sorry," I said. "I had no idea."

She gave me the closest thing to a smile she could manage. "It gets worse, Kathleen," she said.

"What do you mean, worse?"

"That first day that everyone involved with the festival arrived, Hugh asked me to meet him back at the theater after supper. I hadn't seen him in years." She started picking at the skin on the side of her right thumbnail. "He said we were still married."

"What do you mean, 'still married'? I thought the whole thing was a fake."

Abigail nodded. "So did I. Hugh claimed it was because of some loophole in the law about solemnizing marriage. He had documents from a lawyer." She kept picking at her thumb. "He wouldn't let me keep them, but they looked legitimate."

I felt my chest tighten as though I'd tried to put on a sweater three sizes too small. "What did he want?"

"Money. He was broke. He knew I'd inherited some when my father died. He said since we'd been husband and wife at the time, he wanted his half. I think he took the directing job with the festival just to have a way to get out here and blackmail me."

I shook my head. "I wish you'd said something."

She looked away for a moment. "I was embarrassed."

I put my hand over hers. "It's okay," I said.

She looked at me then. "I faked a marriage, Kathleen. My brothers don't even know that."

"Okay, so not the smartest thing you've ever done." I squeezed her hand. "We do dumb things when we're young. That's how we learn not to do dumb things when we get a little older."

She gave me a small smile.

"Do you remember when Andrew told you we broke up because he accidentally married someone else?"

"I remember."

I shook my bangs back off my face. "He didn't tell you that he was drunk and the someone was a waitress he'd met in a fifties diner while he was on a fishing trip with two of his buddies. One of which was the best man at the ceremony. The other one was the flower girl."

"Seriously?"

I nodded. "Seriously. There are pictures. That's partly how I ended up here. The point is, Andrew wasn't nineteen and he did something really, really stupid. So don't be so hard on yourself."

She sighed. "It's not the only stupid thing I did."

"It's okay," I said, giving her an encouraging smile. "Dumb mistakes are not limited to one to a customer. What else did you do?"

"Hugh had our original marriage certificate and the vows that we wrote. He said he even had a Polaroid that one of his friends had taken of us with the minister. I thought if I had those things maybe I could prove that neither one of us had taken the marriage seriously."

She folded one arm across her chest like she was hugging herself. "I figured they had to be in Hugh's room at the hotel. I needed to keep him away long enough for me to find everything. I managed to get his keycard out of his pocket." She lowered her voice. "Burtis loaned me his truck. I convinced Hugh to go out to the lookout with me. I told him we could work something out about the money. I haven't told anyone other than you, but the police are going to figure it out. Somebody probably saw us. I left him stranded out there, Kathleen. It's my fault Hugh's dead."

"No, it's not," I said, shaking my head for emphasis. "Abigail, the person who killed Hugh is responsible. Not you."

She started picking at her thumb again. "He would never have been out there if it hadn't been for me."

"He wouldn't have been in Mayville Heights at all if there hadn't been a fire at the theater in Red Wing. Does that mean the person who inspected that faulty circuit breaker and passed it is responsible for his death?"

"That's not the same thing."

"I think it is."

"I lied to get Hugh out to the lookout. How's that going to look to the police?" she said. "I heard Detective Lind's taken over the case. What am I supposed to say to her? 'Yes, I did lure the victim out to Spruce

Bluff, but I didn't kill him. I was busy ransacking his room instead'?"

"Actually, that's exactly what you do tell her."

She looked at me like I was crazy. "Why? You think she'll just take my word on it?"

"What time did you get to the hotel?"

"I don't know. Sometime just after six, I think. I had the radio on in Burtis's truck and they were just finishing the news update."

Ben had said that Hugh had tried to send him a text around six thirty.

"Detective Lind may not take your word on where you were, but she will believe the security cameras. They're on every floor in every hallway in the hotel. Little tiny cameras, part of a state-of-the-art security system they put in when they did the renovations."

"I didn't see any cameras."

"They're there," I said. I took my cell phone out of my pocket and pushed it across the table.

"Hugh tried to text Ben about six thirty, right about the time you were in his hotel room. Call Detective Lind, Abigail. Once she knows how Hugh ended up at Spruce Bluff, maybe she'll be able to figure out who killed him."

Abigail nodded and picked up the phone.

I felt a huge sense of relief that Abigail's secret wasn't that bad, overall. Now that I knew what she'd been hiding, all I needed to do was figure out Hannah's secret.

Abigail left to talk to Detective Lind at the police

station and I covered the circulation desk while Susan and Mary had lunch. I ate mine outside on a bench overlooking the water while Hercules nosed around the gazebo. The ground was dry and he seemed to have a fine time poking his whiskers into every nook and cranny.

I expected him to give me a hard time when we had to go back inside, but he climbed into the cat carrier with no complaint. I stopped to leave my coffee mug in the staff room and Hercules poked his head out of the bag and looked around.

"I'm not fooled," I said to him as I rinsed the cup. "I know you've been in here before."

He gave me a look of green-eyed kitty innocence.

"You don't really think I believe you stayed in my office all morning, do you?"

He continued the innocence ruse, staring unblinkingly at me. "So you're going for plausible deniability," I said, giving him a little scratch behind one ear. "Good choice, but I know you were roaming around this morning. You heard what Abigail said to me, didn't you?"

He was good. He kept his eyes fixed on my face as though he had nothing to be guilty about.

"I saw your tail when you were by the door," I whispered. "There was a scrap of paper stuck to the tip."

He turned to check it out, forgetting for the moment that the rest of him was still in the bag.

"Busted!" I hissed. I never won a staring contest

with either Hercules or Owen. I wasn't sure what it said about my character that I was tickled I'd won this one.

I should have known I'd pay for this victory. I stepped into the hallway and Hercules wriggled his way out of the bag. He jumped to the floor, flicked the end of his tail at me and disappeared through the door to the workroom.

"Oh, for heaven's sake," I said.

I put the empty carrier in my office and grabbed my keys. When I opened the workroom door Hercules was sitting on top of a cardboard box piled on a wooden storage crate, underneath the small stained-glass window in the far wall.

I crooked my finger at him. "Get over here," I said sternly.

The only movement he made was to tip his head to one side. The distance between us made it look as though he was smirking at me.

"I'm not kidding," I warned. "Get over here right now or there will be consequences. Serious consequences."

The cat lifted one front paw, gave it a couple of licks, and looked at me again.

I could see my ultimatum hadn't scared him one bit.

He scratched at the top of the cardboard box.

"Hey, don't do that," I said. "There might be books inside and you could tear the covers." I actually had no idea what was in the box. I hadn't put it there under the window and I didn't know who had.

Hercules scraped the flap of cardboard again and meowed at me. I realized that maybe he was trying to tell me something. I threaded a path around a couple of partly assembled easels and the top half of the puppet theater that Abigail and Maggie had built and made my way over to the window. "Is there something you want me to see?" I asked him.

He jumped down off the box onto the wooden crate and looked expectantly at me.

I pulled open the top flaps and looked inside the carton. It was filled with papers. I knew at once they had nothing to do with the library. I recognized the tight, angular writing. The papers had belonged to Hugh Davis.

"How did this box get in here?" I said to Hercules.

He had no more idea than I did.

I sat down on the edge of the packing crate and the cat climbed onto my lap. "When he showed up, all he had was that big pilot's case. Marcus sent people over to get that and all the papers Hugh had spread on the table and the desk."

Hercules murped his agreement. I'd already told him that.

"So where did this come from?" I shifted him sideways a little so I could take a closer look at the box. The contents may have belonged to Hugh Davis, but the box was one of ours. I could see Mary's handwriting on the side. It was one of the cartons we'd used for packing books for the library book sale.

I picked Hercules up and set him on the wooden crate. "Stay here for a second," I said. "I just want to look for something."

Of course he followed me, jumping down to nose around the boxes and bags and other detritus that had accumulated in the space. In the end, he was the one who found the books, stacked underneath a pile of folded tarps.

For some reason Hugh Davis had emptied a cardboard box and used it to hide his papers in my library. Why?

"So what's in here?" I said to Hercules, opening the top flaps on the carton again. He stood on his back paws, put his front ones on the edge of the box and peered inside. I took a look as well. On top I could see a couple of yellowed pages covered with messy handwriting. Were those the wedding vows Abigail had been looking for? "Do you think Abigail and Hugh's marriage license is in here?" I asked.

The only response was a muffled meow. It could have been a *yes* or a *no*.

Was that what Hugh had done? Hidden his important papers here at the library where no one would think to look for them? Pretty devious, hiding them in the building where Abigail worked.

I nudged Hercules very gently with my arm and after a moment he pulled his head out of the box and looked at me. His left ear was partly turned inside out.

"Ear," I said, touching the side of my head.

He sat down and swiped at the ear with a paw, turning it right side out again, then made a move to take another look inside the carton.

I put my hand in front of him. "No," I said. "Now that we know what this is, we have to call the police. We can't go through it. It might have something to do with Hugh Davis's death."

Hercules glared at me for a moment. Then he jumped down and stalked off to my office. At least I hoped that's where he was going.

I closed the top of the box, resisting the urge to see what else was in it. In all good conscience I didn't want to lie to Detective Lind if she asked me if I'd done anything more than look inside. After I locked the door I went downstairs to tell Susan, Mary and Mia that the workroom was off-limits until the police came and decided whether there was anything important in that box.

I was about to go up to my office to call Detective Lind when Marcus walked into the library.

"Do you have a minute?" he asked.

"Sure," I said. "I just have to call Detective Lind."

His blue eyes narrowed. "Why?"

"I found a box in the workroom that I think belongs—belonged—to Hugh Davis."

He put his hand on my arm and steered me toward the stairs. "What's in it?"

"Papers, as far as I can tell," I said.

Marcus patted his pockets. I knew that gesture.

He was feeling to see if he had a pair of disposable gloves.

"No," I said, moving to stand in front of the steps.

He frowned at me. "What do you mean, 'no'? I didn't say a word."

"I said no because you were looking for gloves so you could go upstairs and go through those papers."

"I'm a police officer, Kathleen," he said.

"Who's been taken off this case," I replied. "Don't do something stupid."

He looked around. "Could we go talk in your office?"

I nodded. "All right."

We went upstairs. I saw Marcus glance in the direction of the workroom, but I knew there was nothing he could do. The door was locked and I didn't think he'd try to wrestle the keys away from me.

On the other hand, I didn't have quite as much control of Hercules. He wasn't in my office and I had a sneaking suspicion I knew where the little fur ball had gone.

Marcus stood in the middle of the floor. I leaned against my desk. "Kathleen, I went to Red Wing this morning. I know the building inspector, Jeff Harris. He said Hannah was there on Friday to collect some boxes that hadn't already been picked up."

"So Andrew didn't see her drive by the marina." Either Andrew had been mistaken about the color of the SUV or someone else had the same car as Marcus.

"Jeff told me that she was there Friday afternoon. No one remembers seeing her Friday *night*." He stressed the last word.

My stomach seemed to flip over and tie itself into a knot.

"He was at the theater. He helped her load everything in the back of the SUV. She told him she was heading back here, but she let me think she was in Red Wing all evening, including when Davis was killed."

"She didn't shoot Hugh Davis," I said.

He took a deep breath and slowly let it out. "I know that. But if she was here when he was shot, maybe she saw something or she's protecting someone."

I didn't have an answer for him and I was very aware how much he sounded like me. I walked over to him and laid my hand on his arm. "Have you talked to her?"

He looked down at me and his blue eyes were troubled. "I tried. She was angry when she found out I'd been to Red Wing. She said I was a jerk and I'd been a police officer too long and then she left."

"So let Detective Lind figure this out. Just be Hannah's big brother."

He gave me a wry smile. "That sounds like something I'd say to you."

I squeezed his arm. "Must be good advice, then."

"It's been a long time since I saw Hannah that angry."

"She'll get past it."

"Are you sure?" he said.

I smiled at him. "Positive." I wanted to throw my arms around him but I didn't. I gave his arm another squeeze and then I dropped my hand and stepped back. "I didn't always do everything right," I said. "Maybe you can learn from my mistakes."

The start of a smile played across his face. "Are you saying you should have listened to me?"

"I decline to answer on the grounds that . . . I don't want to."

He did smile at that. Then he reached out and touched my shoulder, just for a moment. "I'm going to go so you can call Detective Lind. Maybe I can find Hannah somewhere."

"Give her a little bit of time," I said.

He nodded. In the doorway he stopped and looked back over his shoulder. "Kathleen," he said, "maybe you can learn from my mistakes, too."

I took a deep breath and exhaled slowly. Then I went down the hall to see if I could find Hercules. I unlocked the door to the workroom and looked inside. I couldn't see him anywhere and I really didn't think he'd be stubborn enough to walk through the door—so to speak—just because I'd told him not to. That was more Owen's style.

I relocked the door, went back to my office and called the number I'd memorized from Detective Lind's card. She told me she would send someone over for the box. When I stepped back into the hall, Hercules was standing in the staff room doorway.

"What were you doing in there?" I asked.

He looked back over his shoulder.

"Let me guess: being nosy, looking for something to eat that Roma has not okayed, and walking through walls just because you can."

He gave an offhand meow. I took it as a *yes* to all three.

I leaned forward. "Come here. You need to go back into my office. The police are on their way."

Hercules leaned sideways and looked toward the stairs.

"No. Marcus is gone. Someone is coming to get that box." I wasn't sure if that was what he'd been asking, but I like to keep him in the loop.

He yawned and walked past me into the office. I knew there was no point in locking the office door, but I did it anyway.

"Stay here. Please," I said as I left. Hercules was sitting in the middle of my desk again, meticulously washing his face. He gave no sign that he'd heard me say anything at all.

The afternoon passed in a blur of activity. When school let out there was a rush of eighth-grade students from two middle school history classes whose teachers had specified they had to use at least one real book as part of the research assigned for an essay on the First World War.

"Is there a DVD or something?" I heard one boy ask Mary as she handed him a book I knew was a young soldier's diary from the last days of the war.

"Read five pages," she said, holding up one hand. "And use your imagination."

"I wouldn't have to if there was a DVD," he muttered.

She shooed him toward a chair by the window and rolled her eyes at me. Half an hour later he was still in the chair, bent over the book, engrossed in the story.

I put my arms around Mary's shoulders and gave her a hug. "You're good," I said.

"Consider me a superhero of reading," she said with a grin.

About half an hour before closing I went upstairs to clean off my desk. Hercules wasn't sitting on top of it anymore, but he was in the room, curled up on my desk chair. He jumped down when I came in.

"Where are you going?" I said.

He ignored me, stopping only long enough to open the office door a little wider with one paw. At least he hadn't walked right through it.

I followed him down the hall to the lunchroom. "There's nothing in here you can eat," I said.

He shot me a condescending look and kept going. Inside the room he went immediately to the metal shelving unit against the wall. It was going in the workroom one of these days. I made a mental note to get Mia to start sorting through all the stuff piled on the shelves.

Hercules put one paw under the bottom shelf, which was only a couple of inches above the floor, and batted a piece of paper into the middle of the room. It was almost as though he'd known it was there.

I bent down to pick it up. It looked like part of a page that had been torn from a magazine. The paper was crumpled and damp, like it had been in a cat's mouth.

"Did you steal this from the box that was in the workroom?" I asked, even though I knew the answer.

Hercules, to his credit, didn't even try to bluff me. He looked at me, head up, furry chin jutting out, obviously proud of himself.

I studied the torn page, wondering what about it had caught the cat's attention. Was it the image of the bowl of steaming *jajangmyeon* in the Korean restaurant ad? Or was it the article written by a young woman who worked with teenage alcoholics? I couldn't see what either one could have had to do with Hugh Davis's death.

I looked down at the little tuxedo cat. Just because he could walk through a solid wooden door into the workroom and swipe a piece of paper didn't mean that piece of paper was important. Both Hercules and Owen had found "clues" before, but I didn't see how this scrap of a magazine page was going to help me figure out what Hannah was hiding or who had shot Hugh Davis up at the Spruce Bluff lookout.

I bent down and picked the cat up. "Let's go home," I said.

He twisted in my arms and swatted the paper with one paw. "Yes, I see that," I said. I frowned at him. "You shouldn't have taken it."

He made a huffy sound of indignation in his throat and refused to look at me. I folded the page, put it in my pocket, and went back to my office with my sulky cat.

I couldn't help wishing that Hercules had found something that would help me make sense of everything. What I didn't realize was that he had.

17

Maggie had moved tai chi class from Tuesday evening to Monday, so I didn't have a lot of time when I got home. I put the crumpled magazine page on the counter.

Hercules was still miffed. I crouched down next to him. He stared past me, aloof and unmoving like a black-and-white statue. I scratched his head just above his nose. "I'll look at what you found when I get back tonight. I promise," I said.

He made a disgruntled noise to show he still wasn't happy with me, but he stayed for the head scratch so I knew I was pretty much back in his good graces.

I took the truck to tai chi class instead of walking, which meant I had to find a parking spot. That should have been easy on a Monday night, but I ended up on a side street partway up the hill and made it to the tai chi studio, half out of breath, just before Maggie was about to start class.

Everyone had made it, even with the change of

day. Maggie was going to Minneapolis on Tuesday afternoon to present her application for a grant so the artists' co-op could renovate the store. If they got the money, they would be adding space where the various artists could give classes in the summer and fall, along with a small workspace so tourists could stop and see an artist at work.

Ruby had come up with the idea and Maggie had spent hours and hours on the grant application. I could see Ruby had lots of nervous energy—probably because of the upcoming presentation. She was walking around the studio space swinging her arms and flicking her fingers.

Maggie, on the other hand, was the picture of Zen-like calm, standing in the center of the room in a green tie-dye tank top and yoga pants, talking to Taylor King.

I walked over to them. "Taylor, that book you requested about accessories from the 1960s came in," I said. She beamed at me. "That's great. I could probably come get it after school tomorrow."

"It'll be at the front desk," I said.

Taylor had a good eye for vintage bags. She'd found several classic bags at different flea markets and thrift stores in the area. She was trying to learn more, she'd confided to me, because she wanted to start selling bags online. She was determined to show her dad that her interest in fashion wasn't just some teenage girl thing, but could actually be a career for her.

"Is there anything else I could do to help with the festival?" she asked.

"I'm not certain," I said. "But Abigail might need some help with the costumes she got from the theater in Red Wing."

Maggie made a face. "Everything probably smells like smoke."

"It does."

"Kitty litter's really good for getting the musty smell out of purses and things you can't put in a washing machine," Taylor said. "I use it sometimes if I find a bag that's been stored in, like, a basement or an attic for a long time."

"Abigail could probably use you, then," I said. I fished an elastic out of the pocket of my yoga pants.

"Do you think it would be okay to call her and ask?"

"I think she'd be very happy to hear from you."

Taylor smiled. "I'll call her right after class. Thanks, Kathleen."

Maggie looked around the room. "I think everyone made it," she said. She clapped her hands and called, "Circle, everyone."

Just then Hannah appeared in the doorway. She was wearing gray sweatpants and a white T-shirt. Since she was dressed in workout clothes I guessed she'd decided to take Maggie up on her offer to try a class.

"I'll go," I said softly to Maggie.

"Thanks," she mouthed, touching my arm as she

moved to take her place in the circle that was already forming in the middle of the room.

I walked over to Hannah. "Hi," I said. "I'm glad you came. We're just about to get started."

"I haven't done any tai chi in a while," Hannah said, looking around. "My form is a little wobbly."

I smiled. "Come stand next to me, then. My form is a lot wobbly."

We joined the circle, Roma moving sideways to make room for us.

"Everyone, this is Hannah," Maggie said. "She's here to try a class with us."

Hannah raised one hand in a little wave of acknowledgment.

Maggie worked us hard. She got Ruby to practice Push Hands with me. I was getting better, but I was still having problems shifting my weight forward and back. Maggie stood behind me for a couple of minutes, making tiny adjustments to my stance with just two fingers. I wasn't sure I was ever going to be as fluid as she and Ruby were.

Hannah wasn't nearly as rusty as she'd claimed. At one point I looked over to see her standing between Rebecca and Taylor, all three of them moving smoothly through Repulse Monkey.

When we finished the form at the end of class, Maggie smiled at all of us. "Good work, everyone," she said. "I'll see you all on Thursday."

I walked over to her, wiping my forehead with the

sleeve of my T-shirt. "What time are you leaving to-morrow?" I asked.

"Late morning." Maggie stretched her arms up over her head. "That way I'll have time to get lunch and get to the grant meeting early."

I held up my right hand. "My fingers are crossed and Owen sends his love."

She smiled. "Thanks, Kath. Give the fur ball a kiss from me."

I hugged her. "Call me when you get back."

"I will," she said.

Ruby walked over to us and I went out to change my shoes. Rebecca was by the coat hooks pulling on a cream-colored sweater. She smiled when she caught sight of me. "Hello, Kathleen," she said. She held out a canvas bag with blue handles.

"What's this?" I asked, peering inside.

"I heard your mother is coming tomorrow. I made you some bread and a dozen blueberry muffins."

"Thank you," I said, taking the bag from her.

"And there's a little treat for the boys in there as well."

I shook my head. "You're as bad as Maggie. The two of you are spoiling Owen and Hercules. And you're spoiling me, too."

Rebecca made a dismissive gesture with one hand. "A little indulgence once in a while isn't going to hurt them—or you." She gave me a slightly mischie-vous grin. "Everett says it's not fair of me to pressure you to stay with us. So I won't say a word about that. I'll just say one of those loaves is cinnamon raisin bread."

I wrapped her in a hug. "You are the nicest person I know."

"No, I'm not. I'm turning into a nasty old woman trying to get this wedding planned."

"You couldn't be nasty if you tried," I said.

She started buttoning her sweater. "I came close to it today. Everett suggested we have the wedding at the Basilica of Saint Mary in Minneapolis. It's a beautiful, beautiful church, but neither one of us is Catholic." She shook her head. "I don't want to wear a lacy dress with a train, or have a seven-course sit-down meal or, heaven forbid, hire a choreographer for our first dance. I just want to get married."

"So tell Everett that."

She adjusted the scarf at her neck. "I don't want to hurt his feelings. All of the trappings are so important to him. He has Lita looking for someone to set off fireworks after the reception. Fireworks, for heaven's sake."

I gave her hand a squeeze. "Rebecca, he loves you and he wants the whole world to know that. But you're the most important thing to him. I think he'd understand that you just want something small and quiet if you explain that to him."

She sighed. "I wish we'd eloped weeks ago."

"You'll work it out." I gave her an encouraging smile.

"As long as I don't end up in twenty pounds of handmade Belgian lace."

I slipped my tote bag over my shoulder and we started down the stairs. "I'll tell you what," I said. "If it looks like that's going to happen the boys and I will help you grab Everett and elope. I have a tarp in the basement, lots of gas in the truck and I'm very good at knots."

She grinned and gave my arm a squeeze. "Thank you, my dear. I just might take you up on that."

Hannah was standing outside on the sidewalk, looking at her cell phone. She looked troubled, but when she saw me she smiled. "Your form didn't look that wobbly to me," she said.

"Thanks," I said. "Neither did yours." I looked around and didn't see Marcus's SUV anywhere nearby. Since they'd argued, I guessed that Hannah wasn't driving it. "Could I drop you somewhere?" I asked. "I'm just parked a little bit up the hill." I pointed in the general direction of the truck.

She hesitated.

"Really, I don't mind."

She still had her phone in her hand. "I've been trying to get in touch with Abigail," she said. "I was hoping I could get a drive out to Marcus's with her." She looked at the phone. "Could I get a ride over to the theater? Maybe I can catch her."

"You don't need to," I said. "I'll take you to Marcus's."

She shook her head. "I don't want to put you out of your way."

I smiled. "Hannah, that's one of the great things about Mayville Heights—nowhere is out of the way. Let's go."

I saw a little of the tension in her body ease. She smiled back at me. "Okay. Thank you."

We started up the sidewalk. "How are rehearsals going?" I asked.

"Not that bad, under the circumstances, although I'm glad your mom's going to be here tomorrow. Did you know Ben organized a little memorial for Hugh?"

I nodded.

"I thought it was nice, considering Ben didn't really like him. Anyway, Chloe and I have been trying to help Ben as much as we can—the two of us have the most professional experience after him." She stuffed her hands in her pockets. "Have you met Chloe?"

I nodded. "I have. I like her."

"Everyone does. She's a genuinely nice person, even after everything. And I think she could direct if that's what she wanted to do. She has good instincts. Chloe and I supervised a run-through of all of the short plays that are going to be performed on the street. I just felt like I was stumbling in the dark, but she knew what she was doing."

We turned the corner and started up the hill. "That's my truck," I said, pointing a little way up the grade on the other side of the street. We looked both ways and crossed the street. "So you don't want to direct someday?" I asked. "I thought that was something a lot of actors wanted to do."

She nodded. "It is, but no, I'd rather stick to acting and writing."

"Writing for the stage or a screenplay?" I asked as we reached the truck.

"Stage."

I unlocked the passenger door and walked around to the driver's side. "You should talk to my mom. She's been a judge in several script-writing contests." I grinned and raised my eyebrows at her over the hood of the truck. "She does have some 'strong opinions' on what sells and what doesn't."

"I don't mind," Hannah said. "That's a lot better than someone who'll waffle because they don't want to hurt my feelings."

That made me laugh. "Don't worry," I said, inserting the key in the ignition. "One thing my mother doesn't do is waffle."

I checked for traffic and pulled out. I heard Hannah give a soft sigh. "Is everything all right?" I asked, keeping my eyes on the road so she wouldn't feel she was being interrogated.

For a moment she didn't say anything. Then she spoke, her voice soft and low. "Have you talked to Marcus today?"

"Yes," I said.

"So you know what he did."

I nodded. "I do."

"I told him I was in Red Wing. My word wasn't enough for him. He went into police officer mode and checked up on me."

I noticed she'd said she'd been in Red Wing, not that she'd been in Red Wing Friday night. I glanced over at her. Her face was flushed with annoyance.

I put on my blinker and turned right, toward Marcus's house. "Hannah, you know Marcus a lot better than I do, so you probably know this. Being a police officer is wired into his DNA." I let out a breath. "It took me a long time to understand that and for what it's worth, I don't think he was in police officer mode. I think he was in big brother mode."

"I'm not six," she said stubbornly and something in her tone made me think of her big brother.

I glanced over briefly at her again. Her head was up, shoulders rigid behind her seat belt. Hannah and Marcus were so much alike.

"Doesn't make any difference," I said. "I have a younger brother and sister—twins. I was fifteen when they were born and if you asked either one of them I know they'd say I still treat them like they were six."

"So are you saying you'd do the same thing Marcus did?"

I slowed down to let the car in front of me make a left turn. "I'm saying that if I thought Ethan or Sara was mixed up in something that might hurt them, I'd do just about anything."

She let the silence hang between us for a moment. "I didn't kill Hugh Davis," she said softly.

"I believe you," I said. "And so does Marcus." I hesitated. "But you haven't been completely honest, either. Just now you said you were in Red Wing."

I heard her shift in the seat. "Because I was."

"You didn't say you were in Red Wing Friday night."

The silence lasted so long this time I thought she'd just stopped talking to me. "No, I didn't," she said finally.

Marcus's house was just up ahead. As I pulled into the driveway I could see him, cleaning out the flower bed underneath the living room window. He got to his feet, wiping his hands on his paint-spattered jeans.

"Kathleen, could you stay for a minute?" Hannah asked.

"All right," I said.

Marcus walked over to us and we both got out of the truck. "Hi, Kathleen," he said with just a touch of a smile.

I nodded. "Hi, Marcus."

He turned to Hannah. "I'm glad you're here."

"Marcus, I'm not six anymore," she said, folding her arms across her middle.

"I know that," he said, frowning slightly.

"So don't treat me like I am." She held up a hand

to stop him from speaking. "I'm not finished. Kathleen pointed out that it doesn't matter whether I like it or not; you're always going to get involved in my life. So since I can't stop you, at least be straight with me from now on."

Marcus's eyes flicked over to me for a second. "Okay," he said, "but it goes both ways. I expect you to be straight with me."

"You want to know where I was Friday night."

"I do." He didn't seem to know what to do with his hands. He swiped them on his pants again.

Hannah glanced at me and I hoped the look I gave her seemed supportive.

"I was getting drunk," she said flatly.

I don't know what I'd been expecting, but that wasn't it. On the other hand, I did believe her.

Marcus closed his eyes for a moment. "You don't drink," he said when he opened them again.

She swallowed and fiddled with the strap of her tote bag. "I do a lot of things you think I don't do. Don't worry. I didn't drive." She pressed her lips together. "I'm not the perfect person everyone always expects me to be, but I wouldn't do that."

She turned to me then, laying a hand on my shoulder. "Thanks, Kathleen, for the drive and . . . everything." She looked from me to Marcus and shook her head. "Sometimes you miss what's right in front of you, big brother." Then she disappeared around the side of the house.

I waited until Hannah had disappeared around the side of the house, and then I turned to Marcus. "I believe her," I said.

"So do I," he said. "Whatever you said to her, thank you."

He was standing so close to me I could smell his aftershave mixed with the loamy smell of earth and plants. "All I said was I would have done the same thing if I thought Sara or Ethan were connected to a murder."

He smiled. "Feels good for us to look at something the same way. Different, but good."

I wanted to reach up and smooth the hair back off his forehead. No, I was kidding myself. I wanted to grab the front of his sweatshirt, pull his face down to my level and kiss him just the way he'd kissed me the last time we'd stood in his driveway next to my truck. I didn't, of course. I was good at imagining those kinds of scenarios, but I was just too practical to carry them out. Or maybe too chicken.

"You're right—it does," I said. I put a hand on the side of the truck to remind myself I was in the real world and not some fantasy. "I should get going."

He nodded. "Thanks, Kathleen, for driving Hannah home and for talking to her and for . . . just . . . thanks."

I couldn't seem to stop looking into those gorgeous blue eyes. "I'll, uh, see you," I said. I walked around the truck, got in and backed carefully down the driveway. He stayed where he was, watching me, and even when I was out of sight around the curve in the road, I could still feel his eyes on me.

I was almost home before I started to weigh Hannah's words. She'd said she'd gotten drunk. I believed her. The way she'd said the words, her tone, her body language—everything told me she was telling the truth, not acting. But the fact was that Maggie had seen Hannah not long after Andrew and I found Hugh Davis's body. And Andrew had seen her drive by the marina.

So she got drunk a little later that Friday night. What had happened earlier that made her want to?

18

There was no sign of either cat when I got home. I kicked off my shoes, hung up my sweater and set the bag Rebecca had given me on the counter. Inside I found the promised loaf of her cinnamon raisin bread, a round loaf of honey sunflower and a dozen blueberry muffins. There was also a tiny brown paper bag from the Grainery that I knew had to hold a catnip Fred the Funky Chicken for Owen. And there was a tiny cardboard box from the same store. By the process of elimination it had to be for Hercules. I wondered what was inside.

I put a piece of bread in the toaster and a cup of milk in the microwave. Usually the sound of the toaster would make both cats show up, and after a moment Owen's gray tabby head peered around the living room doorway.

"What were you doing?" I asked, getting the peanut butter and the cocoa mix out of the cupboard.

He gave an offhand meow, cat for "Not much."

Hercules's black-and-white face looked around the opposite side of the door to the living room.

"And how was your night?"

He made a motion that kind of looked like a shrug.

"I saw Rebecca at tai chi," I said as the microwave beeped. I held up the two loaves of bread. "She brought me some bread." I saw the two of them exchange glances at Rebecca's name.

Owen crossed the floor, sat down in front of me and meowed, cocking his head to one side. I knew what he was asking.

"Yes, she sent something for you," I said. "She spoils you."

He blinked a couple of times as though he couldn't understand what I'd said.

I opened the top of the little paper bag and set it on the floor. Owen sniffed cautiously and then a blissful expression spread across his face. He poked a paw inside the bag and batted out a neon yellow Fred the Funky Chicken. For a moment he just inhaled the scent of catnip, a lot like the way Maggie did when I took a pan of brownies out of the oven. Then he picked up the toy and retreated under the table with it.

Hercules had watched the whole thing from the doorway. "Come over here," I said. "Rebecca sent something for you, too."

His green eyes immediately darted to his brother, who was already sprawled on the floor, chewing happily on the chicken.

"No, it's not a catnip chicken," I said.

The toaster popped then. I held up a finger. "Give me a minute," I said. I put peanut butter on the bread and cocoa mix in my milk and set everything on the table. Then I grabbed the little cardboard box.

I crouched down next to Hercules. He looked at the box and then looked at me.

"I have no idea," I said.

I took off the lid. Inside was a tiny stuffed purple mouse. There was a tag attached to its tail. *Shake for thirty seconds. Set on flat surface and press down on mouse.*

"Let's try it," I said. I picked up the mouse and shook it, counting to thirty slowly. Then I set it on the floor in front of the cat and pressed down on its purple back. When I took my hand away the mouse began to skitter around in a circle.

Hercules watched it for a moment. Then his paw darted out and landed on top of the mouse. When he lifted it again the mouse ran in the other direction. He caught it a second time. This time when he took his paw away the little purple critter went in a figure eight and when the cat tried to stop it he missed.

He leaned forward, watching intently. He didn't miss twice. He looked up at me and I swear I could see satisfaction gleaming in his eyes. I had no idea how the mechanism in the little mouse worked, but it was obviously a hit with Hercules.

I pulled out a chair and sat down, propping my feet on the seat of the chair opposite mine. While I ate

I told the cats what had happened at Marcus's place. Neither one of them seemed to be paying attention, but it helped me to sort things out if I said them out loud. Except it didn't seem to be helping this time.

After a few minutes the purple mouse ran out of steam and stopped with a little whizzing sound. Hercules poked it a couple of times and when he decided it wasn't going to move, he took a few steps toward the counter, looked up and meowed.

"What? Do you want a cracker?" I asked. He looked at me over his shoulder and then turned back to the counter.

I got to my feet. The magazine page that Hercules had appropriated from the box Hugh Davis had hidden at the library was still lying there. I picked it up and Herc meowed again. Was he really trying to tell me it was connected to the director's death?

I smoothed out the wrinkles in the paper. It wouldn't hurt to get my laptop and look for the original article. The magazine's name and the date of publication were on the top of the page.

I put my computer on the table and as soon as I sat back down Hercules jumped onto my lap. "So you're helping?" I said.

He put one paw on the edge of the keyboard. He was definitely helping. I glanced under the table. Owen was stretched out on his side, eyes half closed, chewing on Fred the Funky Chicken with a loopy look on his face.

A quick search and I found the issue of the magazine online. The article was the grand-prize winner in a contest called Share the Change, Be the Change, sponsored by a soft-drink company. It was about a program for teen alcoholics, written by a young woman the program had helped.

I was hooked at the first sentence. The language was raw and compelling and when I got to the end I wanted to jump up and cheer for the teenager I didn't even know.

"Wow," I said to Hercules. He meowed softly in agreement. Then he batted a paw at the keyboard, clicking on a link to another article.

"Paws off the keys, fur ball," I said. He was staring at the screen almost as though he was reading and ignored me.

I glanced at the link he'd taken us to and about halfway down the page I saw Hannah's name. I looked at Hercules. "How did you do that?" He was still intent on the screen. I didn't even get a whisker twitch.

This article was about the stage play, inspired by the article that had won the grand prize. The stage play Hannah was up for a role in and Hugh had wanted to direct. But Hannah had a closer connection than that. She was a volunteer with the program. She'd been the one to urge the teenage writer to put her story down on paper and enter the contest.

I leaned against the chair back and curled one arm around Hercules. He turned his head to look at me.

"This means something," I said. "I just don't know what."

He made a face, wrinkling up his nose. I wondered what he knew that I didn't.

I was up early the next morning. I scrubbed the bathroom, vacuumed up the cat hair and started a pot of split pea soup with ham in the slow cooker. Then I walked around the house, trailed by Owen, and wondering what it would look like to my mother. It was home, I realized, just as much as Boston was. Maggie, Roma, Rebecca, the Taylors, Susan and Eric—they were my family, too. I wasn't exactly sure what Marcus was.

I looked at the picture my mom had sent to me just a couple of weeks ago. I'd hung it behind the big chair in the living room. It was a drawing of a tiny cottage, with two cats sitting on the front steps and the caption "Home is anywhere you are." I got a lump in my throat looking at it. It was Mom's way of saying she would support whatever choice I made. I knew that it had to be hard for her not to tell me to come back to Boston.

"As long as you're happy, I'll be happy, Katydid," she'd said to me more than once on the phone.

I scooped Owen up in my arms. "Why does it have to be so complicated?" I asked.

He licked my chin. If he had an answer, he wasn't sharing it.

I'd calculated that it would be late afternoon before Ben got back from the airport in Minneapolis with Mom. Still, I couldn't seem to stop looking at the clock as the arrival time for her flight came and passed. I pictured her walking to baggage claim, finding Ben, heading to the car. Did Ben drive the speed limit? Go faster? Or slower?

I passed the checkout desk and Mary called my name. "Kathleen, go upstairs and make some coffee," she said. "Everything's fine down here."

I shook my head. "Thanks, Mary, but I don't really feel like a cup right now."

She put her hands on her hips and frowned at me. "Well, I do. You're making me crazy walking in circles, not to mention you're going to wear out all those little tiles Vincent Gallo and his boys worked so hard to replace."

I rubbed the space between my eyes with two fingers. "I'm sorry. I feel as if time has somehow slowed down today."

" 'We are time's subjects,' " a voice said behind me.

I turned around to see my mother standing just inside the door, smiling at me. She was the only person I knew who could quote a line or two from Shakespeare in the middle of a conversation and not sound pretentious.

" 'And time bids begone,' " I said, grinning back at her. I didn't give her a chance to quote anything else from *Henry IV*, though. I crossed the few feet between us and threw my arms around her. "I'm so glad you're here."

She smelled like lavender and she didn't look like she'd spent close to four hours on a plane and more than another hour in a car. She was wearing black trousers, a soft cloud gray sweater with a wide, flat collar and heels. Her silver hair was a bit shorter, chin length. If anything, it made her look younger.

"I'm so glad I'm here, too," she said. She pulled out of the hug, kept her arm around my shoulders and looked around. "Oh, sweetie, this is even better than the photos."

She caught sight of Mary then and smiled. "You must be Mary," she said, walking over to the desk and offering her hand. "I'm Thea Paulson."

They shook hands, Mary smiling back. "I'm glad you're here," she said. "We've heard a lot about you."

"All of it good, of course," Mom said, a sly look in her eye.

Susan was coming from the stacks with an empty book cart. Mary made the introductions. I heard my mother ask a question about the building and I knew that within five minutes she'd have its history and a fair amount of Mary's and Susan's as well.

I turned to Ben. "Thank you for picking her up."

He shook his head. "The pleasure was truly mine. I can't tell you how glad I am she agreed to come."

"Me too," I said.

Abigail breezed through the door then.

"Hi," I said. "What are you doing here?"

"I came to fill in for you so you can take your mom

home." She held up a hand. "Don't even think about arguing with me."

I held out both hands. "Okay, I won't."

I introduced Abigail to Mom and she was immediately pulled into the conversation with Susan and Mary. I'd given Ben my keys so he could put Mom's suitcase in the truck. "I'm just going up to my office to get my things," I said.

"Could I see your office before we go?" she asked.

"Of course," Susan said. She had a pink plastic cocktail fork stuck in her updo. I was never quite sure if the odd things she used to secure her hair were her way of thumbing her nose at convention or if she really did just grab the first thing she saw on any given morning.

"Kathleen has a beautiful view of the water and of course the gazebo that's at the back," Mary said.

"You have a gazebo?" Mom said.

Abigail nodded. "One of the performances is going to take place out there."

Mom's eyes lit up. "What a wonderful idea! I love performing outside. John and I did Bard in the Park last year. How big is this gazebo?"

"It's about, what, twelve feet across?" Abigail looked at Mary for confirmation.

"Fifteen," I said.

"Small, but not impossible to use as a stage," my mother said. "Could I take a peek at it?"

Susan nodded. "Like Mary said, you can see the gazebo from Kathleen's office."

"Splendid," Mom said. "Let's go take a look."

They all moved toward the stairs.

I cleared my throat. "Someone has to stay at the desk," I said.

Mary shook her head. "I'll stay." She leaned forward and smiled at Mom. "It was wonderful to finally meet you, Thea."

"You too, Mary," Mom said, reaching out to squeeze her hand. "As soon as I get my schedule sorted out I'll call you and we'll have tea."

"Looking forward to that," Mary said. She brushed past me on her way to the checkout desk. "I like her," she said softly as she went by.

Susan and Abigail gave Mom a quick tour of the second level and showed her the gazebo from my office window. I gathered my briefcase and jacket and only managed to steal her away from them by promising to bring her back the first time she was free.

"I like your library and I like your staff," she said as she settled on the passenger side of the truck. Her carry-on was at her feet and her suitcase was in the bed of the truck, covered with a tarp because it was spitting rain.

"You cut your hair," I said as we drove up the hill.

"What do you think? It was the executive producer's idea."

"I like it."

"I'm supposed to look rich and ruthless," she said with a laugh. "When I e-mailed your father a photo, he said I looked like Helen Mirren."

I shot her another quick look. She actually did look a bit like the British actress. They had the same hair now and the same beautiful posture. "Maybe a little," I said.

She brushed a bit of lint off her sweater. I hoped it wasn't cat hair. "He's just trying to charm me into doing a British accent. He's always thought a British accent is sexy."

I shook my head. "Way, way more information than I need to have."

She laughed and the sound filled the truck.

I smiled at her. "I'm so glad you're here."

"Me too, Katydid," she said.

Owen and Hercules were waiting for us in the kitchen. Mom walked over to them, stopping a couple of feet in front of them. "Hello," she said. Both cats eyed her, whiskers twitching.

"Merow," Owen finally said.

"It's nice to finally meet you, too," Mom said. "You're even more handsome than your pictures."

Owen knew what the word "handsome" meant. He did his I'm-so-modest head dip, watching her with one golden eye.

"And, Hercules, you look like you put on your best tuxedo to welcome me. Very dashing."

Hercules wasn't immune to compliments, either. He sat up a little straighter and gave Mom a look of kitty affection.

"What would you like first?" I said. "A bath or a cup of tea?"

She straightened up and stretched. "Oh, sweetie, a cup of tea would be wonderful."

I reached for the kettle.

"Is it all right if I look around?" she asked. "I do like your house."

I nodded. "Of course."

She headed to the living room with Owen and Hercules right beside her. I put tea bags in the little china pot I always kept for Maggie and set a couple of Rebecca's blueberry muffins on a plate. By the time Mom came back to the kitchen the tea was ready and I'd made a cup of cocoa for myself.

She sank into the chair opposite me and reached for her cup. "Umm," she said after taking a sip. "That's lovely tea."

"It's Maggie's favorite, so I keep some in the house," I said.

"When do I get to meet Maggie?"

"Probably tomorrow. She's in Minneapolis at a meeting." I reached for one of the blueberry muffins. "What time are you meeting Ben in the morning?"

Mom pulled up one leg and tucked it underneath her. "Eight thirty. That's almost civilized compared to the time I have been getting up."

"We could ask Maggie to join us for breakfast," I said.

"Yes," Mom said, putting the other muffin on her plate.

I got up and went to the cupboard for the small bottle of orange marmalade I'd gotten for Mom from the Jam Lady. I gave her the jar and watched her unscrew the lid, put a dab on her plate with her knife and then take a tiny taste with one finger. She reminded me of Owen. He and his brother were sitting between my chair and Mom's, probably hoping one of us would drop something.

Mom took another taste of the marmalade. "This is good," she said. "Where did you get it?"

I sat back down. "There's a woman who lives farther out this road called the Jam Lady. She made it."

She smeared a thick layer of marmalade on half her muffin and took a bite. "Tell me about Hugh Davis. You didn't say much and when I talked to Abigail on the phone, I noticed she very skillfully changed the subject. So did Ben, for that matter."

I picked up my mug and threaded my fingers around it. "He was shot."

"Shot? What happened? Was it some kind of robbery?"

"I don't think so," I said. "He was shot down by the marina. There's a lookout by the water." I set my hot chocolate down on the table again. "There's something I didn't tell you on the phone."

"Let me guess," she said. "You found Hugh's body."

"Actually, I did," I said. "But that wasn't what I need to tell you." I took a breath and let it out. "Andrew's here."

She frowned and put down the piece of muffin she'd been holding. "Andrew? Your Andrew?"

"He's not my Andrew anymore, but yes."

"Why?"

I folded my arms over my chest. "He wants me to come back to Boston when my contract here ends and give us another chance."

"And you said?"

"I said no." I glanced down at Hercules and Owen. The bag of sardine crackers was on the counter. I leaned sideways, snagged it with a couple of fingers and gave each of them two crackers. "I care about Andrew," I said, straightening up and brushing off my fingers. "But I'm not getting back together with him. I've changed."

"I know you have," she said, adding a little more tea to her cup. "And Andrew's not Detective Gordon."

"What?" I said. I could feel my face getting red. I'd told Mom about feeding the cats with Marcus, but I hadn't said anything else.

"Remember the pictures you brought when you came home?"

"I remember." Ethan had teased me because I'd printed copies of the photos instead of just showing them on my phone.

"There was one of the detective. Whenever you were showing the pictures to someone, when you got to that one of him, you smiled. I don't even think you know you did it, sweetie, but you did." She leaned forward and smiled at me. "Is there something going on between the two of you?"

I shook my head. "No, there isn't. We had dinner a few times, but Marcus is a police officer." I sighed. "And that just keeps getting in the way."

She put her hand on mine and gave it a squeeze. "I'm sorry to hear that. Are you sure you can't find a way around it?"

"I don't think so. Marcus can be pretty black and white about some things."

She put a hand up to her mouth, but I could still see the smile.

"What's so funny?" I asked.

She laughed, shaking her head. "Sweetie, you can be pretty black and white about certain things, too. Detective Gordon sounds like he's perfect for you."

"I'm not rigid about things."

"Really?" Her eyes were sparkling. She picked up her teacup. "All right. I'm not going to argue with you." She took a sip from her cup. "Could we change places?"

"Why? Is something wrong?" I said.

"The light coming through the door makes me squint." She patted her cheeks. "I don't need any more wrinkles. HD already makes me look like I'm ninety."

I pulled out the chair to my left. "You can sit here."

She gestured at me. "You just scoot over and I'll sit at your place. It's easier."

I narrowed my eyes at her. "I know what you're doing," I said.

"What am I doing?"

"You're trying to show me that I can be stubborn and rigid because I don't want to switch seats with you."

"So slide over," she said, making a move like she was going to get up.

I got my cup and moved to the chair beside me.

Mom smiled and sipped her tea.

"So are you going to sit there or not?"

She shook her head. "No. I think I'm going to sit here after all."

She put more marmalade on another bite of muffin and popped it in her mouth.

I shifted in the chair, trying to get comfortable. It shouldn't have been a problem. All four chairs were exactly the same, but this one didn't feel right. I moved back to where I'd been sitting. "This doesn't prove you were right," I said.

"Of course not," she said solemnly.

"Tell me what you know about Hugh Davis," I said, mostly to change the subject.

Mom yawned and stretched. She reminded me of the cats. Owen was leaning against my leg now, while Hercules was still watching my mother with interest. "I'd heard his name, but I really didn't know anything about him, so after I talked to you I made a few phone calls."

"And?"

"And he was a decent enough director, although he hadn't done much that was significant in the last year and a half."

That would explain why he'd been pushing Hannah so hard.

"Do you know why?" I asked.

Mom set her cup down. "He may have been a decent director, but it appears he wasn't a decent person."

"Not a decent person how?" I asked. "Did he drink too much? Cheat on his taxes?"

She shook her head. "I heard from an unimpeachable source that he pushed one of his leading ladies so hard she started cutting herself and another ended up having some kind of breakdown."

"Wait a minute. Did Ben know that?"

"I don't think so," she said. "At first all anyone would say was that Hugh could be 'challenging.' That can mean anything from 'he throws things in rehearsal' to 'he likes to wear frilly undies.'"

I pulled both feet up under me. "Those are pretty serious accusations. Are you sure your source is accurate?"

"Very."

I blew out a breath. "Do you know who the two actresses were?"

She poured the last of the tea into her cup. "That I don't know. But it strikes me that they'd have family and friends. If someone treated you that badly, I don't know what I'd do." She smothered another yawn.

"How about you go fill the tub full of hot water while I make you a fresh pot of tea?" I said, getting to my feet.

"Umm, that does sound good." She stood up as well and wrapped me in a warm hug. "I'm so glad I decided to come, Katydid."

"Me too," I said.

I put the kettle on to boil again and took Mom up to her room. When the tea was ready I poured a cup and took it up to her. She'd already put on a fuzzy yellow robe and taken off her makeup. With her face scrubbed clean and her hair pulled back in a messy bun, she looked more like she was my older sister than my mother.

"Take your time," I said, kissing her cheek.

I went back to the kitchen and started clearing the table. Owen was sniffing Mom's purse, which she'd left on the floor next to her chair. "There's nothing in that for you, nosy," I said. One ear twitched, but that was the only indication I got that he'd heard me.

Hercules wound his way around my legs and I bent down and picked him up. "So Hugh Davis wasn't a very nice person," I said.

He murped his agreement.

"Mom's right, you know. Those women must have family and friends who wanted Hugh to pay for what he did. So how do we find out if that's what someone did?"

19

Maggie called about eight thirty that evening. She sounded tired but not at all worried. "It went well," she said. "Now it's in the hands of the universe."

"My fingers are crossed." Owen had climbed onto my lap when I answered the phone and he put one paw on the receiver. "And Owen sends his love."

Maggie laughed. "Thanks. I know they'll both help. Give Owen a scratch from me."

Mom poked her head around the doorway to the kitchen. "Ask Maggie to join us for breakfast," she stage-whispered.

"Mom would like to know if you can meet us for breakfast," I said.

"Yes," Maggie immediately said.

"Are you sure you don't want to think about it?" I teased.

"I have been thinking about it," she said. "I really want to meet your mother. I've heard so much about her from you. The fact that she's on my show is just a bonus."

We settled on a time and said good night. I gave Owen a scratch under his chin. "This is from Maggie," I said. His golden eyes closed to slits and he started to purr.

It was the alarm clock that woke me in the morning, not a furry face with sardine breath. When I went downstairs I found Mom, sitting on the floor by the refrigerator. She had a fork in each hand with half a sardine speared on each one. Hercules was methodically licking fish oil off one chunk. Owen was biting off bits from the other and setting them on the floor so he could eat them.

Mom looked up and smiled. "Good morning, sweetie." She gestured at the counter. "I made you coffee."

"Oh, umm, thank you," I said. Mom could do only two things in the kitchen and making coffee wasn't one of them.

"My internal clock is completely out of whack," she said. "I made some tea and fed the cats. I hope that's okay. Owen seemed hungry."

"What did you feed them?"

She tipped her head in the direction of the counter, where an empty can sat waiting to be washed and recycled. "That canned food." Her right hand moved and Hercules's head bobbed up and down as he tried to keep licking without missing a beat.

"They're very intelligent cats," Mom said. "Hercules took me right to the cupboard with the cat food and Owen showed me the sardines in the refrigerator."

"Yes, they are something," I said darkly, eyeing both cats as I moved to the fridge to get the cream for my coffee. "Why are you feeding them sardines like that?" Each cat was less than a foot away from my mother. Most people, with the exception of Maggie, didn't get that close.

Mom looked up at me, frowning. "You did tell me not to touch them, Katydid."

"I mean why are you feeding them sardines at all?"

She shifted slightly. "I was having my tea and half of one of those wonderful blueberry muffins. It just seemed wrong for me to have a treat and them to have nothing."

Owen made a little murp of agreement.

"I didn't think you'd want me to feed them a blueberry muffin. I can't see how that would be good for them."

Hercules glanced over at me then. Unlike his brother, he at least had the good sense to look a little guilty.

I got a mug out of the cupboard and poured a cup of the coffee for myself. It didn't smell burned or have the consistency of molasses. That was good. As I added cream and sugar I realized I didn't care if the coffee tasted . . . well, as bad as every other cup of coffee my mother had ever made. I was happy just to have her in the middle of my kitchen floor feeding sardines to my cats.

Owen had pulled the last bite of fish off his fork. Mom leaned sideways, set the fork on the table and grabbed her tea. "Cheers," she said, holding up the cup.

"Cheers," I echoed. I took a sip, aware that I was suddenly being watched by three sets of eyes. The coffee wasn't too watery or too strong. It didn't taste like it had been filtered through a pair of old sweat socks. "This is . . . good," I said. I didn't mean to sound so surprised but, well, I was.

Mom gave the boys a conspiratorial grin and got to her feet. She came over and kissed the top of my head. "See, sweetie?" she said. "You can teach an old dog new tricks."

Herc's head came up and he gave her a green-eyed glare.

She held up a hand. "I'm sorry, Hercules," she said. "I meant no offense."

The glare smoothed into a kitty smile. If offense had been taken, it had already passed.

Maggie was waiting for us at Eric's, sitting at our favorite table in the window. She stood up to greet us when we came in the front door.

"I'm so happy to meet you," Mom said, taking both of Maggie's hands in hers. "I've heard nothing but good things about you."

Maggie smiled. "I'm glad to meet you, too, Mrs. Paulson. I've heard good things about you also."

Mom gave her a sly grin. "Well, then, you haven't heard the best stories," she said. She gave Maggie's hands a squeeze and let go. "And please call me Thea."

As soon as we sat down, Eric himself came over with the coffeepot and I did the introductions.

"I hear you make a chocolate pudding cake that's almost as good as my favorite Death by Chocolate cheesecake," Mom said.

Like everyone who met my mother, Eric was already charmed. "Come back for lunch and you can judge that for yourself," he said.

She smiled. "I will."

Mom ordered an omelet for breakfast while Maggie and I both chose our current favorite, Eric's breakfast sandwich.

Eric went back to the kitchen and Claire came over with hot water and a couple of small teapots for Maggie and Mom. Once Mom had a cup of tea steaming in front of her, she reached for her bag and pulled out a small package wrapped in lavender paper and tied with silver ribbons. She handed it across the table to Maggie.

"I hope you don't mind," she said. "I brought this for you."

Maggie looked from my mother to me. "Uh, thank you," she said. She set the package on her lap, untied the ribbon bow, and carefully unfolded the tissue paper. When she saw what was inside, she put a hand to her mouth. She looked at Mom across the table. "I can't believe you did this."

She held up a T-shirt, the same pale lavender color as the wrapping paper. Across the front it read LIFE IS WILD AND WONDERFUL. The rest of the fabric was covered with signatures scrawled in permanent black marker.

"It has to be the whole cast," Maggie said. "There's Billy and Jack and Nicole. I just . . . oh wow!"

"Kathleen told me you like the show," Mom said. "I thought you might enjoy the shirt."

"I will." She couldn't stop smiling. "I can't decide whether to wear it or frame it."

Mom took a sip of her tea. "Wear it," she said. "Enjoy it. Life is meant to be lived, not looked at from a distance."

"Are you and Jack really having an affair?" Maggie asked, holding the T-shirt against her chest with one hand. "I mean, your character."

Mom propped one elbow on the table. "Can you really see me with him?" she asked, eyebrows going up.

"I knew it," Maggie said.

They started talking about the show and I leaned back in my chair with my coffee and let their voices wash over me. Having Mom and Maggie sitting at the same table was the best of both worlds. I wished I didn't have to choose between Boston and Mayville Heights, and I was uncomfortably aware that I was going to have to make that choice soon.

The front door of the café opened then and Marcus stepped inside. He smiled when he saw me.

"Excuse me," I said, getting to my feet. "I'll be right back."

"Hi," he said. He gestured toward the table. "Is that your mother with Maggie?"

I nodded. "Do you have time to meet her?"

"I'd like to, but do you have a minute first?"

"Sure," I said. "What is it?"

"Hannah was telling the truth. She was at Barry's Hat on Friday night. I talked to a friend of Liam's." He made a face. "He took her keys. Some of the crew from the festival were there. One of the women wasn't drinking. She drove Hannah home."

"You went to Barry's Hat?"

"All I did was have supper at the bar," he said. "I was talking to the bartender and he said he'd met my sister." His eyes kept sliding off my face. He wasn't a very good liar.

"Of course. Because you go to bars all the time to have supper." Maybe my mother was right. He'd done exactly what I would have done and was saying just what I would have said.

"I can't do nothing, Kathleen," Marcus said quietly. He closed his eyes momentarily and shook his head. "And yes, those words do sound familiar."

"Then I don't need to say 'stay out of it,' do I?" I glanced over at the table. Maggie and Mom were still deep in conversation. "Well, at least now you know Hannah was telling the truth." *As far as it goes*, I added silently. "That's good."

"Yes and no," Marcus said. "Liam said Hannah got there about eight. Where was she between then and the time she left Red Wing? She says she wasn't anywhere near the marina."

There were deep frown lines between his eyes

and I wanted to rub them away. "Do you believe her?"

He shook his head. "I want to." He let out a long breath. "I know you don't."

"I'm sorry," I said.

He forced a smile. "I can tell you Abigail Pierce is in the clear. She's on the hotel surveillance, breaking in Hugh Davis's room at almost the same time Davis was making a call on his cell phone."

"You'll notice I'm not asking you how you know this."

"I met her and her lawyer coming out of the station. She told me."

"Marcus, please don't do anything—"

"—stupid?" he finished.

I shook my head. "I was going to say don't do anything that might get you in trouble." My mouth was suddenly dry. "Call me instead."

We stood there, eyes locked, for a long moment. Something we seemed to be doing a lot of lately. I cleared my throat. "Come meet my mother," I said.

I took Marcus over to the table and made the introductions.

Mom stood up and held out her hand. "It's very good to meet you, Detective," she said. Her expression was serious. I knew her well enough to know she was appraising him, making a hundred tiny little judgments in just a few seconds.

"You as well," he said.

Claire was on her way to the table with a loaded tray.

"I'll leave you to your breakfast," he said. He smiled at Mom and Maggie. "Have a good day, Kathleen," he said quietly to me.

"'From forth the fatal loins of these two foes, A pair of star-cross'd lovers take their life,'" Mom recited softly as Marcus walked away.

"Marcus and I are not star-crossed anything," I said as Claire reached the table. Out of the corner of my eye I saw Maggie look across the table at Mom and nod, ever so slightly.

After breakfast I dropped Mom off at the Stratton and made my way to the library. There was more than half an hour before we opened, so I sat at my desk, turned on my laptop and started researching Hugh Davis's history as a director. Mom had said he hadn't done much of significance in the previous eighteen months, so I went back a year and a half and started from there.

What I very quickly found out was that there were just too many productions with too many actors for me to figure out who the two women were that Hugh had bullied. I leaned back in my chair and swung around to look out the window. There had to be a better way.

Chloe Miller came in just after ten with the book of poetry she'd borrowed. She walked over to the desk and held out the book. "Thank you," she said. "The poem was perfect."

"You're so welcome. How are rehearsals going?"

"They're going well. I met your mom, by the way. I like her." She smiled. "Everything's coming together."

"That's good to hear."

Every time I'd seen Chloe she was alone. It struck me that the polished, put-together actress was a little shy. I remembered I'd heard that she'd sat down in the middle of the seniors' reading group and answered their questions when she'd been in the building the other day. "Susan told me you spent half an hour the other morning getting peppered with questions when you were here. Thank you."

"I didn't mind," she said, playing with a hammered-gold ring on her left middle finger. "They were fun. They asked some great questions about staging a production."

"Chloe, are you free around one o'clock?" I asked. "I'd love to take you to lunch."

"For taking a couple of minutes to talk to a few senior citizens?" She shook her head. "It's not necessary, Kathleen."

"It wasn't just a couple of minutes or just a few senior citizens. But if you don't have time, I understand."

"I do have time," she said. She smiled. "It would be fun to have lunch. How about I meet you here at one o'clock?"

"Perfect," I said.

Around eleven thirty Susan poked her head around

my office door. I was deep into the budget and started when she said my name. "Sorry," she said. "Andrew's here with some kind of panel thing that's supposed to go in the gazebo. I thought we should check with you first."

"I better take a look at this," I said. "I'll come down."

Abigail and Andrew were in the parking lot with Burtis Chapman's truck. There was a large lattice-work panel tied down in the bed of the truck.

"Hey, Kathleen," Andrew said. "This is supposed to go at the back of the gazebo. Is that going to be a problem?"

Abigail came around the side of the truck. "Ben wants to use it as a backdrop," she said. "If that's okay."

"How are you planning on keeping it in place?" I asked. The wooden panel was long and wide and I didn't want the gazebo damaged in any way.

"Bungee cords," Andrew said. "It's actually two pieces, hinged. It stands up by itself. The cords are just for added stability."

I leaned over the side of the truck bed. The back-drop looked sturdy enough. "How are you going to keep someone from just walking off with it in the middle of the night?" I said to Andrew.

He grinned at me. "You mean not everyone in Mayville Heights is a law-abiding citizen? I'm shocked."

"Oh, people who live here are honest and law-abiding," Abigail said. "It's just that sometimes we get some 'undesirables' from out of town." She said the whole thing with a completely straight face.

Andrew looked at her a little uncertainly. "Okay," he said. "I'll unload this and we can see if it's going to work."

Abigail caught my eye and winked.

He'd brought a wheeled dolly with him and with a little help he got the backdrop on it and around the building to the gazebo. It took only a few minutes to set it in place.

"What do you think?" Andrew said to Abigail.

"I'm just going to see how it looks from each side," she said, heading across the grass.

He came to stand beside me and look at his handiwork.

"It looks fine to me," I said. "But you didn't answer my question. What are you going to do at night?"

"Oren says there a basement and it's dry."

I nodded. "That would work."

"I saw your mother," Andrew said. He brushed some sawdust off his denim shirt.

"And?"

"She told me to go home. She told me I was a year and a half too late. And she called me a dipwad in Hungarian. At least I think it was Hungarian. And dipwad."

I couldn't help smiling at him. He was trying so hard to fix things between us. Once again I caught myself wondering if I was crazy not to give him a chance. He was funny and handsome, and unlike Marcus, he didn't make a secret of how he felt about me.

He glanced over at Abigail, still studying the backdrop. "Have lunch with me, Kath. Take the afternoon off and we'll play hooky and drive into Minneapolis."

I shook my head. "I can't play hooky. I have budget numbers to go over."

"Then at least have lunch with me."

I stuffed my hands in my pockets and took several steps away from him on the pretext of looking at the gazebo from another angle. "I can't do that, either. I'm having lunch with Chloe Miller."

"The actress from the festival?" he asked, running the palm of his hand over the stubble on his chin.

"Uh-huh."

"Did you notice she has a bit of a limp?"

"I did," I said. "I'm kind of surprised that you did, though. It's not the kind of thing you used to pick up on."

"You're not the only person who's changed, Kathleen," he said.

I raised my eyebrows. "Touché."

He smiled. "Okay, so I didn't actually notice the limp; Abigail did. But I did notice Chloe had scars on her arm. She was helping to waterproof the backdrop. I asked her what happened and she said she was in a car accident. She spent weeks in the hospital."

"I didn't know that," I said.

"Didn't know what?" Abigail asked, coming back across the grass toward us. She glanced at Andrew. "That's fine, by the way, but I think Ben should take a look just to be sure."

"Andrew said Chloe Miller was in an accident. I wondered why I hadn't seen her in anything for so long."

Abigail nodded. "Ben told me that about two years ago she just seemed to drop out of sight. For months no one knew where she was." She rolled her eyes. "You know the kind of stories that start going around. People said she had a drug problem. They said she was in rehab."

Andrew gestured toward the gazebo. "I'm just going to double-check those bungee cords. I'll be right back."

Abigail and I started toward the parking lot.

"So Chloe was in a car accident?" I said.

"She was visiting family in Florida, driving to the beach in a convertible with the top down. A glass-repair truck ran the light and hit the car broadside. There was a lot of broken glass and Chloe was cut all over." Abigail shook her head. "Ben said it was a miracle her face was okay."

"That's horrible."

"Remember when we were talking about how some people think *Yesterday's Child* is jinxed?"

I nodded.

She gave me a grim smile. "Chloe was in a production of *Yesterday's Child* right before her accident."

"C'mon, don't tell me you're starting to believe in the jinx?"

"I don't know. Maybe."

"Really?" I said.

"Originally *Yesterday's Child* was going to be part of the festival lineup." Abigail held out both hands. "There was a fire at the theater in Red Wing and now Hugh's dead."

"No." I shook my head. "I don't believe in jinxes or curses or anything like that."

"Normally I don't, either, Kathleen. But you have to admit there's been a lot of negative energy associated with this festival."

"Hugh Davis isn't dead because of a play," I said.

Abigail looked thoughtfully at me. "Then why is he dead?" she said.

That was the problem. I still didn't know.

20

Chloe arrived at the library at five minutes to one. We walked over to Eric's and settled at one of the quieter tables against the end wall. After Claire had poured coffee and taken our orders, Chloe took off her jacket and folded her fingers around her mug.

"I like this place," she said, looking around the room with a smile. "It reminds me of this little place in Florida called Alexander's."

"Florida's home?" I asked.

She nodded. "What about you?"

"Boston," I said. "My parents are there and so are my brother and sister. Mom's been in LA doing *Wild and Wonderful* and Ethan is about to go on the road with his band, but Boston is home. We all end up back there eventually."

"This is a beautiful little town," she said. "Everywhere I turn I see something that looks like a postcard. Did you see the sun coming up over the water this morning?"

I nodded.

"The other day I saw three sailboats anchored in the water and the surface was so still it looked like glass. I've taken dozens and dozens of pictures and I only got here Saturday."

"I did the same thing when I first got here," I said with a smile.

Chloe tipped her head to one side. "Do you mind if I ask why you're a librarian and not a performer?"

I laughed. "No. I don't mind. I'm not a performer because I have absolutely no talent. I couldn't carry a tune if it came with handles. I have two left feet and calling me wooden when I'm onstage is an insult—to wood."

Chloe laughed. "Kathleen, there's no way you can be that awful."

"Sadly, there is," I said with a grin. "I just didn't get the performer gene. What about you? Did you always want to be an actor?"

She traced a finger around the rim of her mug. "You know, I never thought about it that way. It's just what I've always done. I was onstage before I could walk."

Claire came back then with our orders of Eric's beef noodle soup and thick slices of sourdough bread, still warm from the oven. As we ate we talked about our favorite plays. I was surprised to find out Chloe had done several musicals.

Claire brought the coffeepot around for refills as we finished our soup. "Dessert?" she asked. "Eric made chocolate pudding cake."

"I shouldn't," I said.

"I didn't ask whether you should," Claire said with a sly grin. "I asked if you wanted to."

"Okay, I want to," I said. "Please."

"Me too, please," Chloe said.

Claire smiled. "I'll be right back."

Chloe glanced at her watch.

"What time do you need to be back at the theater?" I asked.

"Not until two thirty, for a fitting." She leaned forward to brush part of a dried leaf off her pants. I noticed she was wearing a pair of gray spike-heeled leather boots. They added a good three inches to her height.

"Chloe, is the festival really going to be ready to open next week?" I asked.

"Absolutely." She took a sip of her coffee. ""Don't tell me you believe all that silliness that the festival is jinxed because of *Yesterday's Child*?"

"No," I said. "It's just that with the fire and Hugh's death there's a lot to come back from."

"You know the old saying: The show must go on."

I nodded as Claire served our dessert. "I know. I also know a lot of actors are very superstitious."

Chloe picked up her spoon. "I'm superstitious about some things, but not about *Yesterday's Child*. I was in the very first production. Hugh directed. You probably knew that." She tried the pudding and smiled across the table at me. "Mmmmm. This is good."

I reached for my own spoon. "So how did all the rumors start that the play is jinxed?"

"The script is very dark in places. Hugh is . . . was pretty intense as a director. One of the actors quit the first week of rehearsals. Then there was the fire at the theater." She shrugged. "That was really all it took. After that, the idea that the show was jinxed just took on a life of its own. You know how those things go."

I nodded. I'd been around enough theaters to know how quickly rumors spread in a closed community like a production in rehearsal.

Chloe licked a bit of chocolate from the back of her spoon. "Every production has issues, but every time there was a problem with *Yesterday's Child*, someone would start talking about the jinx."

She set her spoon down, pushed back her left sleeve and extended her arm. It was etched with a web of fine scars.

"Abigail told me you'd been in an accident," I said.

Chloe pushed the sleeve down and rested her arm back on the edge of the table. "Do you know what people assume when they see those scars? They think I did it to myself."

What had my mother said about Hugh? *I heard from an unimpeachable source that he pushed one of his leading ladies so hard she started cutting herself.* If Abigail hadn't told me about Chloe's accident, I might have thought it had been Chloe.

As if she could read my mind, she tipped her head forward and brushed her hair away from the left side of her face. I could see more scars snaking up her neck into her hairline, scars that clearly had been stitched by a doctor. They hadn't been made by Chloe cutting herself. I felt my face flush with embarrassment.

"I was in an accident right after the play finished its run," she said. "That was the jinx, people said. Another actor had problems with his voice and had to have surgery. More so-called proof." She shook her head. "Even though Ben had dropped *Yesterday's Child* from our schedule months ago, when the fire happened at the other theater it was enough to get the whole idea that the play somehow has a black cloud over it resurrected. Maybe if the four of us from that original production hadn't been part of the festival, all the talk wouldn't have started again. I don't know."

I frowned at her. "What do you mean, the four of you?"

"Hugh, me, Hannah and Ben."

I stared at her, my spoon halfway to my mouth. "Hannah and Ben were part of the original staging of *Yesterday's Child*?"

Chloe scraped a bit of chocolate from the side of the heavy stoneware bowl. "Uh-huh. Ben was the original director. So I guess technically he wasn't really part of the show."

"He was replaced by Hugh?"

She nodded. "Before we started rehearsing. The producers didn't like Ben's interpretation of the script. Rumor has it that Ben showed up before the first rehearsal and he and Hugh had a screaming match backstage, although I didn't hear anything." She reached for her coffee. "Of course that just added to the myth that the production was jinxed."

"I've been thinking about doing a display at the library with information about the plays and the main actors," I said. "I might need to pick your brain."

"Anytime," she said with a smile. She folded her fingers around the stoneware mug. "I was surprised that Ben offered the festival job to Hugh. There was a lot of bad blood between them, from what I heard."

"I don't think Ben is the kind of person who holds a grudge."

"Life's too short for that kind of thing," Chloe said.

"So Hannah had a part in the play, too?" I asked. The pudding cake was delicious, but I was getting distracted by the conversation.

Chloe held up her thumb and index finger about a half inch apart. "Very small, but she was very good. I remember because she was working on a script herself then, something to do with some volunteer work she was doing with a program for teen alcoholics. She used to pick Hugh's brain whenever she got the chance." She drank the last of her coffee and set the mug on the table. "I'm sorry, Kathleen. That was a very long-winded answer to your question. The festival is going to be wonderful. There's no jinx, no black cloud over our heads."

"I'm glad to hear that," I said. "And I'm looking forward to seeing you onstage."

We finished dessert and Chloe glanced at her watch again. "I really need to get going now," she said. She reached for her purse and I put out a hand to stop her.

"You're my guest," I said.

She hesitated.

"Please," I said.

She smiled. "All right. Thank you."

We both got to our feet. "I enjoyed this, Kathleen," Chloe said. "I hope we can do it again while I'm here. Next time my treat."

"I'd like that," I said.

I picked Mom up at the Stratton at the end of the day. Her hair was pulled back in an unkempt knot, her reading glasses, lenses smudged with fingerprints, were perched at the end of her nose, and there were papers poking out of the top of her large woven tote.

She got in the truck, fastened her seat belt and slumped against the seat with a groan.

"Good day?" I asked.

She turned her head and gave me a huge smile. "Wonderful," she said.

I heated up the remainder of the pea soup for our supper with some of Rebecca's bread. We sat across from each other at the table, Owen and Hercules parked beside Mom. I figured they thought she was the best possibility for a little ham from the soup.

"Mom, do you know anything about Ben directing the very first staging of the play *Yesterday's Child*?" I asked.

"Does this have anything to do with the silly idea that the play is jinxed?" she said.

"Not really, no," I said. "I just heard that Ben was supposed to direct the original production but he was replaced by Hugh Davis, and there was some animosity between them. I wondered why Ben offered Hugh a job if he couldn't stand the man."

Mom dipped a bit of bread in her soup and popped it in her mouth before she answered. "First of all, the theater community is a very small world. If we didn't work with people we don't like, we'd never work at all." She smiled at me. "And second, Ben is not the kind of person to hold on to hard feelings. I've known him for years. Whoever told you that got it wrong."

She broke off another piece of bread and dropped it in the bowl. "I like your detective."

I held up a finger. "Number one, he's not my detective." I put a second finger up with the first one. "And number two, you said two or three sentences to the man. How can you decide you like him just based on that?"

She waited a moment before she spoke. "Is there a number three?"

"No."

She smiled then. "He's definitely your detective, Katydid. The way you two look at each other makes that much very clear. And as for how I can tell I like him, well, I'm a very good judge of character." She scooped a chunk of ham from her dish and ate it while two furry faces followed her every move. "The two of you are lousy actors, by the way."

"Excuse me?" I said, dribbling soup onto the back of my hand.

"You're acting like you're not crazy about him. He's acting like he's not crazy about you. But the rest of the world, the audience, can see right through you."

I wiped my hand with my napkin and frowned at her across the table. "This is the real world, not a production, and Marcus and I aren't acting."

"'Quod fere totus mundus exerceat histrionem,'" she said, waving her spoon for punctuation at the end.

"Did you just quote 'all the world's a stage' to me in Latin?" I asked.

"'All the world's a stage, and all the men and women merely players.'" She smiled at me. "No, I didn't. But you're close. I quoted Petronius to you. 'Because almost all the world are actors.'"

"Thank you," I said dryly. "That was so helpful."

"It could be if you thought about it." Mom put her spoon down. "When I'm part of a production, what am I doing?"

I shrugged. "Acting. Directing. Trying to entertain people. Maybe make them think."

She nodded. "I'm trying to get the audience to look at things a certain way. Just for a little while. I want them to forget that what they're really looking at is just actors in costume on a stage." She leaned back in her chair. "Do you remember the first time you saw *Peter Pan* onstage?"

I nodded.

"Remember the scene when Tinkerbell is dying and Peter yells, 'Clap if you believe in fairies'?"

I smiled at the memory. The clapping had begun slowly and spread through the theater like a wave of sound. I'd been enchanted when Tinkerbell came to life again and soared over the stage.

"The audience claps every time," Mom said. "But there's always someone who doesn't. There are always one or two people who can't get past the fact that Tinkerbell is just an actor being pulled through the air in a harness. They can't stop looking at the wires long enough to see the magic."

She reached up and took off her earrings. "That's what you and your detective are doing. You're too focused on the wires to see the magic."

She got to her feet and kissed the top of my head. "I have to brush my teeth before I go back to the theater."

I drove Mom down to the Stratton and told her I'd be back in a couple of hours to get her. There was no sign of either cat when I got home. I wandered into the living room, thinking maybe I'd call and see if Roma was back from her visit to Eddie.

Owen was lying on his back in the middle of the footstool, feet in the air.

"Owen!" I snapped. "What are you doing?"

He rolled over, jumped to his feet, and immediately hung his head. For months I'd suspected Owen was napping on the stool. It was old and I knew the fabric wouldn't stand up to a cat's claws, so the only time either cat got anywhere near the footstool was if he was sitting on my lap or sprawled across my legs.

I glared at him. "Get down," I said.

He jumped to the floor and slunk past me to the kitchen.

Mom had been sitting in the wing chair before she left, talking to my dad on the phone. She'd left her purse behind and it had slipped to the floor, spreading its contents all over the polished hardwood.

I bent down and started picking everything up. Mom's wallet felt like it had a couple of pounds of change inside. And why did she have a little tin of bacon-flavored mints?

I thought about what she'd said. Was she right? Were Marcus and I focusing on the wrong thing? Were we getting too distracted by our differences?

A clump of gray cat hair floated down from the top of the footstool. Owen was losing his touch. I knew he'd been lounging up there for months, but he'd always managed to be sitting on the floor, the picture of innocence, when I walked into the room.

And then I got it. I looked at the tin of bacon mints in my hand and suddenly I wasn't trying to push a square peg in a round hole. I'd been had. By a small gray tabby cat, and not for the first time.

I sat back on my heels. Owen let me catch him on the footstool to divert my attention from the greater sin of rummaging through my mother's purse in search of the almost irresistible smell of bacon. Could a cat really be capable of that much subterfuge and misdirection? I was fairly certain this one could.

Suddenly it was as if everything had shifted just a little to the right and now everything was lined up properly, every peg sliding into the right hole. If Owen could misdirect my attention, why couldn't someone who'd spent their life creating a fantasy, making people believe in fairies and forget about the wires, do the same thing?

I put everything back in Mom's purse except the little white tin and then I went to the kitchen. Owen was under the table doing his shamefaced act. I leaned down and looked at him. "Come out from there," I said. "I know what you're up to."

He came to stand in front of me and I held out the little tin. "Were you looking for these?"

He meowed and reached out a paw before he remembered he was supposed to be pretending to be guilty over rolling on the footstool. He hung his head again.

I patted my lap. "Give it up, Fuzz Face," I said. "I know you went through Mom's purse and spread everything all over the floor looking for these and then you couldn't get them open. You left teeth marks on the package."

He understood either my words or my tone because he gave up the act, climbed onto my lap and leaned over to lick the plastic wrapping around the tin.

I shook my head. "That's just sad," I said. "These are not for cats." I set the mints on the table.

He got a sulky look on his face. "They're breath mints with the taste of bacon. No real bacon." I shook my head. "No bacon."

He clearly understood the "no bacon" part. He leaned his head against my arm and made a sound a lot like a sigh.

I stroked his fur. "You should be in trouble," I said. "You should be on the kitty equivalent of bread and water for the next couple of days."

He lifted his head and looked at me. We both knew that wasn't going to happen.

I gave him what I hoped was a stern look. "What you did was bad. Very bad. You don't go through people's things just because you think you smell bacon. Are we clear?"

"Merow," he said after a moment.

I picked him up and got to my feet. "The only

thing that's saving you is that thanks to your little stunt I think I know who killed Hugh Davis and maybe even why."

Owen nuzzled my chin, looking very pleased with himself. I kissed the top of his head. "Now all I have to do is prove it."

21

My laptop was in my briefcase. I set it on the kitchen table. The moment I sat down Owen jumped onto my lap. Clearly I was going to have help with the research I needed to do.

He squinted at the screen as I brought up my favorite search engine. There was a lot more information about the play *Yesterday's Children* than I'd expected. I scanned several articles written about the first production of the play. Then I typed in Ben Saroyan's name to narrow the search. Owen stayed perched on my lap, eyes on the screen as though he was reading as well. And for all I knew, maybe he was. It didn't take me long to find what I was looking for.

There was one more thing I wanted to check on. "Cross your paws that these archives are online," I said to Owen.

He looked down at his feet and then up at me.

I scratched the top of his head. "Never mind," I said.

Some newspapers have their entire archive of back issues searchable online. The paper I was interested in turned out to be one of them. It didn't take long to finish my search.

I leaned back in the chair. Owen shifted on my lap and tipped his head to one side, eyeing me with curiosity. I stroked his fur. "I know the who," I said. "And now I think I understand the why."

He meowed softly in what I decided to believe was agreement.

I stretched and looked at my watch. It was almost time to head down to the Stratton. I set Owen on the floor, put the computer away and ran upstairs for a sweater.

I thought about calling Marcus and decided that part of the puzzle could wait until later.

Ben and Abigail were in the production office at the theater. "Hi, Kathleen," Abigail said, getting up from her makeshift desk. "I think your mom's upstairs. I'll go tell her you're here." She gave my arm a squeeze. "She's wonderful."

"There's no rush," I called after her. I leaned against the door frame.

Ben got up and poured himself a cup of coffee. "Would you like a cup?" he asked.

I shook my head. "No thanks. How did rehearsals go today?"

"A lot better than yesterday. Your mother's a good director. I think we're going to be ready for next week."

I grinned at him. "So the festival's not jinxed."

He exhaled loudly and shook his head. "Why do people believe in that rubbish?"

"I don't know. Maybe because it's easier to believe in a jinx or a curse than it is to accept that bad things happen and sometimes we don't have any control over that."

"The first time Hugh mentioned *Yesterday's Children* I should have said no," Ben said, adding sugar to his coffee.

"Weren't you supposed to direct the original production?"

He nodded. "The producers replaced me with Hugh before rehearsals even started. His vision was a lot darker than the way I saw the script. That's why I considered adding the play to the lineup here. It would have been my chance to show a different interpretation of the script. I don't see it being as bleak a play as Hugh—and pretty much every director since—did."

The door frame was digging into my back and I shifted sideways a little. "So you weren't mad at Hugh because he took your job?"

Ben's blue eyes narrowed. "What?" he said.

"I've heard a couple of rumors that you two didn't speak for a long time because he got the *Yesterday's Children* directing job."

He gave a snort. "Hugh and I stopped speaking more than once, but not because of that play. He was a good director, but he could be a first-class prick."

He picked up his coffee. "Getting replaced was the best thing that could have happened to me. I did *Lesser Mortals* instead. I spent a semester teaching at Tisch. It was all good."

That was pretty much what I'd put together from my Internet search.

"So why did you offer him the festival director's job if you thought he was a jerk?"

He sighed. "Sentiment. We went to college together. He lobbied hard for the job and I figured I could keep him from making a total ass of himself." He swiped his hand over his chin. "Maybe I was wrong."

I heard a noise behind me then and saw my mother coming down the stairs, pulling bobby pins out of her hair. She smiled as she caught sight of me.

I smiled at Ben. "Have a good night," I said.

"How did things go?" I asked Mom as we drove up the hill.

"Good," she said, rubbing the back of her neck with one hand. "I have to say it's a little peculiar to step in like this at the last minute, but everyone's trying to pull it all together."

"They like you," I said, slowing down to let a man walking a golden Lab cross the street.

Mom leaned her head against the back of the seat. "I mean no disrespect to the man, but that's because they didn't like Hugh."

"Ben said he was a good director." I glanced over at Mom, who turned her head to look at me and rolled her eyes.

"Ben sees the best in people, Katydid. He's that kind of man. And to be fair, I think Hugh Davis was a good director. But he got results through intimidation. Plainly spoken, he was a bully."

From the corner of my eye I saw her lean her head back and close her eyes. "I don't work that way."

"Why do you think someone as nice as Chloe Miller was involved with him, then?" I asked.

She lifted her head to look at me. "Chloe Miller and Hugh Davis? I don't think so, sweetie. In fact, I was surprised to see her here, but Ben said she lobbied hard for the part. Anyway, she isn't Hugh's type. She doesn't have the attributes he went for."

I put on my turn signal and pulled into the driveway. "And those would be?"

Mom put a hand to her mouth and yawned. "What your brother euphemistically refers to as 'big teeth.'" She shook her head. "The man was such a stereotype. He was canoodling with the wardrobe assistant and she's all of twenty. Very . . . toothy."

"Canoodling?" I said as we walked around the side of the house.

"I was trying not to be crass, sweetie," she said, reaching over to pat my cheek. "Would you rather I say he was—"

"Never mind," I interrupted, holding up both hands.

"What can I get you?" I asked as we stepped into the kitchen, where Owen and Hercules were waiting. "Another cup of tea?"

She nodded. "That would be wonderful. I want to take a look at both scripts before I go to bed." She smiled down at the cats. "Hello, you two. What a nice welcome to come home to."

"The big chair in the living room has the best light," I said. "I'll bring your tea in when it's ready."

Mom took her overflowing tote bag into the living room, trailed by her furry fan club.

I put the water on to boil and fished my cell phone out of my bag. Marcus answered on the third ring. "Hi, Kathleen," he said.

"Hi, Marcus," I said. Why did I smile whenever I heard his voice? "Is Hannah there?"

"She just walked in the door. Do you want to talk to her?"

I slid the container of tea bags across the counter. "Would it be okay if I came over for a few minutes?"

"You figured something out," he said.

"I think so."

"We'll be here."

"I'll see you soon."

When the tea was ready I took a cup in to Mom, along with two of the brownies I'd taken out of the freezer earlier. She was in the wing chair, feet tucked underneath her, with her glasses on her lap. Owen and Hercules were curled up on the floor beside the footstool.

"Umm, how did you know I needed some chocolate?" she said when she saw the brownies.

"I know you," I said.

Two furry heads swung around at the word "chocolate."

I wiped my hands on my jeans. "I need to go out for a little while," I said. "Could I get you anything else before I go?"

Mom shook her head. "Are you going to see Detective Gordon?"

"Yes," I said. "But not for anything . . . romantic."

She leaned forward and set her glasses on the footstool. "Katydid, do you know why I married your father?"

"Which time?" I said dryly.

She laughed. "Okay. I deserved that." She shifted in the chair. "The first time we were married he drove me crazy. I didn't see how I could ever live with him for the rest of my life. I was sure I wasn't going to make it to Tuesday. But when we were apart I hated it. I didn't want a man I could live with. I wanted someone I couldn't live without."

She looked at me for a long moment and then she reached for her glasses again. "I appreciate you not rolling your eyes," she said.

I leaned down and kissed the top of her head. "I love you," I said. "I'll see you later." I thought about her words all the way to Marcus's house. It wasn't as simple as she made it out to be.

If I went back to Boston with Andrew, things would be easy—no complications, no turmoil. It was tempting. Marcus and I couldn't seem to get a relationship started, let alone keep it going. But if Andrew was a man I could live with, did that mean Marcus was the man I couldn't live without?

Marcus was sitting on his back steps, elbows propped on his long legs.

"Hi," I said.

"Hi." He gestured at the back door. "Hannah's inside."

"Did you tell her I was coming?"

He nodded. "You know who killed Hugh Davis, don't you?"

"I think so. I know who and I think I know why. And I can't prove any of it."

He looked up at me. I could see the stubble on his chin in the light from the kitchen window. He looked tired. "You figured out how Hannah is tied up in this." He didn't phrase it as a question.

"I did." I shifted from one foot to the other. "I can just . . . I can just go."

"No." He exhaled slowly. "Somebody killed the man. I know it's not my case, but I can't do nothing and take the chance that maybe *that* somebody is going to walk away." He stood up and brushed off his jeans. "C'mon in."

Hannah was in the living room, curled up in one corner of the sofa with a script. She was wearing gray sweatpants and a red hoodie. Her bare toes were tucked down between two sofa cushions.

"Hi," she said. She pulled her knees up to her chest and wrapped her arms around them.

Marcus sat on the arm of the chair and I took the chair.

"Hannah, do you remember telling me that Ben didn't really like Hugh?"

She nodded.

"Who told you that?"

She frowned. "Chloe, I think. She's worked with them both. Why?"

I rubbed my fingers over the arm of the chair. "It's not true."

She looked at me, clearly puzzled. "Why would Chloe lie about something like that?"

"Because it made Ben look like a suspect in Hugh's death," I said.

Her blue eyes widened. "You think Chloe killed Hugh? That's crazy. Why would she want to kill Hugh?"

I took a deep breath. "Because of what happened when you were all working on *Yesterday's Children*."

The color drained out of her face. "That stupid play," she whispered.

"Hugh bullied his actors, didn't he?"

Hannah nodded. "He did. He pulled some incredible performances out of people, but I didn't like the way he went about it. "

I glanced over at Marcus. I couldn't read his expression. "I heard a story that he rode one actress so hard she started cutting herself."

Hannah pulled at the fabric of her sweatpants. "I heard that, too. I don't know if it's true."

"I think it is," I said. "I think the actress was Chloe. I think that's how she got those scars on her arm."

Hannah shook her head. "No. She was in a car accident."

My palms were sweating and I wiped them on my jeans. "I don't think so. I did a search in the archives of the newspaper in Chloe's hometown in Florida. I can't find anything about an accident. I don't think there was one."

"Why did she lie?" Marcus asked.

"I'm not positive, but I think probably because she didn't want anyone to know she'd had psychological problems. She probably thought she wouldn't get hired if word got around."

"She wouldn't have," Hannah said. She looked at me and something changed in her face. "You think Chloe killed Hugh." She shook her head again. "No. Not Chloe."

I leaned forward, arms on my knees. "I think she lied about when she got to town. She told me that Hugh wanted her to take part in the festival when really she was the one who went after the job."

"Why would Chloe want to kill Hugh? It doesn't make any sense."

"It does when you know that Chloe had to back out of a movie role because of her psychological issues—issues that Hugh contributed to. That same part turned out to be the breakout role for the actress who replaced her. There's already talk of an Oscar nomination for a movie she has coming out later this year."

"Chloe thought that could have been her life, if it hadn't been for Hugh," Marcus said. He shook his head.

I steeled myself for my next question. "Hannah, did you see anything that night at the marina?"

"I already told you, Kathleen. I wasn't there." Her eyes never left my face and nothing in her expression gave her away, but I saw her left hand clench tightly into a fist.

"I know about the Share the Change, Be the Change contest," I said.

"What contest?" Marcus asked.

I didn't say anything. I kept my eyes fixed on Hannah and waited for her to answer.

"How did you figure it out?" she said in a low voice.

"Chloe told me you were working on a script when the two of you were rehearsing *Yesterday's Children*. She said it was based on your volunteer work with a program for teenage alcoholics."

Hannah nodded. "Hester's Girls. It was a terrible script," she said softly.

"But it was a winning article."

She gave me a small smile. "They'd all heard about the Share the Change, Be the Change contest, where people could vote online for the most deserving project. They needed the money so badly." She chewed the corner of her lip. "There's never enough money.

It's a program for teenage drunks. There're no cute little puppies or big-eyed seals, just kids who get into fights and puke on their shoes."

She shrugged. "Deidre—the piece was her story— had them all convinced she could write an article that would get Hester's Girls enough votes to win. When I read what she'd written, I knew it was a pipe dream. And I knew I could do better."

"How did Hugh find out?"

"He didn't. Not for sure. He'd seen a rough draft of the piece I was working on back when I was in *Yesterday's Children*. He read the article that won. He was suspicious." She shook her head. "The thing was, he didn't need proof. All he had to do was raise the suspicion. Deidre would have caved. They would have lost the money."

"He thought you would help him get the directing job before you'd let Hester's Girls lose the money," I said. Hugh had been willing to blackmail Abigail for money. Why not Hannah?

Hannah closed her eyes for a moment and nodded. Then she looked at Marcus. "I couldn't tell you."

He reached over and grabbed her hand. "You could have," he said, his voice raspy. "I'm sorry you didn't know you could."

"Hannah, what happened the night Hugh was killed?" I asked.

"I got back from Red Wing sometime between five thirty and six. I came in the side entrance and I heard Hugh and Abigail talking. It was like she was flirting with him. I knew there was something going on between them—I'd seen them whispering about something more than once. I followed them. I thought maybe I'd catch them in some kind of compromising situation and I could . . . hold that over Hugh's head."

"Except you didn't," I said.

"I didn't even drive into the marina parking lot. I like Abigail. I couldn't do that to her. I pulled over and sat on the side of the road for a while. You're right—I did drive past the marina. And I really did go up to that bar and get drunk. I thought . . . I thought it was all going to come out."

She looked at me, tight lines around her eyes and mouth. "You're really certain it was Chloe who killed him?"

I nodded. "I just don't know how to prove it."

22

Hannah went to take a bath. Before she left, Marcus wrapped her in a hug.

"I'm in trouble," she said. "What I did was fraud."

"We'll figure it out," Marcus said, kissing the top of her head.

Hannah turned to me. "If Chloe killed Hugh, it's because she's sick."

I nodded.

"I'm not making excuses for her, or saying he deserved what happened, but Hugh helped make her that way."

"I know that," I said.

"Thank you for . . ." She shrugged. "Thank you."

After she left the room, Marcus turned to me. "What are you going to do?"

I rubbed my wrist. It was starting to ache, which meant rain no matter what the forecast said. "I don't know. I don't have any real proof, just a lot of maybes and guesses."

My cell phone rang then. "I better check that," I

said. "I left my mother home with Owen and Hercules. Who knows what the three of them could get into."

I pulled the phone out of my bag. CHLOE MILLER, the screen read. I held it up so Marcus could see as well.

He frowned. "Why is she calling you?"

"Let's find out," I said.

"Hi, Kathleen. It's Chloe," she said. She sounded warm and friendly and I wondered how much work it took to keep up the act.

I sank down onto the arm of the sofa where Marcus had been sitting. "Hi," I said.

"At lunchtime you mentioned you were thinking about putting up a display with photos and background on some of the people involved in the festival. Are you still going to do that?"

"I think so," I said. "I have a friend who's an artist and I think she'll help."

"I have something you might be interested in," she said. "I found some pictures in my bag. I have no idea how long they've been there. They're from a rehearsal of *Yesterday's Children*. There are a couple with Hugh and Hannah and me. If you'd like to use them, it's fine with me."

"I would," I said. "Thank you."

"I'm sitting in the lounge at the hotel. Could you join me right now?"

"I could be there in about fifteen minutes," I said.

"Perfect," she said. "I'll see you soon."

I ended the call and looked at Marcus. "I know

what you're going to say. There's something off about Chloe calling me now. And then we're going to argue back and forth about whether I should go and whether you should go with me."

"That pretty much sums it up," he said.

"So can we just fast-forward through all that and go?"

He hesitated. I had no idea what I was going to say if he said no.

But he didn't.

Chloe was sitting at the hotel bar talking to the bartender. I could tell by the goofy smile on his face that he was charmed. I swallowed the lump in my throat. Hannah was right. Chloe wasn't a bad person. She was sick. Part of me hated that I was about to go knock down all the walls she'd worked so hard to put up around herself. But she had killed someone. I knew I was right about that. And no matter what Hugh Davis had done, he hadn't deserved that.

I walked over to Chloe and touched her shoulder. "Hi," I said.

She turned. "Hi, Kathleen," she said. "I'm glad you came." She looked back at the bartender and flashed him a smile that probably made his week. I thought about Andrew, who did the same thing to women. "Thanks, Charlie," she said. "You have a good night." She slid off the stool and said, "Let's go."

I looked at her uncertainly. "Where are we going?" I said. "You said you had some pictures for me."

She nodded. "I do. I left my briefcase in the car. C'mon."

She knew. Somehow she'd guessed that I had figured out she'd killed Hugh. I knew it was a very bad idea to go anywhere with Chloe Miller.

"It's been a long day, Chloe," I said. "I'll just order a cup of coffee and wait here while you go get them."

She moved a step closer to me so her arm was pressed against my side. She looked at me and smiled. "I have a gun in my pocket," she said, just the same way she might have said, "I like crème brûlée."

I swallowed down the sour taste in my throat. "Are you going to shoot me?"

She shook her head. "As long as you come with me, I'm not going to shoot anyone. If you don't, I'm going to have to turn around and shoot Charlie, the very nice bartender." She smiled again. "I don't think you'd want that on your conscience."

Chloe was a lot sicker than I'd realized. But Marcus was waiting outside. Once he saw us come out the front doors he'd know something was wrong. All I had to do was stay calm. "I'll come with you," I said.

We moved toward the door. To anyone who noticed us we probably looked like two good friends, heads together, catching up on old times.

"This way," Chloe said, turning toward the back of the hotel when we stepped into the lobby.

"I thought we were going outside." I motioned toward the wide glass and metal doors.

"We are," she said. "But we're going this way." She narrowed her green eyes at me. "Hannah's big brother's out there, isn't he?" She shook her head. "That's a little obvious, Kathleen. You might as well have put Big Bird out there with a badge."

I told myself to remember that when I got out of this, so I could tell Marcus. *Because I was going to get out of this.*

Chloe led us down a hallway and out a side entrance that opened onto a narrow alleyway and then the street. She pulled her hand out of her pocket. She was holding a gun. "Just in case you thought I was bluffing."

"Where are we going?" I said. My hands were shaking, but she couldn't see that and so far I'd managed to keep the shaking out of my voice.

"We're going to go for a walk along the river."

"And what?" I said. "I'll have an unfortunate accident and fall in?"

"Something like that," she said with a smile. She made an offhand gesture with one hand. "I know it's very clichéd, but things become clichéd for a reason. Because they work."

We crossed the street and headed for the boardwalk. I wondered if I could run and then roll behind one of the cars parked along the street before she could shoot me.

"You can't," she said, nudging me with the gun. "I know what you're thinking. I saw you look at those cars. You're wondering if you can get to one of them before I could shoot you. You can't—and I would shoot you. I'm a very good shot. I wouldn't miss."

"You can't get away with this, Chloe," I said. "It's crazy."

She shook her head and gave me a look of pity. "Of course I can. We went for a walk—your idea. You got too close to the edge of the embankment and went over. I'll be distraught. I'll try to crawl down and save you. No one will doubt my grief." She sighed. "Sadly, you'll be dead, head cracked open on those rocks like a pumpkin falling off the back of a pickup truck."

She nudged me again with the gun. "And don't use the word 'crazy,' Kathleen. It's disrespectful. 'Psychologically challenged' sounds much nicer."

We crossed the boardwalk and cut across the grass. I concentrated on breathing, trying to keep the panic down so I could think clearly.

"How did you know?" I asked.

She was scanning the shoreline as we walked. "That you guessed what had happened to Hugh? Ben. He told me you asked him about a rumor you'd heard that there had been bad blood between Hugh and him. He wondered how it had gotten started." She looked at me then. "I told him I had no idea."

We were almost at the edge where the grass gave way to the rock wall, huge boulders that protected the shoreline from being eroded by the water.

I needed to buy time. I glanced back over my

shoulder. There was no sign of Marcus, or anyone else. "What I don't understand is why you shot him. Why now?"

"He deserved it," she said, as though the fact were obvious. "I should have shot him years ago, but I just never got the chance. I couldn't let this opportunity pass."

"Because of *Yesterday's Children*. Hugh pushed you so hard you ended up . . ." I hesitated, not wanting to push her any closer to the edge—physical or psychological—than she already was.

"I ended up in a hospital," she said. Her free hand played with the scarf at her neck. "You can say the word, Kathleen. I was in the hospital because I was sick and that was Hugh's fault."

"You didn't have a car accident."

She smiled. "I should have guessed that you'd have good research skills."

I needed to keep her talking. "How did you get the scars?"

She ran her hand over her wrist. "These ones are Hugh's fault," she said. "The other ones . . ." She exhaled slowly. "I banged my head against a window . . . a few times."

"I'm sorry," I said softly.

Chloe had stopped walking. "Hugh wasn't sorry," she said. "I had a part in a movie. Jessica Lawrence replaced me. You know what they're saying about her now? She's probably going to get an Oscar nomination." She stared up at the sky, a canopy of inky darkness sprinkled with stars. "That was supposed to be me. That was supposed to be my life." She looked at me. "I wanted him to apologize. He laughed at me. He laughed. It was the wrong thing to do. It was rude." She shrugged. "So I shot him."

I looked over at the rocks piled on top of each other, seemingly all sharp, jagged edges. About six feet down, off to the left a little, I could see what looked like a flat ledge. Maybe, just maybe, I could land on that flat space and get back against the rocks so Chloe couldn't see me. I swallowed the lump in my throat, except it wouldn't go down.

Chloe looked around. There was no one on the boardwalk, nearby or in the distance, no one chasing a dog across the grass, no kissing teenagers getting busy under a tree.

I thought about what I'd learned from Maggie about visualization. I could hear her voice in my head: *See yourself there.*

I saw myself on that narrow rock ledge. I saw myself alive. And then before I had a chance to think about what I was going to do, I did it.

I jumped.

23

I flung out my arms and caught nothing but air for a moment. Then I hit the rocks and started to slide, almost out of control. I wasn't sure which way was up. I scrambled for something, anything to hold on to while gravel pelted me like rain and above me on the embankment Chloe screamed.

And then my feet connected with something solid. I bent my knees and shifted all my weight forward, trying to hug the rock wall. Jagged bits of rock jabbed through my clothes and scraped my skin. My right foot slipped on the slick face of the rock ledge, but my left one held. The top half of my body kept sliding. There was nowhere to find a handhold—and then suddenly my fingers caught an edge of rock. I held on for dear life with one foot and one hand.

There were rocks in my hair, dirt and bits of gravel in my eyes and mouth, and I was scraped and bruised, but I was alive. I eased my free hand down and wrapped my entire arm around a large rock that jutted out beside me. Over my head I could hear

Chloe calling my name. I hoped that meant she couldn't see me. I fought the urge to cough and pressed myself tighter against the rock face.

Slowly I bent my right knee and pulled my leg in closer to my body. My hands were trembling and my left leg was cramped, but I had no intention of letting go. I closed my eyes while my breathing slowed to normal—or as close to normal as I could get.

I turned my head to the right, the only direction I could really see anything. I was less than five feet from the riverbank. If I could get down without Chloe spotting me, I could run to the marina for help.

A stream of gravel skittered down the slope and hit my shoulder. I tipped my head and looked up. Incredibly, Chloe was starting to climb down. I had to start moving. I knew that once I did she'd know where I was. I was banking on the idea that she wouldn't be able to climb and hold a gun at the same time.

I shifted my weight, the way I would in tai chi class, and felt below me with one foot. After a moment I found a foothold. I loosed my death grip on the rock to my left and began to climb down. That started another slide of rocks and gravel, but I kept moving, feeling for a handhold and then another place to put my foot.

I didn't think about the palms of my hands, scraped raw, or the stab of pain in my right ankle every time it pressed against the huge boulders. I just kept moving downward, down to the riverbank and safety.

A rock as big as my fist bounced off my shoulder. I sucked in a sharp breath as pain ran from my shoulder to my wrist. My fingers went numb and lost their hold on an edge of rock. My body shook, holding on with four fingers and one foot to just inches of rock. Then my free foot found an edge and I caught my balance again.

A smooth piece of stone bounced off a boulder beside me and arced out into the water. I looked over my head in time to see an arm launch another rock, about the size of a turnip, down the embankment. It hit a rock maybe a foot over my head, sending a stream of gravel into my face. Chloe had stopped climbing and was throwing rocks, trying to knock me off the rock wall. Caught in a place where the wall curved, I couldn't see how far away the ground was. I was guessing less than three feet. I pushed away from the rocks and jumped out and back, hoping there would be something soft to land on.

My feet hit a patch of scrabbly bushes and long grass. My left ankle gave way and I landed hard on my hip. But I was down and I was safe. Staying low to the ground, I crab-walked farther down, onto the riverbank, squeezing myself into a space between a massive boulder and a patch of tall grass.

I wasn't sure I could run to the marina. I wasn't even sure I could walk. And I'd lost my phone.

Chloe was moving again, working her way slowly down the rocks.

Where was Marcus?

I felt around on the ground for something, anything, I could use to defend myself. I found a piece of stone about the size of my hand, edges smoothed by the water. I curled my fingers around it and slowly eased upright, grateful for the sound of falling rocks dislodged by Chloe that masked any noise I made.

She made it to the ground. I saw her look down at her feet and I realized too late that she could see my trail, marks that my hands and feet had made as I scrambled to what I'd thought was safety.

I was out of choices. I ran at her, or maybe fell at her was closer to the truth. I swung the rock, catching her on the right side of her head, just above her temple. She crumpled like a wet paper bag. I lunged for the gun, threw it in the general direction of the water and heard a reassuring splash.

Chloe was breathing but knocked out. I had no idea how long she would be unconscious or if I had hurt her. I pulled the scarf from around her neck, rolled her onto her side and tied her hands together behind her back at the wrists. Then I pushed her onto her stomach and sat on her legs. I kept the rock on my lap. If she tried to move I wouldn't have any problem hitting her with it again.

I heard someone calling my name, up at the top of the embankment. When I opened my mouth to answer, it triggered a coughing fit. Finally I managed to take a breath and call out, "I'm down here." My voice was raspy and raw, but whoever it was heard me.

"She's here," I heard him yell.

"Kathleen, are you all right?" I heard after a moment's silence. *Marcus*.

"I'm okay."

"Where's Chloe?"

Chloe was starting to stir. I leaned sideways and dug my elbow into the middle of her back. "Don't move," I hissed. "Because I will hit you again."

"She's right here," I yelled. "She's not going anywhere."

I could see movement at the top of the rock wall and after a moment someone started climbing down. Whoever it was was much better on the rocks than I'd been. It wasn't until he was almost to the ground that I realized it was Officer Derek Craig.

He had a rope fastened around his waist and underneath his armpits. He slipped out of the loop of rope and made his way over to me.

"She had a gun," I said. "I threw it in the water."

He nodded. "We'll find it." He glanced at Chloe's wrists, trussed by her scarf.

"That's pretty much every knot I know," I said.

He had the good grace not to smile.

When I stood up, my ankle buckled. "I'm not sure I can climb."

Derek helped me step into the loop of rope and pulled it up under my arms. "You don't have to.

Hold on. They're going to pull you up." He looked to the top of the rocks and gave the rope a yank. "Ready," he yelled.

And then I was moving up over the rocks, slowly but surely. I tried to help as much as I could, pulling with my hands, pushing with my good foot. And then the edge of the grass was just above me. I dug my fingers into the ground and pulled as hands reached for me. I threw myself into a pair of strong, warm arms.

Andrew's arms.

The next hour was a blur of activity. Paramedics checked me out and then I was taken across the street to one of the private meeting rooms on the main floor of the hotel. The palms of both my hands were bandaged and my left ankle was wrapped. It wasn't broken, just badly sprained.

I gave Detective Lind the bare bones of what had happened. She narrowed her eyes at Marcus. "Remind me to say no next time you come to me with some harebrained scheme," she said.

It had taken all of Marcus's persuasive powers to convince the detective to go along with my plan to get Chloe to confess. None of us had realized how deep her mental illness went. When Chloe and I had disappeared from the bar, both detectives had come in. What they didn't know was that Chloe had told Charlie, the bartender, that she was helping me plan a "romantic" surprise for Marcus. She'd asked him to stall as long as he could.

By the time they found out we'd left the hotel, I

was already over the embankment. The only reason Marcus and Detective Lind knew which way we'd gone was that Andrew had seen us headed in the direction of the Riverwalk.

"Here," Andrew said. He handed me a cup of coffee.

"Thank you," I said.

He hadn't left my side since he'd helped Marcus pull me up over the rocks. I hadn't seen Marcus since. I kept eyeing the door, hoping he would walk in. Detective Lind had sent someone up to get my mom. The first thing I was going to do when she showed up was send her to find Marcus.

Andrew pulled out a chair and sat beside me. There were tight lines around his eyes and concern was written all over his face. "You have to come home, Kathleen," he said. "You can see that now, can't you?"

I shook my head. "Andrew, this isn't the time."

Anger flashed across his face. "It's exactly the time. You almost got killed tonight. That crazy b— woman had a gun!"

I took a breath, struggling to keep my emotions in check. "I'm fine, Andrew," I said.

He shook his head. "You're fine? Take a look at yourself. You've got bandages on your hands. You can hardly walk. This isn't fine."

"Stop," I said. If he heard me, it didn't make an impression. I didn't want to deal with any of this now. All I wanted was to see Marcus.

He exhaled loudly. "I get that you have friends here. I get that. We'll come back for visits. They can come see us in Boston. We can work it out."

"No," I said, a lot louder this time. "No."

That got his attention. "Kathleen, you're not thinking straight," he began.

"Yes, I am." I set my coffee on the table. "We can't work it out, Andrew. I'm sorry, but we can't. I do care about you, but we're not getting back together and I'm not coming back to Boston, because I already am home. Here."

"You're picking him." There were tight lines around his mouth.

I nodded. "If you mean Marcus, yes. I am." Maybe if I hadn't met Marcus I could have married Andrew and been happy. But I had met him.

"You're making a mistake."

I looked at Andrew and shook my head. "I'm sorry I hurt you."

Without warning he leaned over and pulled me against him, his mouth hot and hard on mine. Out of the corner of my eye I saw Marcus appear in the doorway—and immediately turn around.

I shoved Andrew as hard as I could away from me and struggled to my feet, resisting his attempts to help me. I hobbled out the door and across the lobby, looking for Marcus.

There was no sign of him. My chest was tight and I could barely suck in a breath, but I kept going, out the front doors to the sidewalk. I looked around.

There was no sign of him anywhere. I clenched my bandaged hands. I wasn't giving up this easily.

And then I saw him, across the street, leaning against the front fender of his SUV. I started across the street to him, dragging my foot like Quasimodo coming from his bell tower.

"It wasn't what it looked like," I said. "Andrew kissed me. I didn't kiss him. I'm not going back to Boston. I'm staying here." The words rushed out of me.

"I know," he said.

I stopped a couple of feet in front of him. "You know? What do you mean, you know?"

He was standing with his feet apart, hands stuffed in his pockets. His hair was falling on his forehead the way it always seemed to and there was dirt on the front of his shirt. He was gorgeous.

"Earlier, at the Stratton, when I went to pick up Hannah, I talked to your mother."

"What did she say?"

"She told me if I ever made you unhappy again she would make me *very*, *very* unhappy." He smiled. "She didn't exactly word it that way. And then she told me to get the stick out of my, well, you know, and be grateful that I had you." His smile faltered. "Do I have you?"

"Oh, yes, you do," I said.

Then I pushed him back against the car and kissed him until his knees went weak, just so there was no doubt.

ABOUT THE AUTHOR

Sofie Kelly is an author and mixed-media artist who lives on the East Coast with her husband and daughter. In her spare time she practices Wu-style tai chi and likes to prowl around thrift stores. And she admits to having a small crush on Matt Lauer.

CONNECT ONLINE

www.sofiekelly.com

Also available from
Sofie Kelly

Cat Trick
A Magical Cats Mystery

The local businesses of Mayville Heights hope to convince Chicago-based company Legacy Tours to sell a vacation package for their town. Legacy Tours partner Mike Glazer grew up in Mayville Heights, but he's no longer the small-town boy people once knew. Everyone seems to have an issue with the bossy loudmouth Mike has become—until someone shuts him up for good.

When Kathleen Paulson discovers Mike's body on the boardwalk, she can't help but get involved in the investigation. With a little help from Owen and Hercules, it's up to Kathleen to make sure the killer is booked for an extended stay in prison...

Available wherever books are sold or at
penguin.com

facebook.com/TheCrimeSceneBooks

OM0115